FLOWERS FROM THE VOID

HORROR

Copyright © 2024 by Gianni Washington

Cover by Joel Amat Güell

ISBN: 9781960988249

CLASH Books

Troy, NY

clashbooks.com

All rights reserved.

This is a work of fiction. Unless otherwise indicated, all the names, characters, businesses, places, events and incidents in this book are either the product of the author's imagination or used in a fictitious manner. Any resemblance to actual persons, living or dead, or actual events is purely coincidental.

No part of this book may be reproduced in any form or by any electronic or mechanical means, including information storage and retrieval systems, without written permission from the author, except for the use of brief quotations in a book review.

Printed in Colombia by Editorial Nomos S.A.

For you, dear Reader.

I rehearsed emotions, naming them: joy, peace, guilt, release, love and hate, react, relate; what to feel was like what to wear, you watched the others and memorized it. But the only thing there was the fear I wasn't alive: a negative, the difference between the shadow of a pin and what it's like when you stick it in your arm...

— MARGARET ATWOOD, *SURFACING*

Even so, why can't I do what others have done—ignore the obvious. Live a normal life. It's hard enough just to do that in this world.

— OCTAVIA BUTLER, *PARABLE OF THE SOWER*

CONTENTS

Prelude: The Glass Terminal	1
Redemption Express	6
Go, It Is the Sending	22
Under Your Skin	49
Hold Still	87
When I Cry, It's Somebody Else's Blood	110
Intermission	121
In Between	123
Homunculus	140
Take It From Me	146
Barroom Blessings	167
Mr. Hide	179
Epilogue: And Now, Back to Your Regularly Scheduled…	209
Acknowledgments	211
About the Author	213
Also by CLASH Books	215

FLOWERS FROM THE VOID

GIANNI WASHINGTON

PRELUDE: THE GLASS TERMINAL

You got a lighter?
I think so. Yeah—here.
Ooo, a Zippo. Fancy.
Damn.
What's wrong?
This thing's dryer than your scalp.
Girl, shut up. I think I have some lighter fluid under the sink.
Is it the whole complex? I can't see lights on anywhere.
Probably. It's happened before. Maybe we got a wannabe Frankenstein up in here somewhere, blowing the power out with his nonsense. I hope they find him and evict his ass.
Me too...

Oh yes—let there be light.
The scrawniest light ever. I can't just carry it around like this.
Why not? Better than nothing.
It's fire, fool. You got any candles? I'd rather have more than an inch and a prayer between my thumb and this open flame.

If you lose your thumb, I'm sure Frankie'll sew it back on for you.
Pshh.
Hahaha. Hold on.

Woo-wee! Got ourselves a lil séance in here!
Don't say that shit, Denise.
Why not?
It creeps me out. I'm glad you found votives. Otherwise we'd be holding a lighter between the two of us like idiots. Why do you have so many candles, anyway?
Oh, you know. It helps, when I speak to the darkness. The flames carry my messages whenever I ask for a little guidance.
From who?
Whoever's listening.
Okay, you're really freaking me out now.
Girl, I'm just messing with you. Don't worry; this house is safe from "demonic forces."
Except the ones you already let in.
Nothing bad's gonna happen! Damn! I thought you were a grown-up.
I am! I just... don't like sitting in the dark.
We can watch something on my phone.
And waste the little bit of juice you got left? No, thank you. We'll need it if something happens. Anyway, I do *not* wanna have to press my eyeballs to that tiny-ass screen. Too much blue light is bad for you.
That why you don't have a smartphone?
Bingo.
Whatever. If my laptop weren't dead we could watch something on that.
Is that all you do in life? Watch stuff?
Nope. Sometimes I watch other people watch stuff and react to it. Then I react to their reactions.

I am officially done with you.

What else is there to do?

Um... read? Talk to the friend who came to visit you in this janky-ass apartment complex?

BO-RING.

You know what...

I'm KIDDING! Jeez! You're like a different person when the power goes out.

I told you—I don't like it.

Look. You wanna pretend something's on TV, like we used to when we were kids? We can act like we're watching that show you like about people pretending to buy a new house they've already bought. And no electricity means no blue light.

No. That's creepy.

What is?

Watching a TV that's not on. The screen is just... black.

So are you.

Shut the hell up.

Hahahahahaha!

I'm serious! Isn't it weird?

It's just a blank screen. See?

What is you staring at it supposed to prove? It's not like we share a brain. If it's creepy to me, it just is.

It proves that you're a whiny bay—

What?

You see that?

Man, I swear to God, if you're tryna scare me...

No, really! Don't you see that? Look. There's... something there.

I slap her arm, but she doesn't say anything else; just smiles wide enough to split her skin, and I almost laugh until I notice how vacant her stare has become. I wave a hand in front of her and call her name but she doesn't move, except to gurgle sounds that aren't quite words. I seize her hand before the signals from my brain grow stale, but what I'm clutching has no life in it. I want to call for help, but there is a buzz mounting in my brain that won't stop. This is my fault. I broke my own rule.

I looked.

When I'm alone, I do my best to avoid reflective surfaces because I know, with an itching certainty, that if I look long enough, I'll see something I don't want to. Have you ever caught them watching? Shapes with no center, chittering at the edges of everything. I take pains to distract myself because it is vital (if living is something you enjoy) to keep your attention away from the corners they call home. No one seems to clock the things that beckon from the outer rim of creation. Our collective consciousness spins past them, axis tilting forward. Like we can sense in that deep-down place we all have, the tower receiving unseen signals, that perpetual motion is key. Pause long enough, and the monsters make themselves known.

I wanna drop everything, grab Denise, and get the hell out, but I can't move. We paused for too long. Now the abyss has claimed us in the name of every creeping, border-dwelling thing. Swirls of pixels shimmer in ribbons across the television screen. It undulates, a puddle made of glass, boiling with life. We are swimming in the cells that make it up. We live here. It is primordial, this ooze I am peering into. Am part of. As un-there as a breeze and as hard as a diamond's teeth. I've lost my purchase on this world; there is only static here.

Laughter and squeals rend the nothing like knives shearing through fog. I open my lips because I am hungry for the noise. As I pull this scene apart and let its pieces revolve in my mind, I detect a figure being drawn before me. When his outline reaches the swarming floor, he is instantly whole and I am ashamed because he has been there all along—waiting for me. Unlike the rest of us, he has a center. It shifts with his thoughts. I watch each dart of cognition streak across him, alive. He is talking to me. *We tell stories here*, he says. *It's a nice way to pass the time.* What's that? I think to myself, and he laughs. *The time until?* I ask, and he laughs louder, inspiring the tittering chorus to swell. I join in without meaning to. It's a hollow sound that ends when he wants it to.

Let us begin, he says. Underneath the thick layers of puppetry that now command me, I don't actually want to hear anything he might say. I don't want any part of this, including sharing myself in slices with the eyes that now sting us with their never-ending regard. Their greed is bottomless. They want. They need. And I am not enough.

My neck won't turn; I can't look for Denise, though I feel her life-force crackling somewhere, just out of reach. *Don't worry*, he says. *She is preparing for her role.* I wonder what parts he intends for us to play, and whether there will be others, strangers in costume yanked from their lives, waiting in the wings for their cue. I curse Denise for inviting me over, and myself for agreeing to come. If I hadn't, maybe we both would have spun on, seen and unseeing. But the shapes are growing more distinct and so, too, are the instructions transmitting from his mouthless head. He is speaking loud and clear, directly into my uncovered ears, and I can only nod. Yes. Tell me more.

Tell me everything.

REDEMPTION EXPRESS

I ONLY KNOCK TWICE. THAT SORT OF THING IS OFF-PUTTING TO HEAR, isn't it? Most brains are conditioned to a third knock, so their heads jerk left and right, poised like a prairie dog's, searching the airwaves for it. It would quiet their thudding hearts to hear it, but that wouldn't be fair. I'm doing them a favor by nudging their paintings askew; I'm preparing them. The only way to set things right is to open the door.

Seeing me tends to go a long way in quieting the disturbed flow of their thoughts. Their limbs slacken and their stomachs ooze forward, their gazes clouded briefly by the bliss of relief. I guess if all they're worried about is whether or not they're hearing things then, technically, yes—everything *is* "fine." No, you're not hearing things; yes, I am really here. But soon you'll wish you were, and that I wasn't.

This one is pale, bald, and stern. His face prunes in confusion, adding about five years he doesn't need. I watch him redirect his tongue away from *What do you want?* to the more polite *Can I help you?* just in case I'm holding a petition it would make him look good to sign. I always wait to speak so they can take in the sight of me. White t-shirt, white overalls, white sneakers with white laces. A white ball cap shading the amused quirk of my eyebrows. I don't want them to think I'm laughing at them, even if I am. Even *though* I am. Why lie? I don't need to lie to you.

The bald man spies the orange bandana hanging like a drowsy flame from my front pocket and, almost as soon as it clicks on, the cartoon lightbulb hovering above his head winks out. I wear the bandana like a thuggish pocket square because I've seen people on TV who paint houses do the same thing. I'm not sure why that memory sticks in my mind, or where it came from, but I like to wear one myself because it makes sense to me with the overalls.

I've got one arm behind my back, but I'm sure he hasn't noticed seeing as I'm dressed like an emissary from the light side of the chessboard, which is probably distracting. Maybe he assumed I only had one arm since his eyes bug when I pull the other seemingly from nowhere. I hold my hand out to him and he looks down. It's a brown package with cream-colored twine. The kind people get in the movies. I folded the paper just like he did once upon a time, but he gives no sign of recognition. It was a long time ago, after all. Every package corresponds directly to its recipient, though it doesn't always arrive when people think it should. Don't look at me—not my department. The bald man takes his from me more readily than expected, all things considered, and starts turning it every-which-way. There's no name or address. No *to* or *from*.

"Who sent this? Do you know?"

I shrug.

"How do you know it's for me?"

"It's for you," I say, his little mynah bird, but with a special kind of emphasis that makes him stop turning the thing and look up. My smile is smack in the middle of reassuring and threatening. I know because I've practiced. We have a staring contest as I stand there, wondering if he gets it yet. Maybe he's blocked it all out. Or considers that chapter (man, I hate when people say that) of his life long over. He was a young man with a young man's zeal. When he got away clean, the memory went to work obscuring itself like an odd dream whose morning wisps were too thin for his tired mind to keep hold of.

He is warier now than when he first took the package from me. Moisture bubbles up through the pores in his scalp, little globules that soften him into a lesser Pinhead. Now it's me he's turning over and over with his eyes, looking for any detail he might have missed. I have no connection to what happened, so I'm no kind of clue; I wasn't even around back then. Not in this body, anyway.

He's staring at my hat. The thread embroidered there is the exact same hue as the cap itself, so most people don't notice it. They just want what I'm there to give them, so they grab it and turn their backs, which doesn't offend me. It's easier if you want what's meant for you. I'd rather not chase anyone down. And what reason could they have to run unless they know why I'm there?

He squints. "FedEx?" Close. He searches me all over for any familiar sign, then shakes his head. "Major uniform upgrade, huh? Pretty big change, and I never heard a word about it! Guess I should get out more." He's waiting for me to join in, to confirm or deny. Why not? Let's have some fun.

"No one ever sees this kind of thing coming," I say, stretching my smile like taffy. He takes this as confirmation of one of those things that sometimes happens. A random choice made by the marketing wing of a ubiquitous company that ultimately doesn't affect him as a consumer, but is still pretty strange. He won't even let himself suspect we might be talking about two different things.

"No idea who the sender is, huh?" he asks, pleading with his eyes for any trade secret I'd be willing to part with. He's making one last-ditch effort, which I can respect. I'd pegged him as a thorough guy. Detail-oriented. He'd have to be. Would have had to be, more like.

I fold my mouth into the shape of regret and shake my

head in a grave way. Kind of shitty of me, I know, pretending sympathy, but this is the role I've been given. It separates me from what's going on in the tradition of worker-bees everywhere. *This is above my pay-grade. I don't make the decisions—I just work here.* It's the kindest, most banal *fuck off* you'll ever get in this life, and it's all lies. No, my colleagues and I don't run things, but of course we know more than we'd ever share.

My face is stiff from holding approximately the same expression for thirty seconds. Not quite a smile, but something verging on warmth that says *I understand how inconvenient this must be, sir, and I am so sorry.* My cheeks are cramping. I'm ready for him to shut the door.

"Well, alright then. Thanks," he says. I stare into his eyes and say nothing. "See you around," he says. He steps backward, the door clicks shut, and we're done. Good. He didn't give me time to lie again.

I have to walk down the porch steps in a way that won't alarm him if he's watching me go. Not too fast, not too slow. Some people like to watch me leave—it extends the transaction and adds to their anticipation. I pick up speed once I clear the last step and reach the empty sidewalk. I don't turn around. Not even when his living-room windows explode, raining scorched glass onto the pavement like old diamonds. I keep walking until I reach my truck, which is maybe thirty feet from his front door. I get inside, but I don't start her up. I've got a clear view, so I think I'll watch for a while. At least until I know whether or not he survived. It's not like I'll be devastated either way, but I can't know these people's fates without watching everything play out in front of me. Usually there's one of us who makes the delivery and another who handles things from there, but I tend to do both. Not that it'll earn me Employee of the Month or anything—I just like to. After so many years, I have to get my kicks how and when I can.

I open my glovebox and grab the little wooden pipe with my true likeness carved into it. Pretty badass, amirite? I've got a dime bag of indica stashed there, too—company-issued to take the edge off. They want us to pay our dues, but to enjoy ourselves in the process. I can appreciate that, even if it kinda muddles their ethics. Not that I'm an expert. I open it and give its contents a sniff. With two fingers, I pack my pipe full. Then I flip my lighter into a small somersault before swiping it from the air as neighbors swarm the sidewalk in front of my unwitting client's house. Most of them have their phones out, but none of them are calling anyone. They're holding the tiny machines up like solar panels, sucking up the energy from this disaster in case the recording catches fire, too, and they get blessed by at least one algorithm with a few hours of interest beyond their pool of relatives and old schoolmates. I light up and breathe deep. He still hasn't come out yet. Considering what he did, I guess it's only fair if he doesn't survive. Then again, maybe he's learned something in the years since about why what he did was unacceptable, and even feels bad about the whole thing. But then *again*, again...

There's a little girl at the front of the crowd using her whole hand to hold the ring and pinky fingers of the woman standing beside her. Her dark brows are furrowed and she's chewing her bottom lip, hypnotized by the flames and the noise. She's practically the only one other than me watching the proceedings without a screen as liaison. If we stood side-by-side, I'd probably be pegged as her big sister in this particular skin-suit. The after to her before. I wouldn't mind playing that part. Holding her hand as everyone points and shouts all around us. Assuring her that she'll be okay, at least for now; it'll be years before her package comes, if she gets one at all.

I always retract what I need to and oil my costume before stepping inside it so nothing snags. The suits are custom-made—you wouldn't believe how tricky they can be to fix. This one is a gorgeous, deep brown. Wide eyes shaped like almonds, with whites that stand out like pearls against the dark pools at their centers. This is a favorite guise I often circle back to, even if it means taking more care to go unnoticed before the cops arrive. As long as I get to my truck in time, I'm good; no one remembers seeing me once I'm inside. The bosses really have thought of everything.

Wearing this little number electrifies me, like I'm tiptoeing across a taut cord between buildings, five hundred stories up. The wire's end is my horizon line, tauntingly out of reach no matter how close I get. Each time I lower my weight onto it with a new step, the wire shudders and droops just enough to make me afraid. The crowd's stares come from too far below for me to gauge their hostility, or lack thereof. In the moments when I'm most unsure of how things will end, I lift the thick mane from the back of my neck and let it go, bit by bit. The box braids hit the space between my shoulder blades in a widening spill and I breathe out a decadent sigh. Whatever your opinion of me, I am thrilling.

I don't think I could handle the strange mélange of optimism and dread 24/7, but I do enjoy a good cameo.

I wonder what the little girl's guardian will tell her about what happened here today. Small scrolls of burnt wood turned to ash are floating through the air and the girl is stretching her fingers out to them. They must look like fireflies with their glowing orange tails, until they land, dead-gray. I wish I could remember what any of this was like. It's why I watch so much TV and listen to the radio and all. When you're out of practice, it can be hard to recall even the simplest things.

My head lolls as dissonant sirens bloom from a pea-sized whine into full-blown whale song. I guess someone called for help after all. Each howling note falls one after another against my ears. I love this part. Eventually, every type of emergency vehicle roars past my foggy window and skids to a halt in front of the house and I feel the thrum of every movement shimmy up through my tires and along the metal skeleton of my truck. A cop car does half a donut that scatters the crowd of oblivious onlookers, waking them at last to the possibility of real danger. Shit... this is just like those crime dramas where the title is all letters that don't spell anything. Anachronistic? No, that's not it. Anyway, you know the ones I mean: where a ragtag bunch of enforcers, each with their own principles, puts their differences aside to form a found family they can kick ass and fight evil with. And "evil" is usually a terrorist who wants nothing more than to destroy the regional way of life. Only this time, the terrorist is me, and it's not their way of life I want to destroy—just this guy's. I actually enjoy their way of life. Especially in this kind of high-definition. Gives me chills.

I can see the eyes of the gathered masses widening from here. Or maybe I just think I can; this stuff's pretty strong. I can't even make out irises in the crowd—just open-mouthed zombies with milky marbles in their heads, knocking shoulders, looking over each other for a way out. I can't see the little girl anymore. Firefighters leap down from the big red behemoth they rode in on, immediately yank the coil of hose from its hook and start to unfurl it. It worms out longer and longer until the guy holding the tail-end reaches a lonely, green-capped fire hydrant I hadn't noticed before. While they fiddle with the hose, a troop of creatures in weird suits covered in pouches and zippers and what look like the military version of Jules Verne diving helmets scurry up to the burning house. They look dressed to walk on the moon, but they're probably bomb disposal. The emergency med techs are clearly itching to leap into action, but the most senior police officer holds out a hand, instructing them to wait. The EMT in the lead flings his arms to the sky as if to say, *Someone could be dying in there!* The cop nods sagely, then offers a reply with his palms held out to placate. *Something has clearly blown the fuck up in there, son. We need to make sure it's safe before you go barreling in like an idiot and get turned bite-sized, alright?* Or something equally dire that makes the EMT's eyes bulge. He hustles back to his team to spread the word.

Gobble, gobble.

I don't know why, but that gaggle over there makes me think of turkeys. In which case, they'd be a rafter, not a gaggle, but gaggle sounds better. I like the way the word feels in my mouth. *Gag. Gul.* Saying it is like juggling boba with my tongue. You ever try that stuff? No matter how much you chew on it, it keeps its shape. It's crazy. Anyway, the term gaggle is the best way to describe the jumble of bodies in the street, and should include the fire, catalyst for the chaos, which is dying under the spray of the now functioning hose. The alien beings in their zip-locked suits have disappeared, though I'm not sure when that happened exactly. Three firemen troop out of the building with a fourth following at a distance. The last fireman carries a bundle that wilts blackly over the edge of each burly bicep. The EMTs try to look alive as they dash over to him with a collapsible gurney. Hm. I just realized. I assumed he was alone in that house, but there's a chance he wasn't.

Oh well. Maybe that'll drive the point of all this home for him.

The lead EMT shakes the gurney's folded legs out in one practiced motion. The charred and crumpled form in the fireman's arms is lowered onto the rolling stretcher so the techs can unbend its joints as carefully as possible, before death is quickly confirmed. Then the remains are covered and hoisted into the back of the waiting ambulance. The emergency workers all clot together in their respective groups while a police officer ties yellow tape across the front gate. As each vehicle pulls away, the crowd lessens. I can just make out a tiny head with tinier afro puffs bobbing at the ear of an adult woman. The little girl, with her chin sunk into her chaperone's shoulder, stares at what's left of the blackened house. I follow her gaze with mine, and can just make out someone standing on the front steps of the destroyed building. They are blacker than soot from head to toe. Skin, clothing—everything. No one from the dispersing crowd notices. They've already decided there's nothing more to see.

The figure heaves itself down each step in such a way that I feel the weight of their movements, like the stairs are made of my own bones. As the being trudges along the snaking path to the sidewalk, something in me expects them to sag to the ground and immediately drift off to sleep. The figure walks on until it reaches the yellow tape. It considers the plastic ribbon, tilting its dark blot of a head, before continuing on as if nothing is there. And the tape stays obediently strung up, as if nothing dubiously corporeal had interrupted its banner-brightness. The little girl is still staring, and the figure stops on the sidewalk to watch her shrink against the horizon. I wonder what their expressions are saying to each other. You'll probably think I'm a monster, but I can't help smiling. Funny—it's always kids who see ghosts.

I could watch the smoke curl in front of me forever, but he won't let me. He's shuffling this way now, slow but steady. His progress is almost painful to watch, but part of me is rooting for him. *Come on. Come to me.* The closer he gets, the slower he seems to move. The echo of his mind is probably unsure despite the confidence of his feet, which toil on. He stops when he reaches a point parallel to my passenger-side window. It seems to take a supernatural effort to turn his body to face the glass, but he manages eventually. It probably took less time than it feels like, but I'm way up into the atmosphere now. Here, every moment stretches until it begins to tear.

He mostly looks the same. Same wrinkled, plaid button-down. Same stiff khakis. Same bumpy nose and bald head. His skin's not as pale, but that's because he's made of shadows now. When I look at him, I realize I'm staring into two empty holes. The explosion must have blown his eyes out of his head faster than he could manage to die. I picture them liquidating before he even has time to consider blinking against the blast. I wish I'd recorded it. That would spice up the old video library for sure. He tilts his head like he's wondering what I'm thinking. I hope he is. It'd be nice to be that important.

"Get in," I say.

He looks at the passenger-side door and does not seem to recognize the concept. No more eyes, but he blinks.

"Come on," I say. "It's part of the deal. Anyway, without eyes, you might fall into a ditch somewhere and get stuck haunting that." It's a dumb joke—I mean, he can obviously see well enough to get to me—but I like to lighten the mood if I can. His mouth balls up; apparently he doesn't find me funny. He arches his neck and I wonder blandly when his head will stop moving. It doesn't, until finally the underside of his chin is held up to me like a shield. His face is now a charred plateau with a pile of ash dropped conspicuously at its center, tunneled moistly through in two places. He leans back farther, then yanks his head forward like a hammer's claw coming unstuck. I take a year to close my eyes. They are shut tight, but my ears are all the way open, waiting for the crash.

Waiting.

I separate my lids the tiniest sliver, pressing them closed as much as I am holding them open. Light slides in, but not enough to see by. I open my eyes all at once and his face is halfway through the window. The window isn't down; he's phasing through it. I knew he wouldn't be able to break the glass, but it's like someone suddenly making like they're gonna hit you, whether they're stronger than you or not, you know? I try to move my mouth, but the weed has dried it to dust. A hacking cough takes hold as I try to say something, anything. He reaches a hand, then an arm toward my thigh and a combination of guttural noises and wheezes tumble from me. As his fingers get closer, I flinch away. I don't like the feel of apparitions. However, instead of going for me, his fingers find the emergency brake. I face front as he hauls himself inside.

Before long, he is upright in the seat next to mine. He

isn't melting through to the ground below because he doesn't want to. Well, that, and the truck makes that sort of thing impossible. Last week, one lady kept trying to phase back through the door and escape after we got rolling, but the truck wouldn't let her. I don't think it's alive, but it honestly wouldn't surprise me if it were. Anyone glancing at us now (to whom we were both visible) would think we were pals. Maybe they'd think I was here picking him up on the way to our favorite spot. Or maybe, since we're sitting very still, eyes front, they'd think we've just broken up. I take one last toke and wonder if I look like the dumper or the dumpee. Weed makes me feel scraggly and unkempt, like my guts are falling out, but not in a clutch-the-sides-of-my-face kind of way. More like... my body is a house that needs tidying and my guts are only on the floor cuz I can't be bothered to pick them up, even if I am slightly embarrassed by the whole thing.

A sound like sacks of gravel being dragged across a sandpaper floor is coming from my passenger seat. His neck is crooked forward and his mouth is in the harshest "o" I've ever seen. He's trying to speak but the ash has grown fat in his lungs, replacing every inch of air with itself like it knows he's already dead and won't need it. It'll never go away—that sensation of being suffocated by smoke. A grinding like rusted machinery comes from him. It sounds like—

Why?

"You know why," I say, doing my best to keep the words dull. He goes quiet; all I can hear are the workings of his laboring chest, like sawdust passing from one alveolian grape to another. Ash to air; water to wine.

I—I didn't know... how many... would die.

"But the point was that someone would, right?" I ask. "Did you stay? For the carnage? Or did you hurry home to catch the highlights on the news?"

His expression hasn't changed, yet shame radiates from

him like heat. Pretty fucking rich of me to say any of this. I guess the system does work. Badum-tsss.

"Everybody pays." My mouth forms the words automatically, the company slogan now seared into my very essence. Whether we go on thinking we're right all along, or turn some type of corner before dispatch, the only relevant thing is the damage done. He could've ripened into the second coming of Gandhi by the time I got here and it wouldn't have mattered—I still would've blown him up. That's how this works. If he'd survived, it would've been just as well. He probably would've been maimed beyond recognition and have to go on wearing the reminder of what he did every single day. Either way, he'd have gotten what the bosses had decided was coming to him.

I glance at the pocket watch tied with leftover twine to my air vent. Fuck. I slam the key into the ignition. The engine shakes my entire body and disguises his breathing, which is a relief to me but I don't know why. The houses in his now former neighborhood look like they were baked in a witch's oven. Icing at the windows. Gumdrops in the garden. Homes fit for dolls with breakable bodies. How nice for you, I can't help but think, and am caught off-guard by my own bitterness. He'll probably be disappointed by where we're headed, but then that's part of it, too. Our grass is just as green, though. We've even got a few gumdrops of our own, swaying red, purple, and yellow in the breeze. He'll see them all. See them, but never touch them.

He doesn't speak in the car and my buzz is dying. A new one's replacing it. My head rings like a bell and I can't stop it. I shouldn't have smoked; I completely lost track of time. I have to get back. My foot grows heavier on the gas pedal until everything passing by is a blur. My stomach hurts from trying to hold my current shape, but the stitches in my shoes have already started to snap apart and air is rushing against my exposed talons. Please, let me make it. Not here.

There is always a road, no matter where in the world I find

myself, that leads to where we're going. I spot a highway exit sign with a dog's-ear bend in the bottom-right corner and squeal over to it amidst honks and shouts and middle fingers. We bump down the potholed ramp like we're on a hayride. Well, *I* bump down it, every so often rising an inch from my seat; he's too weighed down by the events of the day to move. The thighs of my trousers are stretched to capacity as I turn left at the light. The fabric tears just as my red toes begin to curl over the edge of the gas pedal. I can see it, the dirt road a little way ahead. I make the sharpest turn ever to reach it and for half a second I'm impossibly happy because it feels like I'm in a high-speed chase. A crazed laugh escapes me as my shirt rips. Bristles hard as plastic sprout between my breasts and shoulders, shredding fabric as they grow. My tires seem to roll over every rock and into every dip and I try not to bite my tongue. I'm clenching my mouth shut with the organ curled safe inside it like a sleeping serpent, but I yelp because, apparently, I had a bit of bottom lip caught between my teeth without realizing it and they're sharpening and it hurts. The blood trickles warmly down my chin as we pull into the circular drive... and I deflate back into something he might recognize. My suit is ruined.

I turn to my charge and am met with his eyeless stare.

What are you? he asks, and there's some tremble to his smoke-ravaged voice. *Is this Hell?*

I wipe my mouth on my torn collar and grin like the joyless jack-o'-lantern I am. "Probably," I say.

He follows my lead and gets out of the truck, but waits for me to direct his attention or his steps somewhere, anywhere. Some of my teeth are still kind of pointy, so I'll just let him take the place in without any awkward audio-booking from me. Unlike the dirt road and withered trees flanking us on the way here, the grass in front of the building is vibrant and alive, shimmering like water when the wind rolls through it. I can't tell you how many hours I've spent staring at these grounds, scouring them for a seam in the mirage, but never finding one. The building is colosseum-shaped, minus the hollowed-out center, with rows of barred windows watching like a million cross-hatched eyes. He cranes his neck until he can't anymore. It's impossible to see the top. I know—I've tried. I'd hurry him along, but something in me wants to give him a few minutes more of this serene liminality. That's how it's done on-screen, you know. The prisoner gets a few wistful moments to appreciate the jut of a single blade of grass, or a unique crack in the wall that zigzags down to the ground like an errant hair free of its scalp. He sighs heavily, regretting all the details of all the places he's ever been that he realizes he missed during the more carefree days of his life. That would all be fitting now, especially since once Ol' Smoky here crosses the threshold... well. Anyway, he's my last inductee for a while, so this extra time is as much for me as it is for him, even if I'm not the hero of this particular tale. I take in a few robust lungfuls and look around me. It really is nice out here. Every time my turn comes, it feels like the beginning of everything. Like I have more time than I could ever need to do all the things I've spent trillions of hours watching actual people do in their made-up stories. Then when it's over, I inevitably feel cheated, as if I hadn't known all along when it would end and didn't have a disgusting amount of time to prepare. When I'm out here, I always get caught up in watching events unfold. It's like being back in my cell with my pile of tapes, except it's real and I'm part of it.

I fill my lungs again and heave the longest, loudest, yearningest sigh I can. I'd rather not let my time in this scene go to waste. For a split second, I imagine someone else watching me, and laughter explodes from me until my stomach aches. My eyes are shut tight, but still the tears leak out. My body is wracked by every gasp, which makes me laugh even harder until there's no sound coming from me at all. Ghost-man surveys me, the edges of his mouth dangling well past his chin. "What's wrong?" I ask, allowing my laughter to taper off, but still linger.

I don't understand any of this, he replies, turning away from me to lock eye sockets with the windows again. Seeing his smallness against this hulking container of souls drains any mirth I've got left. Part of me wants to pat his arm in a way that means... whatever that means to people. I can't remember.

"Let's go," I say. There's a beat of inaction before his shoulders relax into an even deeper slump. He glances again at the immensity before us, then falls into tentative step behind me as I head for the door.

The inside is pretty unremarkable. Lots of light gray, silver, and subway tile. The staircases wind in every direction to every room, splitting here and there at various, twisting inclines. I don't meet the eyes of any of my fellows as I walk. His paperwork was done before my turn began. I knew that if he died, he'd end up here. A room is always allocated just in case, and the number is clear in my mind despite its impossible length. He can't hear what I hear; if he could, he'd have jumped the railing and run by now. I've learned it's best to keep walking, because this time I know he's watching. Soon, the transaction will truly be over. I come to his navy blue door and hear his Marley-shuffle end somewhere near my right ear. The air beside me fills with his terror, silent and dense, as he waits for the abyss he is sure I will reveal to swallow him whole. I let my eyes rest on him and am not surprised to see his lids closed; he can't even bear to look. My lips curl as I push the door open and stand aside.

The room is empty of absolutely anything. No hair or dead skin cells exist to attract dust. Not even dust exists here. He steps over the threshold, then turns back to me. I nod, which I guess reassures him, so he walks to the center of the room and revolves in a slow circle, searching for a sign. I shut the door just as he is about to face me again. The screaming starts as I descend the stairs.

I've seen this film before, more times than I can count. His victims' last moments will play on an endless loop inside his head, and the devastating grief of their loved ones will seep in, steadily filling all the cracks in his knowing, until it spills from everywhere and he is drowning in it. His transparent teeth will crack against one another, and he will beg for silence. He will try to tear the flesh from his non-existent bones and gouge out eyes that are already gone. He will understand, and wish he had asked more questions, that he had begged to remain outside a little longer. As I take the path that winds back to my own unhappy island, his howls join the violent chorus that is the eternal soundtrack of this place. I slow my pace and close my eyes, until the noise melts exquisitely to static, and I hum along.

GO, IT IS THE SENDING

Her steps made no mark in the snow for She was lighter even than the bird eggs in Her pocket. She would succeed today. The Mothers had asked that She remove Her scroll from its shelf and follow its dictate to the letter if She desired another chance at initiation. Her only remaining chance. She knew that creation was a tenet of membership, but it was difficult. The incantation required faith in order to work, and this had always been Her failing. After all, She had not been raised to practice this sort of magic. As such, all She had managed thus far were singed feathers and the almond tip of an unfinished beak. She pulled Her hood low against the numbing gale, and trudged on.

 She felt the warmth of the hearth even before the cottage door opened. The bottom of the outsized door scraped along the rough wooden floor but She did not hear. The baying winds hid all sound until the door stuck shut behind Her, sealing in the heat. She kept Her head down as She approached the roaring fire. Agnes would have chided Her for leaving such wild flames unattended; Her bottom lip wobbled at the thought. No. There would be time enough for grief. It would be Her reward for a successful induction. She knelt at the fire, palms out. The anise stars sat in their open bowl, mingling their licorice scent with the cinnamon sticks that hung in occasional bunches from the mantel like a garland. She would have had a kiss as soon as She was in from the cold. To warm Her sweet lips and sweeter soul, Agnes would have said. She put Her fingers closer to the dancing flame until it licked at them in earnest. The fire closed about Her hand until She was on the losing end of a torturous handshake. She clenched Her teeth, allowing the pain to continue feasting on Her. She wanted Her skin to blacken more. She would cook from brown clay all the way to coal and lie in the snow to be the beautiful child of lava missing from this alabaster scene.

Pull your hand from the flames, you fool, the ghost of Her great love whispered close to Her ear, warming it so that She could feel nothing else. She obeyed and held the smoking meat of Her hand away from Herself. There was pain, yes, but it did not matter. She could feel no greater misery than had already eaten clean a space for itself within Her. The Mothers could not promise Agnes's return. Agnes herself would never have joined had they practiced resurrection. Some covens did, but Agnes had believed the very notion unnatural. However, the Mothers *did* believe the best spellwork was done with living ingredients. Agnes had summoned the entire town as part of her initiation. She had been young in both age and spirit, with no misgivings about calling the villagers to trek through the woods in search of a grand clearing where pieces of their souls then left their bodies to feed Agnes's midnight workings. All were manipulated into the farce of a Black Mass; the Mothers had each been greatly amused by this. None but one amongst the enchanted citizenry of Salem later remembered the strange theater they had performed. That one man, however, not having shared the blind euphoria of his fellows, had wrenched himself free of the scene and fled, becoming an incurable wretch beset by nightmare even as he lay dying. Though she successfully gained admission to the coven by virtue of her transcendent skill, that one man's unending torment had been enough to turn Agnes permanently away from living ingredients. From the time of his passing onward, Agnes pledged that her energy alone would make her magic work, or there would be none.

Agnes's lover pulled the unmarked jar of honey-colored paste down from the shelf on which many journals and grimoires leaned in drunken unison. Each spine had a remembered brightness underneath the layers of old spider silk and dead leaves. She scooped some of the homemade salve into three fingers and spread it thickly across the shining skin of Her injured hand. Her hand tingled and its temperature dropped little by little until the sensation of sheets of ice began to wrap round each digit. She took the opportunity borne of waiting to lie on Her back, elbow propping the convalescing hand aloft. She stared into the tangle of branches insulating Her home from the weather and let Her face rest, expressionless. The sticks began to quiver and She watched for what they would show Her. The coven already had a seer, so this would never be enough to impress them. She must show them, show them all. Life. Why steal it when you could...

"Come in, Marguerite," She called from the floor.

There was shuffling from the other side of the door amidst Mother Nature's shrieking. "I wish you would not do that," Marguerite yelled through the wool that no doubt guarded her lips against the cold. "'Tis an eerie thing."

She smiled to Herself and rolled onto Her side, cheek resting comfily in Her head's nest of black cotton. "I thought I should save you the trouble of knocking." Snow flurries tumbled almost to Her nose as Marguerite entered. Her friend shouldered the door closed and began to beat her cloak and skirts like rugs. Snowflakes scattered to meet the floor. She opened Her mouth to catch one.

"Are you prepared, then, for your trial?" Marguerite asked.

"Is this..." and Marguerite waved her hands in the air above her friend, "part of it?"

"No," She replied, laughing. "My bones were tired, that's all."

"And your limbs burned purely by chance?" Marguerite asked, bending for a closer look at the hand coated in what looked like a shell of beeswax. While Marguerite looked on, She took the opportunity to make a fist. Deep yellow chunks pelted the floor, and those that fell nearest the grate commenced immediately to melting. The briefly ailing witch sat up cross-legged and brushed the remnants of the salve from Her now healed hand. Marguerite *tsk*ed at her friend, who smiled back like a child.

"All is well," She said.

Marguerite bore her disbelief silently, choosing instead to begin removing cast-off herbs and other used and broken things from the surface of an impressively crowded table. Marguerite picked up an ulna that had once belonged to a fox and peered at it from every angle, allowing her mouth to open some. "I did not think you one for animal sacrifice." Marguerite held the bone out to her friend.

"I found that in the woods," She replied. "Buried."

"You were digging holes?"

"One end bloomed from the snow like a bud," She said, closing Her eyes. "I could not leave it."

Marguerite set the bone back onto the table and wandered over to the mantel. She paused there, before a drawing of Agnes strung tightly to a frame made of twigs. The image was little more than a loose collection of charcoal strokes, but each resultant line had clearly been drawn by fingers that remembered well the real-life counterpart to every contour laid upon the sheet of dried flax pulp, which strained before Marguerite's eyes to keep its shape. Special attention had been paid to Agnes's lips and eyes; the charcoal was a bit heavier where shadow once lurked in life, and impossibly light where the skin had been thinnest and most sensitive. Marguerite had never had the desire to kiss the former resident of this cottage in life, but each time she laid eyes on this drawing, her own lips pouted toward those pictured, and she dreamed, too, the sensation of laying her mouth upon each drooping eyelid. Marguerite turned away from the image. "Does the spell work now?"

Her jaw tightened. She stared into the flames rather than hold Marguerite's gaze. "I haven't... quite mastered it yet."

Marguerite sighed. "You have only until tomorrow night."

Eyes on fire, She did not reply.

"Apologies. I know you do not need reminding. But what will you do?"

"Spend the eve of my final failure in meditative silence."

Marguerite smiled fondly down at her friend. "My dear," she said, quieting her voice as she knelt to the floor. "I know you would not have exerted such mountainous effort in this pursuit if you believed in your heart it could not be done."

"But am *I* capable of such a feat."

"Again I say, and trust, that you would immediately relinquish any pursuit whose ends you did not see yourself reaching." Marguerite took her companion's whole, undamaged hand into the shelter of her own, and kissed above its knuckles. The hand smelled of smoke and melted honeycomb. "Though I am not allowed to provide assistance in conjuring, is there any other help I can give?"

She leaned into Marguerite, who embraced Her, and closed Her burning eyes. In the yellow glow that buzzed behind Her lids, She saw a creature emerge from a breaking egg. Shutting Her lids tighter, She tried to follow the animal's progress as it swirled into the black. "This helps."

Marguerite kissed Her temple and held Her closer.

The circle was drawn in chalk and blood on the wooden floor, which had eaten up even more chalk dust, sigils, pollen, and herbs than the trees of the forest She had marked with Her spells, against which the acorns slept and flower heads leaned. Along the border of the circle were strewn all the winter blooms kindly gathered by Marguerite before her visit. In the center, She set down lightly the bird eggs She had toted home in the pocket of Her cloak. She lifted the top from each eggshell, revealing its hollowness. Her index finger hovered above the first of the three. To that finger, She held the edge of a small blade. She gritted Her teeth and sliced. One heavy drop fell to the bottom of the first eggshell. She squeezed the skin around the cut until another drop fell, then repeated the exercise with the remaining two eggs. Next, She placed found feathers shed from the same species of fowl, one to pad the innards of each blood-bottomed shell. Then, a sprig of southernwood at the circle's center, for birthing anew from nothing as Mary's followers believe she had done. Inside each shell, She placed a plucked, five-fingered leaf from that sprig's same bush. And finally, plump pokeweed berries to nourish each forthcoming bird.

The remaining sigil, She drew in blood with the tips of the first and second fingers of Her right hand. The spell, She breathed into the fire. Each word, She uttered as clearly as the ringing bell tone which followed. The spellwork bell was Agnes's; She would have to earn Her own. The incantation, too, was Agnes's, or at least had been found in the grimoire she'd left behind.

New life from nothing.
   New life to something.
   Peck the air with your beaks.
   Feathers sprouting from skin.
   Drink the blood I have offered.

Become now my kin.
Live.

Smoke rose from the ingredients, now engulfed in conjuror's flame. She carved signs into the air above the magic circle as fast as She could with Her fingers. Dazzling orange gashes in the fabric of time and space danced higher and higher as She flexed Her fingers, using them as quills to write the ancient tongue in ink made only of Her own energy. The color of the ink changed to an electric eggplant, then the special pink of sunsets, and Her heart leapt to Her mouth. It was working. This time—

The bright words blackened before Her eyes and spilled down the air like the blood already spread in shapeless pools on the floor, then evaporated. Her hope fizzled as She looked at each shell. Their contents smoldered. One baby bird's raw skin was peppered with the beginnings of feathers. Another had died with only the bottom half of a beak jutting like a small shelf at the open puncture of its mouth. Its tongue clung roughly to the incomplete beak, like a raindrop unsure of the fall. The sigils had erased themselves, swallowed up by the failure of the spell. She trembled, sadness indistinguishable from rage, and flung the bell away from Her to clang against whatever immovable object it met first.

The effort to maintain Her determination to join the coven had already been tremendous. After all, if She wished, She could immediately practice magic in Her lonely cottage for the benefit of Herself and all those seeking refuge from their so-called purity. Upon Her arrival on a ship which had provided friendly passage at the behest of Her mother, nearly every proper citizen of the new land where She found Herself had believed She, like those She resembled, should belong to them, when Her only reason for plunging Her toes like flags into that soil had been to belong squarely to Herself. Her mother had supported Her desire to see what She could of this great Earth, but had bade Her do so with caution. Their people had protected themselves from harm with sorcery since the very first cries had rung from the first children born to them. But whispers of their cousin-tribes being stolen away had reached their ears. She of course had seen where these unfortunate souls had ended up in Her stealthy travels; She had even used Her magic to free those who were not yet divested from all hope by the fear of greater suffering. Each time She Herself was captured and held, the trapper's life soon ended with a few words taught to Her by Her mother, and off She went again. Her final time spent captive, She had remained. The woman had not actually trapped Her, and never intended to force Her into work of any kind, instead wanting to know everything about Her. With every day, each grew hungrier for knowledge of the other. Knowledge of every kind. She showed Agnes what She could do, and Agnes showed Her the same. Agnes was further along in the formal acquisition of occult education, but She had ancient blood and the collected learnings of Her people, imparted throughout their lovingly shared lives.

She showed Agnes how She could peel the skin away from Her own face and speak to Her captors as blood rolled past Her flayed mouth and down Her naked torso to their wretched floors. She would shut their doors with only words when they tried to flee, and open Herself up with glowing mouth to Her ancestors to let them steal Her voice away and replace it with one of their own. She told Agnes how the sound, like poisoned honey, dripped with such abysmal resonance that Her captors would jab their own eardrums and bellies full of a molten poker's sting until they lay, ruptured and dead, twitching senselessly as their spirits were dragged down to the Hell whose existence they secretly prayed against. Those who did not end their own lives lost their minds. She showed them things, for She was not only a seer, but one who could create visions of such horror as to torture the brains of the deserving into unknown depths of despair. In the end, She would creep past their rocking and drooling forms, out the door forever.

Agnes had hoped to guide her lover in a less gruesome form of practice. Despite the fact that the Puritans had also begun attacking those of their own number whom they wrongly suspected of witchcraft (for the truly magical were often skilled enough to evade their ire). They must save them, Agnes had told Her. They must save the Puritans from themselves by dispelling the stigma of evil from witchcraft, lest the citizenry of Salem, magical and not, become extinct as a result of their unchecked zeal. This could only be done with compassion. *Your magic might not be best for our purposes.*

"And what is *our* purpose, sweet milkmaid?" She replied in Her worst moments. "You felt a speck of empathy over one man's madness, but so what? If I had not defended myself, I would be dead now." And those words always seized the ones poised to leave Agnes's lips, and she would bow her head and say instead, *Yes. Yes I know.*

Agnes had not been the one to string her lover up and make unholy demands of Her. Agnes had not been the one to knock Her senseless for not speaking, working, or opening Her legs as She had been bidden. But She wanted—needed—Agnes to know that not everyone required a shepherd to show them the light. Some would be better served with a hard shove into the brambles, eyes open, and no helping hand after. They would always disagree on this, but that divergence of philosophy never kept them from the certainty that the other was the ecstasy of cold water on days when the Sun was at its highest.

And because She knew that Agnes wanted only what was best for Her, and because She no longer awoke in a puddle of fear, wondering if She could make it through another day without being snatched, She had done things Her lover's way from then on.

She gathered the remains of Her almost-flock with tears in Her eyes. She would bury them beside the others, in soil made hard by the snow.

In the night, Agnes came to Her as she often did. This time, she was one of many. The coven were at their meeting place, lit by the glow of a thousand candles. The women stood in a circle of twenty. Extending their legs in unison, they swept their pointed toes across the dirt floor in ever-widening arcs, back and forth; one leg, then the other. The fabric of time folded about them, blurring the scene, but honing Her emotions to their keenest extent. Hips swayed as each woman glided easily through each step of the ritual. Their arms rose until their palms faced the ceiling, which dripped stone in bubbling spikes to meet them. Every arm waved elegantly in time with the next as they continued to move through the air like ripples in water. Each breath of life in them, each movement, seemed to merge with every other until they were as one gigantic, graceful beast. She found Agnes amongst her sisters and called to her, but Her lover would not turn her head. Determined to be seen, She ran on bare feet and reached for her. A hissing pain, and a powerful force like that of one bush elephant ramming skulls with another knocked the breath from Her body. She was not allowed to disrupt the circle. But the heart beating inside that raven-haired woman belonged to Her. She must be allowed to have it or She would die! She crawled to the edge of their gathering on hands and knees, wailing. *Don't leave me here alone!* Her breaths came slower and slower until the air was thicker than mud. Meanwhile the spellcasters danced on frenzied ankles, truly blurring into one entity. At the center of their circle, specks of white hovered, spinning. The white expanded into domes before Her fading eyes. Four of them, equally spaced in the earth. As the domes took their true form, the spellcasters slowed their manic gambol as if to wade through the muddy air that impeded them. Eventually, they swished to a stop. Through the forest of human legs, She spied four eggs large enough to contain a full-grown fowl of mythic proportions.

It took a spectacular effort to lift Her head and focus. Her reflection gleamed darkly on the surface of the nearest shell. The ground rumbled in such a way that She could be certain the source was not the movement of molten rock leagues beneath Her. A crack like a bolt of lightning split Her reflection jaggedly in half. With each thunderous peck, the Earth shook. Finally, a beak emerged like a spear. Pieces of the fledgling's former home rained down like the hardened salve of Her waking hours. Its beak opened and a piercing shriek rang out, shaking the cave walls and loosing rocks to break upon the floor. Four enormous chicks haltingly absorbed their surroundings with black, blinking eyes as large as turtle shells. She rose to Her feet, astounded and terrified. Is this what the combined faith of twenty women could do? Suddenly it struck Her that the spell was complete and the forcefield no more. She ran to Her beloved to embrace her. When she turned around, though, it was not Agnes, but a friend of Her mother's from the home She had left behind. When She looked around at the other faces, each belonged to a woman She had known and loved as a young girl. These were the women who had raised and taught Her. The women began to move the circle as if along a track, side-stepping so that each might embrace Her in turn. Every caress enveloped Her in an all-encompassing warmth such that Her spirit was fully nourished by the time the circuit was complete. Last in the line was Her mother, naked breasts painted over with golden symbols. As She gazed at them with shining eyes, a sensation of coolness welled up inside Her like a fountain. It was relief. She gasped. Her limbs were lighter than air now that Her burden had finally gone. She looked into Her mother's eyes, which were happy crescents. For the first time in an age, She could remember Her own name.

She woke as though ripped from a nightmare. The darkness surrounding Her was not total as there were still embers clinging to life in the fireplace. Their faint glow outlined Her arms, which were held up in front of Her. Her fingers stretched to grasp the edges of the name that had briefly been restored to Her dreaming mind, but to no avail; it had already slipped away. The fingers curled into fists She then used to pound the straw mattress. Its wooden frame creaked in protest. For one glorious second, She had remembered. A scream burned to be set free, so She released it wildly into the night. Any runaway or bandit unfortunate enough to be passing by just then would have been chilled to their marrow to hear the rage in that howl. They would have believed it must be the recipient of their most shameful wrongdoing come to avenge themselves at last. She fell back onto the goose-down cushion that still carried Her lover's scent in hidden folds here and there.

Agnes had asked Her name only once in the year they had spent together. When She replied that She did not know and could not remember, Agnes had paused, deep in thought, perhaps wondering what amount of suffering could cleave a person's mind so greatly that they could forget their own name. Even unfortunate Mr. Brown had managed to keep hold of the letters that spelled him out amidst his never-ending turmoil. In truth, She had forgotten Her name as soon as She first set foot upon that new land from the ship's gangplank. But alone, there had been no need even to realize its sudden absence from Her mind. And before Agnes, when She was not alone, it was only because someone had deemed Her more useful to their purposes than to Her own. She recalled now Her mother warning that She might forget Herself upon arrival in that new place, but She had assumed Her mother referred to customs and traditions—not the name She had answered to since She was old enough to understand that it was Hers. Agnes had been the first since Her arrival to ask what She was called. The first to care. And that had been enough to release Her of Her need for it. From then on, Agnes called Her "my love" or "dear one" or "beloved" so oft that Her heart could not recall a time when She had another name. Those words, though they might be uttered by others in their own homes and lives and within the cocoons of their own loves, became names that belonged only to Her.

But She had dreamed of Her mother this time. The first to give Her a name. She remembered the symbols painted across her breasts. Eyes squeezed tight, the image swam before Her. No... She did not know what they were. What they meant. But She could see them about as clearly as She could see Her own hand in the glowing dark. She rolled over until Her legs hung off the bed frame and Her soles touched the floor. Then She ran to the shelf and tore book after book from it until She found one with a blank page. A loose feather teetered on the shelf's farthest edge. She snatched it and a small, near-empty pot of ink after ripping loose the page from its woven spine. There was just enough ink left to scratch out the curves and joints of each symbol before they vanished from memory completely. Rather than return to the mattress to flick fitfully back and forth, She crouched before the dying fire and studied the shapes from Her dream. She traced each contour until Her brow throbbed from being pinched into a frown for too long. This was absurd. She had learned to read as a child. Her mother and aunties, always so generous with their time and wisdom, had spent hours each day dipping their fingers in animal blood and drawing words on every available surface to aid Her. But these symbols, though familiar, were unintelligible.

Her chest tightened, the breaths coming faster and shorter with each inhale. Before She knew it, warm rivulets flowed down Her cheeks until She ran out of air to breathe. Her bottom lip shook and She drooled in agony. It had never mattered while Her heart was being cradled by Agnes. But the pain of not knowing Herself now, on the eve of Her pending acceptance to the Salem sisterhood, was too great. Agnes had been a shelter against hardships known and unknown. Now there was nothing to protect Her. There was nothing at all. Nothing but

Darkness.

The solidity of the floor beneath Her back came into focus well after She awoke. There was no sound indoors—only the chirruping of birds inching along the branches and puffing out their chests in their morning glory, and the scritching of land-bound critters happily searching for their rhythm atop the icy crust of this new day. She kept Her eyes closed to better hear the world waking. When She did open them, She began searching the thatch overhead without meaning to. Soon, the sticks began to rattle in the way that signaled a vision of the future. She shut Her eyes tight against it, in case a picture of Her own failure or its aftermath fizzed into view. She hoisted Herself up and sighed, a puff of breath nearly crystallizing before Her. The original plan for the pre-initiation hours remaining was to attempt the spell as often as time would allow until it had been perfected. But She knew it wouldn't be. Not with a brand-new emptiness vying for space beside Her grief. She walked over to the mantel and faced Agnes's portrait.

Forgive me, my love, She said with dour serenity. *I believe I may fail you today.*

Agnes offered neither consolation nor rebuke in return; she smiled flatly upon the whole scene in a way that seemed to merge the meaning of her lover with that of every other object. She paced to each corner of Her one-room cottage, past the cold ashes in the grate, and the table laden with fruit, cheese, and objects found during Her ploddings through the woods, one of which glowed white. She turned to look but could not see, for the glow obscured the shape of the thing. It lay next to a pile of acorns at the edge of the table. She gazed until Her eyes were sore, then blinked and found Herself... on Her back at the mouth of the fireplace. So, She hadn't avoided the vision after all. She rose and strode to the table as She had in Her vision, but without glancing at the portrait on the mantel. She couldn't bear just now to be another fly caught in the glazed web of Agnes's eyes. It was there, beside the pile of acorns, though it was not aglow. It was the fox bone Marguerite had asked about the day before. The one She had found sticking out of the frozen ground like a headstone in the woods. She picked it up and handled it, searching its roughness for some sort of vibration and finding none. She had not practiced the spell with bones. She would have had to rewrite the incantation. Besides, Agnes would not have approved—she would have called it desecration. No living things, nor even things that once had been so. The eggshells escaped that particular difficulty, for they merely housed what lived as it developed.

She replaced the bone on the table... but did not lift Her hand. She ran to the bookshelves and found the forest bestiary complete with anatomical drawings and labelings. Back on the floor She sat and smoothed out the page drawn with the mysterious word, which She had crumpled in Her sleeping hand. She found Agnes's drawing of a fox without skin or muscle, his most vulnerable self laid bare. Agnes had studied many things at the feet of the Mothers, including anatomy. Every bone was labeled, but no label matched what She had written on the torn page. So instead, She set upon every word in every book there present. Nothing matched. She considered that the symbols might be in Her own native tongue, but then, why would She—how *could* She—not understand? By the time She had turned every page in the cottage and wandered the woods thrice, hoping to relax Her mind into a state of understanding, the sun had begun its descent. She splashed Herself with water, scrubbed with a rough rag, and hastily wrapped Her body in the clothing She had set aside for Her initiation that night.

She had not practiced the spell even once that day. Perhaps they would laugh and ban Her from setting foot near their cave ever again. Laughter might be beneath them, but the Mothers were not known for their compassion. She gathered the unused shells of bird eggs, Her other ingredients, Agnes's grimoire and bell, and the ritual dagger before hurrying to the door. Halting at the last second, She turned back to grab the bone and shove it into the pocket of Her cloak. Anxiety was strangely absent as She trudged through the snow. Her fear of being cast out by them, Her only existing network in this particular realm of magical doings, had crescendoed and burst, leaving in its place a powerful numbness.

"Are you ready for your trial, sister?" A familiar voice floated to Her on the back of a breeze. But there were only trees every which way She looked.

"Perhaps, though less so than I should like," She replied uneasily.

Marguerite stepped out from behind a gnarled pine and grinned.

At the sight of a friendly face, She allowed one of the many knots in Her gut to unfurl. "Goodness," She whispered, hand held to Her thumping heart. "Now who behaves eerily?"

"Apologies for the fright. I only wanted to accompany you. I meant to set you at ease. An ill-advised attempt, I see."

She tried to grin back at Marguerite, but decided against disguising Her worry. "I do not know that anything could set me at ease this night, friend. Wait... how are you here? If you travel with me now, surely they will not let you into the meeting place. I am to be the last arrival."

"I am already there," Marguerite said, waving away Her concern.

Ah, She thought. Marguerite was a master of projection, and must have been doing so that very minute. "Are they not aware of your absence?"

"They care not," Marguerite replied. "As long as my body is where they want it, the rest is of no consequence to them." Marguerite held out her hand and She took it. Its warmth and substance were faint, but present. This heartened Her. Together they traveled through the woods until they were but a short distance from the rock face in which the coven now dwelt. She turned to Her friend, who left the ghost of a kiss upon Her forehead.

"No worries, now, my girl," Marguerite whispered, and was gone.

She loitered at the mouth of the cave until the tone of entry sounded. She then stepped across a thick line of ancient sand poured at the threshold to keep out the unwanted. The sand was rumored to be from the isle where Circe spent her days turning men into swine. None knew the actual ages of the Mothers—nor much else about them—so this rumor was not so unbelievable. She followed a gloomy tunnel that wound this way and that. More than once, She was faced with three paths and forced to choose which might bring Her closer to Her destination. Finally, She arrived at the ritual chamber to an immaculate silence. Every head but the Mothers' was bowed; every Child on her knees.

"Come," said the Mothers in unison, as they said most things.

The robed and hooded Children knelt in a perfect circle, leaving a gap just wide enough for Her to pass through. She tried not to search the circle for Marguerite's particular bearing. Her friend's duty as comforter had ended—She must now do what She had come to do. Or at the very least, attempt to hold onto Her dignity no matter the outcome. She strode to the center of the circle and knelt, bowing until Her forehead touched the grit of the stone floor.

"Rise," said the three who were one. "Tell us your business in this sacred place."

"I am here to Create, Mothers. I would be your Child."

"Is..."

"... that..."

"... so?" Each spoke in turn, stretching her neck toward their young hopeful as their words were uttered.

She screamed at Her nerves not to betray Her by causing an involuntary twitch. Truly, the longer She stared into the three pairs of black, unblinking eyes, the more the women appeared to merge into a single being. They were as vultures, their necks hung loosely with skin that looked as soft as freshly churned butter but was somehow held aloft like drooping shawls. Noses sharp as beaks prodded the air in front of them. At the elbows, their arms were linked like the spellworkers in Her dream. The memory of the symbols gleaming across Her mother's chest flashed, then died. She braced Herself to begin.

"Yes, Mothers."

"Do you truly believe yourself prepared to join this family?"

"Yes, Mothers."

"For reasons having naught to do with ego? For instance, to sate your grief?"

Her eyes widened. She opened Her mouth, but made no sound.

"*Well*, child?" asked the one on the right. A harsh smile twisted her face until it was unrecognizable as such. The other two grinned nastily in just the same way, eyes like glee-filled sickles shining with black blood.

"Yes... Mothers," She said, Her voice faltering. One, two, three eyebrows rose, but none spoke. She shook. The Mothers were unflinching, as statues carved from the walls surrounding them. She knew they were watching for any sign of weakness. Tears readied themselves at the corners of Her eyes, but She willed them away and swallowed the growing lump in Her throat. She would not move. She would not satisfy them so easily. After an age, the six eyes blinked for the first time, slowly, deliberately, and only once.

"Proceed," they said, the one on the left sweeping a hand outward in a generous arc.

She bowed again and reached into Her cloak for the necessary items. As She grabbed for the dagger wrapped in cloth, Her fingernails clicked against the fox bone. After laying out Her ingredients, She set the closed grimoire down beside Her magic circle in case, in Her nervous state, She forgot anything. The Mothers frowned, but did not speak. She knew they would view this as terribly childish, but there was no rule against having an external source of knowledge present. She opened a new slit in a new finger and squeezed blood into each prepared eggshell. After the last physical sigil was writ on the ground, She rang Agnes's spellwork bell and spoke the incantation. As the eggs smoked, She drew in the air above them the ancient symbols as practiced. Only this time... nothing happened.

Hurriedly, She mimed again the writing of symbols in the air, and still nothing appeared. Her chest began to tighten. *Please, no.* She had expected to fail, but not even a thousand of the most dreadful fantasies could have readied Her for the horrific vertigo that then took hold. Again and again, She swiped Her fingers through the air, and was met with the same lack every time. She packed each subsequent breath inside Her chest until it pained Her and prayed for the colors to show themselves.

The Mothers straightened their backs unanimously and

shifted their combined gaze to the witch, alone in the circle, struggling once more to contain Herself. "It seems you were not ready after all," they said, their voices ringing throughout the chamber, every echo a mockery.

"But..." She said, still trying to write Her energy into the air. *It could not be.*

"Perhaps..."

"... if it were your *own* spell..."

"... it might have worked."

She shook Her head in disbelief. She looked not at the Mothers, but through them, into nothing.

"Based on such a performance..."

"... we cannot..."

"... accept you."

She slumped, Her mind empty, and wept soundlessly. For months, She had attempted the spell again and again. She had hoped to succeed and to tell Agnes when next they met in Her dreams how it had all gone off, perhaps with a challenge or two, but without any real trouble. If only.

She sniffed and put Her hand in the pocket of Her cloak to find the rag. Her bloody fingers found the fox bone, which burned at Her touch. She screamed, yanking Her hand away. The Mothers, who had begun to turn their backs and dismiss the coven from the chamber, turned back to Her.

Breathing deeply, She returned Her hand to Her pocket and found the fabric that had covered the ritual dagger. This She used to remove the smoking bone from Her cloak. For a time, She could only stare at it. The bone heaved with energy. As the Mothers looked on, She swept the shells aside and bent to place the bone at the center of Her circle. When She stood upright She nearly fainted, overwhelmed by a heaviness—as if something had opened a door in Her to rest its immensity just inside. The image of the swaying women from Her dream reappeared more vividly in Her mind. She moved Her body in the serpentine way of those women, feeling, knowing, that

She should. Raising Her arms and arching Her back, the steps came more easily. She danced and danced, the fox bone still smoking at Her feet, not noticing when one of the bowed heads in the wider circle of witches rose to watch Her. The movements felt more familiar than they seemed in Her dream. She pointed the toes of one foot and swept it in an outward arc. One foot, then the other, over and over. She bent at the waist and increased Her speed, bringing Her elbows in. Then up Her hands flew to the stone sky. As She revolved in place, another of Her appeared. Without pause, the two of them continued to dance, and spun once more; a third appeared. By now, every head in the circle, once bowed, faced the multitudinous woman, agog. The Mothers' eyes sharpened, for three was a sacred number and they would not be supplanted. As one, they moved forward... until another of Her appeared. The Mothers froze, unsure of what they were seeing.

She danced and multiplied on until there were twenty of Her, swishing and winding with a slinky grace. None ever intruded upon another, even accidentally, though every single one, seeming to reside in a state of pure bliss, had Her eyes closed. As the witch spun Her selves into a whirlwind, the faces of each began to change. They slowed to a halt, heads bent to meet their knees. When She righted Herself, so did they all. She opened Her eyes and Her breath caught. Around Her were the women from Her dream... the women who had raised Her. Her bibi, spine curved elegantly in old age, white hair wild about her shoulders. Her aunties, mahogany skinned and shining with the glow of the dance. Their skirts were blood red and gold, threaded with all manner of jewels, for they were the queen's court and had sworn to look after her baby as their own. As She stared around Her into each beautiful brown face, warmth spread from Her chest to every extremity. Finally, when Her gaze fell upon the last woman, Her knees buckled and She could not breathe at all. The woman cut slowly across the center of the circle and wasted no time clutching Her to her wordless breast.

"Mama?" She asked, for how could it be? Her mama, Her queen, rubbed Her back until Her breath returned.

"Sweet child," Her mama whispered, and held Her close. The Mothers and their Children alike were in awe. None dared interrupt.

"I dreamed you." She spoke into Her mama's hair, as coarse with curls as She remembered.

"It is your talent, is it not?" Mama said, a smile in her voice.

She inhaled the complex scent of herbs, clay, charred nyumbu from the spit, and ash. "A vision?" She asked, pulling away to fully take in the sight of Her mama. "But, you do not wear the symbols. I spent the Sun's rise and fall trying to remember..." Her voice died in Her throat as She recalled wailing miserably into the night. She ran over to the circle She had drawn. At its center, the fox bone continued to throb inside a cloud of smoke. Tearing Her eyes from it, She grabbed Agnes's grimoire and yanked out the folded paper upon which the mysterious phrase was scrawled. She ran back to Her mama and held the paper up to her mournful eyes. Mama did not need to study what was written there. Instead, she leaned until her face emerged from behind the crumpled page.

"When did you forget?" Mama asked.

She bowed Her head in shame because it was indeed as She had feared. "When I arrived," She said. She waited to be chastised. Mama's hand appeared before her daughter's lowered eyes, touched Her chin, and brought Her face level.

"I am so sorry, dearest," Mama said.

Her brow rumpled in confusion. "Why?"

"You have forgotten that name because it is no longer yours. Remember what I taught you? When one queen passes from this life, her heir's name also passes from mind and heart to make way for what is new."

"You have... passed on?" The odor of ashes grew stronger as She stared in shock. The smell of charred meat was not leftover from the cooking of a wild beast, but from the ceremonial burning of Her mother's body, and that of her familiar whose soul had departed alongside hers. "Were you murdered?" She asked, clutching the beautiful fabric of Her mama's skirts, as real as could be.

"No, no. The veil began to fall over me long before you left, only slowly." The two sank into another embrace, this one dense with regret.

"Why did you not tell me?" She whispered.

"Because I knew that if I did, you would stay," Mama replied. "I wanted you to see as much of this world as you could without added burden. Our people have a great deal to be thankful for. We have been kept from harm by our gifts, but wider knowledge of this world would surely benefit us. When you are ready to return, you will do so with much to empower our people."

"I must return now!"

"No," Mama said, looking into Her eyes. "You must live, Mbweha."

At that, a clatter came from the magic circle on the ground where the bone rocked madly back and forth. The wider circle of Children finally broke, and the women of the coven gathered about the Mothers to both shield and be shielded. A rope of muscle shot out from within the bone, cracking it. Soon many more followed suit. A sphere expanded like an egg around the bone and the whipping cords of muscle until its top neared the ceiling. From the strange bone, more bones grew like ivy. The resultant skeleton was nearly the length of Agnes's cottage. Each strand of muscle thrashed as organs swelled into being within the ribcage, beginning their activities. The muscles calmed, stretching and wrapping about the skeleton until the whole was encased in living tissue. Hair sprouted here and there until it covered the beast like the finest silken robe. He turned his giant head until he found his mistress, and bowed until the black tip of his snout touched the floor. His ears, like massive mainsails, densely colored at their centers and white along their edges, rotated toward every sound in the echoing cave, and his tail, like the largest paintbrush, dipped in ink, swept the ground endlessly.

Mama backed away to join the women from the intact circle in kneeling. They raised their arms and chanted, *Malkia wa Mbweha! Malkia wa Mbweha! Malkia wa Mbweha!* Surely the past mattered; it had led her here. But nothing remembered or lost could preclude her evolution. No matter who she had ever been—when the sea carried her to an unfamiliar land; when love's richness remade her, and when its loss dismantled her; or when failure drew her into its waiting lap, laughing—she had become the Fox Queen.

Mbweha's giant familiar raised his head, seeking her approval. She glanced at her mama, who nodded, before walking slowly over to him. She held out her hand for him to sniff. When he was satisfied that he would know her scent anywhere, he pushed his nose, like a large wet plum, into her open palm. Mbweha giggled, burying her face in his fur, a mélange of beige and black that seemed to go on forever. His ears were open, pivoting endlessly. She traced their broad outline gently with her other hand.

"Masikio ya popo," she whispered, smiling as his large ear twitched at her touch. She considered alternatives, but knew a better name was unlikely to occur to her. The resemblance was quite striking. Thus she asked him, "May I call you Popo?"

The fox huffed wetly against her fingers, indignant at being compared to something as lowly as a bat. However, he conceded that their ears were indeed much alike. After apparent consideration, he dipped his head in agreement.

"You are bonded now, forever," Mama said, drawing sigils of union in the air, her voice sonorous. Mbweha ran to her mama, for she knew the members of this circle, whom she had summoned, must now depart—the living back to their waiting bodies, and the dead to their graves.

"I will return," Mbweha insisted.

"I know you will," Mama replied. "But not before you have seen what this world has to offer. Our people do not need you to govern them—only to enrich them. So do not return before you have accomplished great deeds, made great friends, and fallen in love."

Mbweha cast her eyes to the Children crowded round the Mothers. Marguerite, her curls now free of their hood and shivering in the wind made by Popo's swishing tail, smiled at her friend whose name she now knew. "I have done, Mama," she said. "But I will continue my journey." The women of her kingdom bowed to Mbweha once more and instantly began to fade, one at a time, from view. As the last of them disappeared, Mbweha hurried to share one more thing with her mother. "My beloved is where you are now. Her name is Agnes. Agnes Gifford."

Mbweha's mother's graying eyes brightened with pleasure. "I will pass onto her as much of your love as I can carry. I fear though that my arms will never be strong enough," she said, laughing and holding those same arms out to her daughter. And then they were gone, along with the rest of her.

Nothing but the sound of Popo's powerful breathing could be heard in the cave. Mbweha returned to his side to stroke his fur, forgetting momentarily that anyone else was there. The clearing of three throats brought her back to herself. When Mbweha turned to look, the Mothers' black eyes were on her, but their cast was somehow different than before. They were incandescent and stretched.

With fear.

The great Mothers, revered by multitudes in that region of the world, and others besides, balked in the presence of the unknown. Mbweha did not speak for she worried she might... laugh. Though Salem and its ways were known more deeply to them than to her, she knew unequivocally in that moment that she did not need their guidance—in magic or otherwise. Even with her mother and her great love dead, her true family remained. The creation of something from nothing was not always necessary. Especially when the essence of that which had been could be called back and transformed, by *her* magic.

"Resurrection?" the right-most Mother squawked, her voice tremulous.

"Blasphemy," said the left-most.

"Evil," whispered the central Mother.

Their Children were cemented in their places. All but Marguerite, who stepped tentatively toward Mbweha, a twinkle in her eye.

"Not exactly as planned, was it?"

And Mbweha did laugh then, noting with deep satisfaction the Mothers flinching in concert at the sound of her voice. "No. But I believe that is for the best."

Marguerite peeked slyly over her shoulder at her skittish coven and allowed herself a smirk. "Yes," she agreed. "I think you are right." She closed the distance between them and held Mbweha in a way that both would surely miss, for she knew what must come next. "Where will you go?"

"I am not certain," Mbweha replied. "There is so much to see and know in this world. Other magics to learn."

"I hope you are not thinking of abandoning your own way."

"Never again. But I am curious as to what I will find."

Marguerite smiled. "Will you return to teach me someday?"

Mbweha took Marguerite's sweet face into both hands and kissed it, hoping to leave some lasting trace of the love she felt. "You may rest assured, dear friend."

Stepping back, Mbweha inclined her head respectfully to the Mothers, who still shuddered faintly at the center of their unmoving flock. After touching Marguerite's hand for the last time in what was sure to be a long time, she returned to the circle drawn in her drying blood to gather Agnes's things from the ground. She would bury them beside the unmade birds in the forest. Popo came to Mbweha without being called. In the glistening pool of his eye, she saw herself far away, the location wholly unfamiliar.

"Where then, darling, will you find me next?" Mbweha wondered aloud to her beloved, her soul alive with what could be. Searching the depths of Popo's eye, she thought she saw Agnes there.

Let us see then, my love, she replied.

UNDER YOUR SKIN

Fluid slid from the little creature's mouth like drool. Its face was balled up, eyes pinched shut and lips mushed together except for two small gaps on either side of its mouth. From those spaces, formaldehyde leaked in a steady rhythm. Phillip imagined the tray in front of him filling with it. Sure, dissections could be interesting, but the smell made him sick. His stomach clenched. Pull yourself together, he thought. Vomiting on their specimen wouldn't be a good look. What would his lab partner think? *Well, something at least*, some tiny, wretched voice inside him said. It would be more than she thought of him now. No one thought anything about Phillip.

Was it wrong, pathetic even, to wish he were already home, alone in his room? It would've been nice to skip over the hours between now and dinnertime. After all, it wasn't like he could look forward to meeting up with anyone in the hall later, or to walking part of the way home with a classmate after school. Phillip often imagined what it would be like to have friends. People you could talk to about things. *What would you talk about, Phillip?* Oh, anything, really, he thought. Everything and nothing.

In any case, all Phillip had to look forward to was being

shunted endlessly between the aggressive shoulders of his classmates en route to his locker. They would shout to one another above him, because he was at least a head shorter than most of them. They would laugh about things that had nothing to do with him, denying him a place in their world as anything other than a nameless extra. And his teachers were no better. Last week, his algebra teacher completely missed their tutoring session. Phillip had sat at his desk with a notebook and pencil for forty-five minutes before the janitor came in to empty the trashcans. He told Phillip he hadn't seen anyone in that part of the school for a while. Drowning in self-loathing, Phillip thanked the janitor and went home. The next day, Phillip asked his teacher what had happened. Turns out she'd forgotten, but—and this was said with a casual wave of her hand—she was sure he would be fine.

It galled him, existing this way. A shadow on the walls that watched all the other boys and girls get recognized as sentient flesh and blood. Meanwhile, he had to make do as a discard, trimmed away from something greater, but he had no idea what. A nudge from his partner brought him out of his daze.

"Sorry," he muttered.

"You pretty much murdered the intestines," she said, laughing.

Phillip looked down at the hand holding the scalpel. The blade was indeed halfway through the unborn piglet's tract, and digging deeper. Phillip pulled the instrument out slowly and handed it to Amy. "You can finish taking them out if you want," he said. "The right way, I mean," he added. Amy grabbed the knife from Phillip and asked him what was next on the worksheet, but his attention was elsewhere.

A boy in the center of the room had an entire table to himself. He was white, tall, thin but muscular, and had a head full of curly, orange hair. Everybody knew him; he was the first ninth-grader to make varsity wrestling in twenty years and, from what Phillip heard while shuffling through the halls on any given day, was chiefly responsible for the team's thus far immaculate record this season. He was also the object of several crushes. Even some senior girls had it bad for this guy. That made Phillip sick, too, but in a different way than pickled dead things did. Girls glanced Phillip's way sometimes, but never did anything more. Even though his mother said the hair on his head was the "good" kind, and his father's genetic contribution prevented Phillip being as dark as she was, tan skin and curly hair had never been enough on its own to make girls pay him any special attention. He sometimes wondered if maybe he just didn't know how to play it up properly. But the real, deep-down truth of it was that he did not have the will to try. Anyway, the school photos at Barringer Country Day—not to mention the mall, or any given aisle at the grocery store in this town—were dotted so infrequently with color that Phillip assumed, for most of the girls there, dating him wasn't really an option. Not on the same level as shooting up in front of your grandmother at her eightieth birthday party, but still something to be avoided if possible.

Phillip only had Honors Biology with this boy, who wasn't a "lifer" like many of the other kids who had attended this school since pre-K. Neither was Phillip, who had been awkwardly enrolled at the start of eighth grade, well after the bonds typically formed in grades one and six at a normal school had been solidified. When returning their work, Miss Carter made a habit of laying the stack of graded materials on whatever desk was nearest at the time. As the mound of papers made its way around the room, each student was expected to find the sheet with their name on it before passing the shrinking pile along. As such, Phillip had seen his classmates' grades often enough to know who had more than generous donors for parents and a pile of rocks inside their head, and who didn't. If his grades were any indication, the boy with the orange hair was one of the smartest kids in class. The other jocks only studied hard enough to be allowed to play since they couldn't if they flunked. They did little more than show up during the rest of the year. It seemed wrong. Why wasn't Phillip allowed to give only the bare minimum and still get what he really wanted? It's true, he didn't have much in the way of natural ability. But he worked hard for every scrap of knowledge he had. Shouldn't that count for something?

Phillip's hands were in such tight fists that they began to ache, so he let them fall open. It was dumb, being jealous of someone he knew almost nothing about. For all he knew, that kid had people lining up to do his work for him. Phillip looked back down at the tray and at Amy's busy hands as she deftly cut organs from their pig, placing each one delicately onto the shining metal surface beside the carcass. The pig's body was nearly empty now. This class was not easy, but he kept up without too much trouble. He could do without the odors that attended dissection, but in general, he was intrigued by the inner workings of the body. Though it wouldn't be happening for another year and a half, he had already decided he would try to swallow his disgust and give AP Biology a try. Physics, too, if he could somehow get his algebra up to snuff.

Phillip looked back at the boy with the orange hair, expecting to see his pig's organs laid out in some absurd order, like longest to shortest or in a sequence that made some sick, gray-scale rainbow. However, there was nothing on the table but a tray and a pig, which Phillip realized was untouched. Class was half over and the boy had done nothing but stare at his specimen the entire time. Maybe he really was stupid after all.

Miss Carter walked over to the boy's table and spoke to him in a low voice. He nodded, but continued to stare at the pig. When he finally moved his right hand, Phillip caught sight of something bright on his wrist before his sleeve slid to cover it. It was a beaded bracelet. Phillip wouldn't have pegged this boy for someone that... whimsical. The flame-haired boy stroked the nipples of his fetal pig adoringly before letting his braceleted hand settle. Suddenly, he plunged a scalpel into the tiny beast's stomach with his other hand. Phillip jumped. In the focused silence of the classroom, the blade made contact with a sound like a small tire being punctured.

Amy had by now removed every internal organ left from their pig and was ready to answer the last questions on the worksheet. "Phillip?" she said. "Helloooo?" She touched his forearm with her fingertips, electrifying Phillip into knocking a pair of surgical scissors to the floor.

As the doors separating the densely packed halls from the outside world opened, Phillip tried to measure his relief. He almost floated over each stair and its carpet of dead leaves to the sidewalk below. The autumn air was crisp enough to suck the moisture from his lips and force his mouth into a trumpeting pucker. Phillip loved being affected by nature. Unlike in his interactions with other people, his passivity outdoors seemed only right. The natural world had existed longer than any person, and would continue long after. The wind pushed him along in a parody of his own mother's occasional impatience with him. The rain clung to his curls and dangled artfully from the tip of his nose before plummeting into a puddle of like-molecules at his feet. And in the fall, the leaves spun and ricocheted off of one another as they fell—brown, red, and yellow jewels—battling for Phillip's attention before resting on the grass, in the hood of his jacket, or in the palm of his hand. It all made him feel small, but in a pleasant way. Like he had permission to be ordinary.

Phillip crossed the street that ran between the school's entrance and the woods. The trees were frozen in poses of utter despair. Some threw their branches to the sky, imploring the tree gods to change their collective fate and keep them from brittle death's edge. Some bent their wooden arms low into the path the humans traveled, seeking pity from beings not scaly with centuries-old bark. There were holes in their middles that opened into a pitch-black not even deemed safe by the squirrels and birds, who appeared to take their chances only upon the sturdiest branches or elsewhere in some other forest altogether. Sometimes it frightened Phillip to walk this trail, which seemed to snake on forever through the trees, perhaps ending in an unfamiliar realm. But because it was the best shortcut home, Phillip swallowed his fear.

When he was a quarter of the way down the path, he heard a twig snap behind him. He turned around, but saw no one. He walked on and eventually heard the same sound, this time much closer, but decided not to look again. He felt a tap on his shoulder, but before he could get the culprit in his sights, a fist collided with his jaw. Phillip's head and body did an abrupt about-face. As he went down, he watched the blurry world zoom up and away. His teeth clacked as his chin hit the ground.

Phillip heard the crush of leaves underfoot as his attacker stepped in front of him. His eyes were askew. One observed the slow-moving shell of a snail in its determined crawl along a blade of grass; the other saw a crowd of tree roots jostling for a place aboveground. Phillip shook his head until his eyes were trained in the same direction. They landed on a pair of tube socks over two legs tinged the red of raw meat. Phillip raised his eyes, past dirty kneecaps and cargo shorts. His assailant's fists loosened. On one wrist was a bracelet that looked homemade. It was just an elastic bit of string wound through big, orange beads made of soft-looking plastic. You could probably mash each little sphere flat with two fingers if you squeezed hard enough. It was familiar, but Phillip was too dazed to make the connection. Rather than use up energy making sense of things, he let his eyes continue to rove. They found a navy blue t-shirt with the white outline of a hand in a rude shape. Phillip stared into the fuck-you-shaped pool, mesmerized.

"Hey, Phillip." The speaker's head was at an angle. Despite the sunlight obscuring his features, it was clear that he was evaluating his quarry.

"The fuck?" Phillip spat, trying out the word for himself. He bared his soil-speckled teeth.

"What?" the boy replied innocently. He might have just shown up.

"*What is your problem?*"

The boy extended a hand to his fallen victim. Phillip folded his brow as the beaded wrist hovered closer. Small domes of blood dotted the boy's knuckles. Phillip remembered his teeth catching briefly on the skin of that hand as the fist first parted his lips. The domes broke even as they formed. Phillip scowled up at the boy, whose hair was a bright orange halo. The face remained invisible, obscured by shadow as the sun burst behind his unholy head. Phillip wondered if maybe that punch had killed him.

As the boy bent forward, rays of light sliced the skin of his eyes apart. His irises were a slyly faceted jade and emerald mosaic. They were prisms, glassy and infinite. Phillip saw himself reflected a thousand times: sticky with dirt-peppered blood, swollen-faced, eyes wide and tired.

"You're angry aren't you, Phillip?" the boy asked. "So fight back."

Phillip knew that, in civilized society, anger often attended something dramatic—spitting, kicking, storming off. Not lying used up on the ground like a piece of human garbage. But people were complicated creatures. Phillip's anger had already begun whooshing out of him. At that moment, he lacked the wherewithal even to glare. Rather than hoist his body from the ground, he made a home for it in the dirt. What could he really do, anyway? He'd never fought anyone before. Even if he managed to land one punch, that would be the height of his luck. He'd only end up deeper underground if he fought back. Phillip pressed his face into the soil and breathed in. He immediately coughed up a spray of dirty saliva that burned his nostrils. He turned his face to lie on his bruised cheek and closed his eyes.

"I'm Martin," the strange boy said.

Of course you are, Phillip thought. Martin Foley. The boy from his Biology class with hair like fire. An image from earlier that day blinked into remembrance: Martin hunched over the corpse of his fetal pig. Staring into Martin's eyes, Phillip recognized the same fascination. "How do you know who *I* am?" he asked.

Martin didn't answer. His eyes had glazed over. They were on Phillip, but somewhere else, too. Maybe he'd stay that way long enough for Phillip to slither off and leave him to wonder, like everyone did, whether he had ever truly been there at all. Too late. Martin's eyes refocused and his pupils shook as they steadied on Phillip. Without warning, he grabbed Phillip's face with one hand. Pressing a thumb against one cheek and mashing his fingers into the other, Martin squeezed and shifted the flesh there like putty. Phillip's nerve endings howled where his battered skin was being worked over, and he jerked away. The sting of his teeth against the inside of his fattening cheek was sharp. Martin brought his own face closer until their noses touched. His breath made Phillip's chapped lips a desert. He didn't know, couldn't decide, if he minded.

"Let's be friends," Martin said with what could only be love. And as the seeds of screams threatened to blossom in Phillip's belly, his body trembled.

Phillip felt the wet warmth of a mouth at the shell of his ear. It whispered words he couldn't make out, but that made his groin throb and stomach ache nonetheless. Martin's tongue entered Phillip's ear and he awoke from his strange dream bewildered. The clock beside his bed told him it was far too late, or too early, to be awake. Sticky with sweat, Phillip swung his legs over and eased out of bed. He moved like a man of seventy from his bed to the hall bathroom. He had become a mutant version of himself. One cheek was so large, the eye above it had been forced shut. Both eye and cheek were purple because Martin had decided to punch Phillip a few more times before helping him up. Phillip's bottom lip had split open to reveal a strip of red shining in a valley of dry skin. He put a finger to it, but yanked it away at the sting of his own touch.

What exactly, he wondered, had he done to deserve this? His reflection seemed as vacantly overwhelmed in the face of such a question as Phillip felt inside. Perhaps the mediocrity of his existence had reached a level so obscene, the mechanics at work in the natural world had moved to correct it. Checks and balances; he had learned about that last year, in Intro to US Government. He stood there a long time, tallying the cuts and bruises, willing an answer to appear from nothing.

As he sidled through the doorway into Bio the next day, he saw that Martin was already in his seat, as were most of his classmates. The two boys locked eyes briefly before Phillip slid silently into a chair beside Amy, who didn't even pretend she wasn't fascinated by the giant lump on his face that was now the color of sewer water. After glimpsing his own handiwork, Martin let his eyes fall to the table before him and smirked. Phillip's face ruddied as pair after pair of eyes fell upon him and the staccato'd whispers of his classmates pecked at the air around him like agitated birds. At least Miss Carter had the decency to look away eventually. Unlike his mother, who had stared all through dinner the night before.

"How did you say you got those bruises again?" she'd asked, unable to believe what she was seeing. Phillip recounted the tale he had come up with on the way home. He told her a group of kids on bikes had sped down the path and knocked him face-first into the nearest tree, where a heavy branch fell on him and finished the job. He sensed his story might not quite account for the severity of his injuries. Phillip rarely got into accidents because he rarely left the house except for school. And even if something happened there, he usually managed to come out of it unscathed. He was surrounded by a bubble of irrelevance so thick that even objects were repelled from causing him harm. She had taken extra care tucking him in that night—something she hadn't done since he was in kindergarten—kissing her fourteen-year-old son tenderly on the forehead. Phillip had closed his right eye tightly (the left was already swollen shut) as a single, warm drop of water fell from her eye to his cheek. He kept it closed until she left the room.

"C'mon, man," Phillip had whispered up at the ceiling, indignant, as he was now. In class, he straightened, arching his back, and cut a hard line through the air with the tops of his shoulders. He set what was left of his jaw in invisible concrete and remained this way until the bell rang, releasing everyone else from the spell of his violent ugliness and him from the weight of their conspicuous glances. He moved quickly to his locker to switch his science book out for his math book. He had a top locker and noticed with a hint of pride that the person with the bottom locker grimaced when he looked up and saw Phillip's misshapen face. He grabbed what he could and scurried away. But Phillip's ghastly smile fell when he shut his locker door and found Martin standing on the other side.

"Feels good, huh?" he asked, like he knew exactly what Phillip had just been thinking. Maybe he did. But Phillip feigned ignorance.

"What does?" he replied without feeling. Martin's eyes were slits.

"You know exactly what I mean," he said. Phillip held his breath as Martin moved in closer. "That kid just now. He jumped when he saw you. A lot better than being invisible, right?"

Phillip gave himself away then, allowing his eyebrows to creep up his forehead. Martin laughed.

"No need to thank me," he said before punching Phillip playfully on the shoulder.

"*Thank* you?" Phillip shouted. A couple of passing classmates turned to look. Hot-faced, he lowered his voice. "Are you insane?"

"No. I just know how you feel."

"You don't know shit."

"I know you don't like being ignored," Martin said.

Any reply that may have followed dried up in Phillip's throat.

"Getting banged up makes you look tougher. People get interested. They respect you more," Martin continued. "You could use some of that, couldn't you?"

Phillip thought he could see it now, what made Martin so powerful in these halls. He had the confidence of someone three times his age. It never occurred to Martin that he might not know what he was talking about, which made you question whether you knew as much as you thought you did, even about yourself.

Phillip's cousins had wasted no time in calling him soft when they found out he went to "that fancy school" but, to his mind, looking tough wasn't a problem in a place like this. In fact, he was sure it didn't even mean the same thing to his mother's family as it did to most of his classmates. Moving according to the definition he'd grown up with would surely steer him toward an altogether different end than what Martin seemed to imagine, or was likely to face himself. Respect, on the other hand, was something Phillip could do with. Though from what he'd gleaned so far, getting the shit kicked out of him seemed to inspire more in the way of pity or concern than reverence. But beggars couldn't well be choosers, could they?

Phillip considered Martin's words. It sounded like he was offering some sort of arrangement, though Phillip couldn't quite work it out. The air around the two of them was dead; they had landed in a private abyss. Certainty settled upon Phillip that he had been shoved into outer space. If he screamed, or if Martin decided to rip him open and eat whatever was inside, no one would ever know.

"So?" Phillip asked. "What's in it for you?"

Martin's awful grin reappeared, and Phillip shuddered without meaning to. "I like you, Phillip," he said. Phillip resisted the urge to back away. "I wanna help you."

No you don't. The words leapt to mind immediately, but Phillip said nothing. He had no idea what Martin really wanted from him, but knew he wouldn't find out if he didn't follow the breadcrumb trail where it led. Besides, even if his nerves were spitting like live wires ripped free in a storm... the attention felt nice.

Phillip's mother's concern over the number of "accidents" her son seemed to be getting into only grew, and he was running out of plausible excuses. Not that it mattered whether he came up with one or not. He knew his mother suspected he was getting jumped regularly and that her phone calls to the school principal were behind the increase in security on school grounds, the heightened number of teachers in the hallways between classes, and his last three invitations to speak with Ms. Sharpe, the guidance counselor. His mother begged him to tell her what was going on, said the principal had called to make clear that they don't accept violence at BCD but could only put a stop to it if they knew who was involved. Phillip wouldn't budge. They had their first argument ever when she sat beside him in tears as he watched television through swollen eyes one night after finishing his homework. She kissed his hands and asked again what she could do to help him. She had always buried her own needs in the shadow of her son's. At six years old, Phillip climbed onto the kitchen countertop to reach the cereal bowls in protest as his mother filled a large pot with water at the kitchen sink. They'd had spaghetti two nights in a row, and that would've been the third. On tiptoe, he reached for the big red bowl that could hold the most, but lost his balance. He fell toward the stovetop and its glowing coils, but his mother got there first, snatching him away and burning her arm in the process. She cried then, too, but soundlessly, eyes as red as the shards of bowl that rocked out of time with one another on the floor. Her own pain meant nothing to her. If he needed to be taken out of school, she would find him another one. Or she could home-school him.

"No!" Phillip screamed, voice scraping with uncharacteristic force against his throat. "I'm already basically friendless! You wanna keep me here like a little baby so you can watch me all the time?"

His mother jerked in her seat, the corners of her eyes pinching slowly together in shock and sympathy. "I just want you to be safe. You may not be a baby, but..."

"DON'T say it!" Phillip shot up and swayed under the sudden rush of his own blood. His mother tried to help steady him, but he snatched himself away from her touch. He saw the rest of her unspoken words in his head. It made him feel like a fucking toddler every time she said it. *You may not be a baby, but you'll always be* my *baby*. If he could smooth out any wrinkle in his brain, it would be the one where that sentence lived. "Bad things happen, Ma, alright? It's fine! Stop hovering all the damn time!" As soon as the words left him, he knew a line had been crossed. His mother had always been compassion itself, but Phillip wasn't stupid. He knew he'd never be too old to be her baby *or* to catch those hands.

"Boy, you better get control of that mouth."

"I—I'm sorry. Just... please, stop asking. Please." And before his mother could say anymore, he went to his room and shut the door.

Martin invited Phillip over for dinner about a month from the time their little deal was struck. Perhaps it was the lingering memory of that argument that made his mother say, after days of taut silence, that he could go. Phillip was sure she thought someone inviting him over was a good sign. Even if his new friend had to help her son stand up for himself, at least someone would be allowed to. She would have dropped her plate of bacon and eggs to the floor had she known Phillip was asking permission to visit the lion in his den.

Martin's place was run-down, and the least charming of those collected in his neighborhood. Instead of an expansive wooden porch like the others, there was just a small, concrete stoop out front on which the scattered remains of a broken flowerpot rested. The long-dead plant inside hung over the top step, beyond classification. There was a clear separation between the Foleys' lawn and that of their neighbors. Where bright green life ended, brown death began. Grass shot out of the cracked ground in tufts of gnarled blades, each too dry even to flex at a finger's nudge. After hearing the anguished crunch of the former flower underfoot, Phillip lifted his shoe a little too quickly, waking the nerves clustered around his latest injury. He slipped a hand under his sweater to caress his side where a portion of the lowest rib had no doubt been cracked by the toe of Martin's shoe a few days before.

After readjusting into the least painful posture he could, Phillip thumped the front door with his fist. A shuffling grew steadily louder until finally the door swung open, revealing a woman only an inch or so taller than he was with a head full of greasy red hair streaked with white that hung in clumps like wasps' nests around her face. She wore an overlarge, long-sleeved t-shirt, and corduroys the color of mustard. She also wore a beaded bracelet on her right wrist in a deep purple. She looked tired, but kind.

"Are you Phillip?" she asked. Phillip decided then and there that he liked her, if only because her voice was so determined to meet the air—despite how worn out it seemed to become in the process.

"Y-yes, I'm—"

"Welcome," she said, wrapping her arms around him. His nose was buried in hair that smelled of earth and cloves. "I'm Molly," she said. Phillip clocked eyes that were the same disturbing shade of green as Martin's. "It's so wonderful to meet you." Phillip winced as her grip tightened. "Martin's told us all about how you two have become such great friends. I was so excited when he said you'd be coming for dinner. He never brings friends over." She let go, reluctantly it seemed, in favor of linking arms with him and ushering him inside. "Miles! Martin's friend is here—come meet him!" She sounded as pleased by Phillip's presence as he suspected his own mother secretly was about his being invited somewhere by a "friend." But Martin must have tons of friends.

Stains crusted the carpets, and piles of out-of-date newspapers lay next to a broken TV set Phillip was sure no company made anymore. Each sunken cushion on the floral-patterned sofa put the intimate knowledge of a different body rawly on display. The condition of the room in no way matched its contents, which looked like remnants of a 70s-era garage sale. Phillip grew more uneasy the farther he advanced into their home. Like he had intruded upon something that could only rightly be captured in a nature show narrated by a deep, hypnotic voice to an audience watching safely from thousands of miles away. Phillip thought of complaining about some made-up illness and bolting. But the woman gripping his arm for dear life seemed so happy to have him there. A great wave of guilt kept his feet moving forward.

"Umm, where's Martin, Mrs. Foley?" he asked. The sides of her mouth drooped.

"Ms., hun," she corrected him and he wondered why. "But call me Molly. He's upstairs in his room."

"Should I go up, then?" Phillip tried. Her stare was incredulous, as though she could not understand why anyone would suggest such a thing.

"He'll come down when he's ready," she said, squeezing Phillip's forearm and resuming their cheerful parade through the house. When they reached the kitchen, Phillip was greeted by the back of a very tall individual who was at that moment rummaging through the refrigerator. There was nothing cooking either on the stove or in the oven, the maw of which hung agape beside the open fridge. At the sound of their footsteps, the man turned around, clutching a number of things to his chest. "Miles, I told you I would order pizza," Molly said.

"At's uhrright, Mahl," the man replied with the twisted end of a bag of bread clamped between his teeth. After letting the bag fall onto the counter, he said, "All I want is a sandwich." In the man's arms were bags of turkey, buffalo chicken, honey-baked ham, salami, olive loaf, Brie, Cheddar, and Swiss cheese. There was also a container of horseradish in his left hand, mustard in his right, and a jar of mayonnaise pinned beneath his chin. Rolled a small way up his forearm was a bracelet with large, white beads. "Who do we have here?"

"This is Phillip," Molly said, smiling warmly at their guest.

"Oh, right, Martin's friend." The man had a face like Martin's, red hair and green eyes, but everything about him was muted. Rather than a fiery orange, his hair was the faded color of a shirt washed too many times. His eyes were so light, they looked almost blue. He did however share his family's uncanny ability to make Phillip feel like all the layers of his skin had been peeled back. Phillip played with the hem of his shirt as he tore his eyes away from Miles in search of a less threatening view.

"How are you, sir?" he mumbled. Since this would normally be the part where they shook hands, Phillip extended his automatically across the width of the table separating them... before remembering that the hand he intended to shake held a condiment. Phillip allowed his unshaken hand to fall awkwardly away. The man's eyes laughed, but his mouth remained a disinterested line above his chin. As easy as it was to think of the woman at his elbow as *Molly*, it was that much harder for Phillip to see Miles as anyone but *Mr. Foley*.

"Well, I'll be in the basement if anybody needs me," Mr. Foley called over his shoulder. Clinging to his haul, he made his way to an opening at the edge of the kitchen through which a faint light could be seen glowing from below. The refrigerator door was left ajar. One of the three chairs around the table had its back to the open basement. Phillip thought the chair looked seconds away from being devoured and made a mental note not to sit there when it was time to eat.

"Miles, we have a *guest*," Molly said, her whole demeanor a sigh.

"Look, Mol, I can't just do nothing and expect the answer to waft down to me from on high like the blasted word of God," he said. His expression read like disdain without changing in any discernible way. "We both know that's not how this works. You of all people should want me to get this right. I know you don't wanna go around looking like *that* forever." Molly lowered her eyes. So this is what Martin's been taking out on me, Phillip thought. He balled up his fists until they shook before letting them unspool at his sides. He very nearly sneered at himself. He couldn't even convincingly argue his own right to exist without being overlooked or undermined; what made him think he could be of any use in defending a grown woman? He chose instead to redirect the flow of conversation.

"Are you a cosmetologist, Mr. Foley?" He didn't seem the type, but Phillip knew better than to assume anything about the people in this family.

Miles paused on the threshold of the doorway and turned around, his face inscrutable. "I guess you could say that," he replied. His tone of voice halted the flow of Phillip's blood. "But more than that, I suppose. I'm something of a chemist. Does science interest you, Phillip?"

Phillip answered in the affirmative with as much enthusiasm as he could, despite the memory of the sometimes nauseating smells that went along with it. It was then that the opaque entrance to the basement, which he had avoided looking at directly until that moment, enveloped his vision. He noticed a familiar scent emanating from the bowels of the house, one he couldn't quite place, but that would not give up its hold on his senses. It was sharp, distinct. *Clinical.* The word emerged in bold at the front of his mind. "What do you do, Mr. Foley?"

Miles unloaded the various fixings in his arms onto the tiny dining table. His smile reminded Phillip of the one Martin had worn that day by his locker. Phillip wasn't sure he really wanted to know what it was Mr. Foley did down there after all, where the air was cold and blew out in gusts, carrying with it the smell of decay.

"I'm a scientist," he replied. Molly pursed her lips as she looked first at Miles, then down at the black and white tile of the kitchen floor and the sticky stains spotting it here and there. "I—"

"He's a mortician." Miles shifted his gaze to the source of the words, and Molly closed her eyes as if preparing to be struck down. Phillip turned to see Martin, his rosy skin and thick frame like a blockade set up halfway down the living-room stairs.

"Ah, there he is!" Miles said. "My perfect boy."

Martin's hair and eyes seemed more intense than usual. Their brilliance against the drab, gray-blue paint on the wall behind him made Phillip feel like his head might explode. Martin finished his descent and stood before Phillip, who had to raise his eyes to meet his classmate's, something he didn't recall having to do since the day Martin loomed over his prone body in the woods. Rather than greet Phillip, Martin turned to stare his wan, outsized doppelgänger down. Miles looked upon Martin with the kind of pride Phillip imagined was usually reserved for the completion of a magnum opus. Martin exuded another feeling altogether —something like hatred. That's when it hit Phillip: the smell.

With recognition came horrific visions of scabby limbs protruding from the cover of a white sheet. Phillip pictured the cloth being pulled away to reveal mouths frozen in a final wail. The eyes watery and bulbous. Crooked noses. Black teeth. The smell of moldering corpses yet to be lowered into the earth.

Phillip searched the faces of man, woman, and child. Feeling his gaze, the family turned their eyes upon him as one, each imparting a different illegible secret without words. Finally, Miles said, "I don't do the embalming here. I just compose the mixtures." Plural, as in more than one. After sensing the follow-up question on Phillip's lips, he continued, "I feel more comfortable working out of my own house."

"I thought embalming fluid was always the same," Phillip said.

"Oh no," Miles replied, definitely smug. "Of course every embalmer uses different percentages of the primary chemicals." He extended a finger for each in turn: "Formaldehyde, ethanol, methanol, blah, blah, blah," he said, opening and closing his hand like the mouth of a puppet. "What makes each mixture truly unique, however, are the additional preservatives the embalmer includes, which differ according to the condition of the body you're working on. Don't they teach you guys about this in school?"

Phillip shook his head slowly. Martin didn't move an inch, save for one twitching muscle near his mouth.

"Ah, well... I guess it wouldn't be every instructor's cup of tea." Phillip couldn't remember meeting another person who so obviously loved their job. He was sure Mr. Foley would be all too glad to guide him in the serious consideration of a future in mortuary work. "In any case, it's been my goal to produce a mixture that can preserve a body beyond the standard length of time. I guess you could say I'm trying to create the ultimate embalming fluid." He smiled and Phillip thought he saw the face of someone much younger show through. Miles fingered the beads on his bracelet.

By this time, Molly stood under the kitchen archway with her back to the three of them. She held herself in a loose embrace and looked with longing at the photographs ascending diagonally beside the staircase. They were the usual family photos. In one picture faded with age, a pair of people Phillip didn't recognize crouched and held hands behind an androgynous trio of children who nested between one another's legs like dolls, oldest to youngest, the youngest being an infant. Martin's grandparents most likely, as there was a distinct resemblance, though Phillip couldn't decide whether they were maternal or paternal. In a more recent photo, the same man and woman, noticeably older, held a laughing child aloft between them, each supporting a leg with one of their shoulders. The child looked to be about Phillip's height with a build similar to Martin's, though far less... filled out. Perhaps the image had been captured a couple of years prior, before Martin was on the wrestling team, or before middle school even. The child in most of these photos did not look like an athlete. Yet, he was Martin. A gentler, happier Martin. One photo in particular caught Phillip's eye. In it, a family posed in a fashion once favored by department store photographers: a woman sat in the foreground, a child at her side and a man behind, each resting a hand on one of her shoulders. She wore a sky-blue dress and her hair fell in slightly uneven layers to her pointed chin. The man fizzed with enthusiasm, light-hearted, almost carefree, with hair a far more vivid shade of maroon than that of the man in the kitchen. The child looked quite small, shorter even than Phillip. And his hair and eyes weren't such violent shades of red and green. His mouth was open, as if he were speaking. He even had freckles, which were currently subsumed by his blushing skin. His naked happiness was beautiful. The word occurred to Phillip naturally as warmth diffused from his navel outward. He shook the feeling off and confusion settled in its place. The family in the photo definitely resembled the one in the kitchen, but the photo looked older than it should. Martin's development was normal enough—Phillip knew plenty of guys who had a better relationship with puberty than he did—but his parents seemed to have aged significantly since then. Was it stress? As Phillip's glazing eyes took in their smiling faces, the word *bodysnatchers* bobbed against his skull's ceiling and he could not blink it away.

Phillip thought of his own mother and the sometimes reluctant ease with which she let him out into the world. He was definitely not a kite whose string ended in a speck for her, but she did trust him. Or at least, she used to. This was because they knew each other the way two people who had only one another must. Phillip recalled their argument and wondered if his arrangement with Martin would be what turned him and his mother into funhouse versions of themselves, too.

Molly did not seem comfortable with the version of her family that existed outside of photographs. She hummed in barely audible tones that Phillip imagined took her back to a different time. She hugged herself tight and swayed, like the dead flower on their doorstep briefly reanimated. The aperture of her movements narrowed until she stilled completely. "I'd better order that pizza," she said, the words soft in their tumble from her lips. Miles took that as his cue and disappeared into the basement. As Molly dialed, Martin stared accusingly at Phillip, as though the awkwardness of the last ten minutes was all his fault. Then he grabbed Phillip's wrist and squeezed, offering a weak smile.

When the pizza arrived, Molly and the boys sat around the table pulling slices from the box and up to their mouths. No plates. No napkins. New drops of oil decorated the tabletop; Phillip thought of them as his own biodegradable tag. *Phil wuz here*. If spied through the kitchen window, they would have looked like a tableau of construction workers, too fatigued from the day to trouble themselves with neatness. Phillip spent the time before the pizza arrived listening to Molly's stories about baby Martin, her parents, and her days as a college student. She painted such a complete picture of her past that Phillip started to feel like he had grown up with her. Martin remained silent, sometimes deigning to shoot Phillip a look that fell somewhere between annoyance and sage forbearance.

When the last slice was gone, Molly said, "Well, that's all, folks! Guess I should take this out back to the recycling." Phillip couldn't believe they recycled anything. Molly rolled up her sleeves like she might take an entire stack of pizza boxes out back. Phillip stared at the livid bruises covering her arms until Molly pulled her sleeves back down. "I'm super clumsy," she said, laying a hand on Phillip's. Martin clenched his jaws. Seeing this, Molly yanked her hand away and carried the box outside.

Phillip had called his mother as soon as the pizza came and told her she could pick him up in a few hours, which turned out to be too long. Martin never offered to show

Phillip his room or any other. He had eaten the most of the three of them, gobbling each slice ravenously, and was rummaging through the refrigerator when Phillip's mother eventually arrived. Phillip answered the door and practically shoved her away from the house. She did catch a glimpse of a disheveled Molly, who waved eagerly at her, insisting that she join them next time. Phillip's mother returned the greeting, but must have been too far from the porch by then to properly make out Molly's hair because she never mentioned it.

"Where was your friend, Martin?" she asked when they were on the road. "Is he shy about meeting people?"

In Phillip's opinion, he wasn't shy enough. "He was doing the dishes," he said instead.

"Oh? Now that's nice. What did his mother make for dinner?"

"Lasagna and green beans with garlic bread," Phillip rattled off immediately, still careful to exhale only enough to make the words heard, in case she caught a whiff of his breath. She was the kind of parent who cooked most nights. Rarely did they eat what she considered "junk food," which was basically anything made outside of their home.

"That sounds good. I should really get back into Italian cooking," she said. "I think enough time has passed that it wouldn't feel bad to do, don't you?" It had been almost a decade since Phillip's father had returned to his home on the Adriatic coast.

"It's up to you, Ma," he replied. His father was nothing more than a fuzzy collection of contours with no real character lost in the attic of Phillip's mind, entire cities of cobwebs constructed around them. None of the photos in their apartment were of him. Maybe if Phillip had known the man, he would have felt more firmly anchored to himself. Instead, Phillip watched his reflection in the passenger side mirror, waiting for the inevitable distortion.

The trees threaded their branches above him in a brown-veined network that would have been thickly flowered if not for winter's dutiful stripping. He kept his eyes on the widest gap, one God could watch him through if He were bored enough to try. See Phillip lie among the toadstools and earthworms. Knees straddled him in the dead grass as the body they belonged to lowered like a ceiling caving in. Hands slid up Phillip's cheeks and temples, into his hair. Their fingers twisted every curl within reach until the hair stretched taut from the scalp, setting it aflame with pain. Martin's lips brushed Phillip's ear and he heard the ghost of Martin's voice as he had in his dreams, absent of meaning. Martin seemed only to throw his breath into the dark canal to catch its echo.

They had reached the point in the beating where Phillip could no longer see for the water that pooled on his irises, waiting to be displaced by a blink. His cousins were wrong. If Phillip had been soft, his body would have accepted every blow without complaint. Maybe lengthening inward like a trampoline before propelling Martin's fists back out into the cold. Instead, each strike landed like a stone. Phillip only became soft afterward, when fluids rushed to inflate him until every bruise rested on a cushion of swollen tissue. The rest of him was smeared with blood. Martin seemed to revel in every hemorrhage, cupping puddles of it in his hands before wiping them onto his own shirt. Making art of Phillip's life-force.

In a perfect world, the beauty of the clearing, a mile or so into the trees from the path he took home, would be enough to distract from what was happening. Phillip forced his mind into pockets of earth, between bird feathers, and under the caps of acorns. God didn't often figure into his imaginings—that was new. And laughable.

. . .

On the day of his appointment with the guidance counselor, Phillip was barely recognizable. Ms. Sharpe's turnaround was stunning. When Phillip went to see her last spring about his feelings of loneliness and invisibility, her best advice had been for him to join a few clubs at school. When he replied that he had in fact joined several organizations since enrolling, but still felt somehow separate from everyone else, she said absently to her computer screen, "Hmm. Well, maybe you should get a haircut or some new clothes. That might get the other kids interested."

This time, she didn't take her eyes off him for a single second. Actually, it didn't seem like she was capable of looking away from his bruised neck and swollen cheeks. He'd been mangled—there was no other word for it. Ms. Sharpe held Phillip's hands inside her parched ones and asked with maddening sincerity what had happened to him. She informed him that she and his mother were in talks about removing him from school altogether. He wanted to laugh in her face. He settled for gathering the largest glob of bloody saliva his mouth could hold, leaning over the arm of his chair, and opening his jaws like the bucket on a backhoe, letting the contents spill in a viscous curtain onto her thinly carpeted floor. Then he got up and left. Her face remained frozen in disbelief for about as long as he used to linger at the edges of a teacher's vision waiting to be noticed. As the sound of his rubber soles disappeared down the hall, Ms. Sharpe left a voicemail for Phillip's mother recommending that he see a therapist.

In Biology, Phillip could only just see the notes Miss Carter had made on the board since his left eye was little more than a bulb that glowed with pain behind his inflamed eyelids. His classmates, repulsed by Phillip's increasingly misshapen face, now resorted to avoiding him entirely. It almost felt the way it used to, only this time, they did see him... they just didn't want to. Of course. It would never be any other way.

He felt a hand on his and turned to meet Amy's stare.

"What's been going on?" she asked. The words *What do you care?* leapt to his lips. That is, until he really looked at her. "Are you getting bullied? Are they seniors?" Her voice quivered on certain syllables and Phillip couldn't understand why.

"No, it's not like that," he said. He was unable to pull his eyes away from hers. Her concern was sticky enough to hold him in place and force him to pay attention to thoughts he had made a habit of shrugging off. Amy always spoke to him in class, but he had thought it was only because they shared a table. Her fingers curled around his wrist as chalk clacked and slid across the board at the front of the room. "It's not a big deal, I swear," Phillip said. But the pleasant pressure of her did not disappear. He looked down at their hands, one on top of the other, and felt the good kind of knot in his stomach. He smiled. "Really, Amy," he said, trying to sound as sincere as possible. She closed her entire hand around his and stroked it with her thumb.

"If you want me to tell someone, I will. You don't have to." Pink circles colored her cheeks. "You're so different now. It's like you're always waiting for something bad to happen. And it is." She fell quiet and moved her hands into her lap. "Sorry if this is weird. I just wanted you to know I'm here, you know? If you ever wanna talk, or whatever."

Phillip had never really kidded himself that life had improved since becoming a punching bag. Sure, he enjoyed everyone's queasy stares at first, but he had also worn dread like a tightening collar. No matter how he tried to adjust, it never settled—just choked and choked. He would grin at his freaked-out peers between classes, then run to the bathroom and vomit up the bile that never stopped churning in the hours before a beating. They didn't happen every single day, but he knew one would, before the last injuries had a chance to stop pulsing with pain. Before Phillip could start to remember what it was he liked about himself.

Amy wasn't looking at him anymore. The pink in her cheeks had spread to her chest. Phillip watched her mouth move as she pretended to read what was written on the board. Her posture was rigid with a sheepishness he recognized. He wanted to tell her not to be embarrassed, that it was really cool of her to care about him like this. To even think of him existing outside this room. That he had never dared to imagine she would. Instead, he laid his hand on her wrist and did not let go until she returned his smile. When he redirected his attention to the front of the room, he refused to look anywhere else. No matter how Martin's eyes dug holes in him.

Phillip told his mother he would be late getting home that day. She was beside herself after listening to the guidance counselor's voicemail. Phillip told her not to worry—he was only staying to tell Martin he couldn't help him practice his wrestling moves anymore. A crackling quiet expanded on the line. Phillip pulled the phone from his ear to check the screen; the seconds of the call continued to tick by. He put the speaker back to his ear just in time to hear his mother inhale.

"Martin? That white boy whose house you went to for dinner? *You let him beat on you?*" Her voice escalated to octaves Phillip had never heard before. He knew she was now re-evaluating every nice thing she had said about *that white boy*, the moniker that would absolutely accompany Martin in her mind from now on.

"It's not like that! I was just helping him!" He knew she would never believe skin had nothing to do with it because it had something to do with everything, every day of her life. It did not matter that Phillip was only half of what she was; he was entirely her son. Phillip pictured the shadows in the corners of his mother's eyes and the twist of her mouth as she asked, "Why didn't you tell me earlier if you were just *helping* him?"

"I didn't want him to get in trouble! I'm not on the wrestling team, so I thought the coach would be pissed if he knew Martin was practicing on me. Plus, I know you don't like fighting, even if it's fake. I didn't wanna disappoint you." The lies came so easily now. There was a trick Phillip had come to understand. You had to add a bit of truth to them—that was the key. Martin *was* on the wrestling team, and even though it was against the rules to straight-up bash your opponent's face in during a match, Phillip was ready to chalk his bruises up to his own inexperience and lack of athletic prowess if she continued to question him. If he had told any of the faculty at school about their arrangement, he would have gone from invisible to hated, having benched the golden boy, as he suspected the principal would have done at his mother's request. He couldn't tell her that he had lain inertly in the grass, on the asphalt, and in the lower school's playground sand, waiting for each strike to fall, not once lifting a hand in his own defense. He truly did not want to disappoint her, but she wouldn't understand what it had all been for. The flimsiness of his existence could never be apparent to her. A mother who had spent her days and nights praying for you to coalesce inside her sees mainly what is best in you. Who you could be. But Phillip could never be whatever it was she thought she saw in him, no matter how she squinted and tilted her head to pretend.

"That so," she said. Her words were splotches of ink. Each time he looked at them, he saw something different. She did not believe him. That much was clear from the pauses that grew longer, punctuated only by Morse code breaths heard above the call's faint electric buzz. She was starting to see it now. Something other than the Phillip she had known. The new, wonky bend in his nose, the too-thin neck, the bulbous knees. He was changing to match the funhouse mirror, and so, too, would she to accommodate his impression of her as it evolved. All this in the name of keeping their conversations civil and her son's love firmly in view. Love was a precious commodity after all, and she had already lost more of it than she could stand. "Well, you tell th— *Martin*," and Phillip almost felt how her lips moved unpleasantly around the name, "there'll *be* no more wrestling practice. One more new bruise, and you're out of that school. Understand?"

"Yes, ma'am."

"Alright then. You come straight home after."

"Okay."

It had been easier than he'd expected to break his contract with Martin, though he'd looked very much like he wanted to punch Phillip in the mouth at first. Phillip confessed to being in danger of being pulled out of school, so there could be no more pummeling. And anyway, people knew who he was now, so maybe their work was done. Martin's expression dulled over the course of Phillip's little speech, though he did smile when Phillip said he hoped they could maybe be friends for real this time. If hard pressed, Phillip could never have described that smile to anyone, but he took its presence as a good sign.

"I didn't think anyone knew I existed," Phillip said. "Especially not someone like you."

"Like me," Martin said, a million miles away.

"Someone everybody likes, I mean."

Something like bitterness interrupted Martin's expression before tranquility resumed. "It's not such a big deal, being liked. It doesn't give you anything real."

Phillip didn't tell Martin how easy it was for him to say such a thing, being someone who actually had that unreality at his disposal. He settled for admitting, "I'd take whatever it did give me."

"You sure about that?"

Martin's eyes were like an eclipse when, lured out of his trance by Martin's voice, Phillip looked into them. From where he stood, a fine film obscured the window into Martin's soul. Or he simply didn't have one.

"I don't know if you know what it feels like. Or if you used to, I don't know if you remember," Phillip said. "Not being seen, ever. It wears you down. Like being ground into the floor over and over until you fucking disintegrate." Phillip had meant to keep his voice down, but the vent had opened wide without his knowledge. "When people look through you long enough, you start thinking *Am I even here? Is there anything for them to see?*" He squeezed his fists against his eyes to stop the headache he had coming on. When he finally gave up and pulled his fists away, the daylight came screaming back. Martin's body was wavy at the edges for a good while. When he came into focus again, he appeared unmoved by Phillip's revelation. Phillip's eyes darted everywhere to escape his nauseating shame.

"You wanna walk with me?" Martin asked. It was as if the last few minutes hadn't happened. Overwhelmed with gratitude, Phillip rushed to nod, then stopped.

"I mean, I would, but don't you live kind of far from here?" he asked.

"I'm not going home. I'm going to the funeral parlor," Martin replied.

"Your dad's job?"

Martin didn't answer. Phillip wasn't sure how he felt about seeing where Mr. Foley worked. It was likely "peopled" with corpses. His skin prickled, but he agreed to go anyway. He made a mental note to call his mother on the way home and tell her his talk with Martin had lasted longer than expected. Despite everything, Phillip couldn't help but be drawn to the version of Martin he'd glimpsed in the photos. He wondered what had caused his classmate's guileless joy to dry up and whether there was any hope of resurrecting it. Or, if it had only ever existed as a possibility, teased into view by a button pressed at exactly the right moment. After several weeks of violent intimacy and even visiting his home, Phillip was still no better acquainted with Martin than when their bizarre arrangement began. Phillip hoped that could change, starting with their field trip to the undertaker's.

The walk wasn't long. Phillip answered every question Martin asked, sometimes lapsing into lengthy descriptions. He talked and laughed so much, he almost didn't recognize himself. Most of Martin's questions didn't probe too deeply. What's your favorite color? Which class is your favorite? Ever been to a concert before? Phillip answered them all and asked Martin the same. Martin's favorite color was green. His favorite subject was science, and he didn't like music.

"Like, at all?" Phillip asked.

"Nah," Martin said. "Don't see the point of it."

They arrived at the Sweet Partings funeral home in about fifteen minutes.

The double doors were a rather cheery shade of blue, and the paint shone like it hadn't been long since a fresh coat was applied. The bushes were neatly trimmed to resemble predatory animals. A lion with a spiked mane roared in their general direction. Martin kicked the torso of a hyena frozen in a state of savage mirth. As they neared the entrance, Phillip took the place in.

"Wow," he said.

"Yeah," Martin replied without looking up from the keyhole. The doors opened on soundless hinges. There was no light except the little that filtered through the wooden blinds at each window. Ten rows of chairs with burgundy cushions filled both sides of a great room. An open casket lay at the end of the central aisle. The tip of a nose was just visible above the coffin's edge. Phillip thought about Snow White as his legs propelled him forward. Passing row upon empty row of chairs, Phillip felt it would be his duty, upon reaching the front of the room, to give the world an answer, though the question remained unclear. When he reached the casket, he looked at the dead woman's face. She must have been in her eighties. The creases in her skin were light, like paper folded and unfolded. Her lips were bunched around her gums, prepared for speech. Phillip wondered blandly if a kiss would wake her. As he gazed upon her peaceful face, her eyelids twitched like a dreamer's. No; that wasn't right. Phillip leaned closer.

Her eyes snapped open.

Phillip jumped backward and fell. His stomach clenched and he waited, to the beat of his drumming heart, for fingers to curl around the casket's edge.

"Come on." Martin beckoned from the front door before disappearing down a corridor.

Struggling to catch his breath, Phillip crawled to standing and ran up the aisle, a time-lapsed evolution of man. When he turned back to look at the casket, the woman lay as peacefully as she had before. Phillip jogged until he caught up with Martin, shaking.

"That woman! She woke up!"

Martin walked on, giving no sign of having heard. The soles of their sneakers scraped the floor as they approached a door with the words "Personnel Only" engraved on a plaque at its center. Phillip grabbed his friend's shoulder. "Martin!"

"What?"

"The woman back there..." Phillip began.

Martin smirked. "What's wrong, Phil, you scared?" He turned the doorknob in front of them. Phillip bit the inside of his cheek until he tasted blood, then shook his head in one firm movement. The door opened onto a staircase that spiraled down to an unseen end. "That woman is dead, Phillip. Stone dead. You're seeing things," Martin said, and stepped through the doorway.

"Where are we going?" Phillip asked, hyper-aware in the dim well.

"Down to where the morticians work," Martin said. "You did say you were interested in this stuff. That true? Or were you just trying to be nice?"

"No, I am interested," he implored. This friendship was too freshly formed to put at risk. Martin leaned in close. Phillip imagined how it might feel to run his fingers along his new friend's jawline. To let them rest there.

"You *are* scared, aren't you?" Martin asked. Phillip felt a magnetic pull to Martin as they stood, nose to Cupid's bow. Martin's lips were stacked cherries—red, full, their edges chapped. So close. They were so close.

"I—" Phillip began, but his mind was a swamp. Everything he had thought or felt since their first encounter in the woods pushed against his insides. He was dizzy. Martin brought his hand to Phillip's face... and flicked him between the eyes.

"I'm just messing with you, Phil," he said, and grinned. "Come on." He started down the stairs. Phillip followed behind, not loosening his grip on the handrail or daring to look back until he reached the bottom.

Martin opened a door and flipped a switch on the wall. After the stairwell, the bright florescent bulbs made Phillip's temples throb. The space was longer than it was wide, and bordered by countertops. There were three large tables in the center upon which, Phillip assumed, the bodies were laid, drained of their own fluids and infused with preservatives. Nearly everything had a metallic sheen. The sterility made Phillip cold inside. Martin strode to the middle of the room with his arms raised and spun around.

"This is it," he said, letting his arms slap down against his hips. "What do you think?"

Phillip didn't know what he thought. It was a weird place. Anything that wasn't silver was white. There were scissors, pumps, tubes. From a tray of instruments, Martin picked up a hooked needle with a short tail of thread tied to one end.

"They use this to sew their mouths shut," Martin said, holding the needle out to Phillip, who wrinkled his nose.

"Really?"

"Yeah. I guess it's so they'll look peaceful. Not like this," Martin said, and stretched his face into a horrified expression, tongue jutting from between his teeth. The boys laughed and Phillip felt himself relax.

"This is wild," he said in awe, moving about the room. He was careful not to touch anything. He wasn't exactly afraid, but the idea of touching someone else's fluids disturbed him in a way he couldn't fully articulate.

"But necessary," Martin replied. His sudden sobriety made Phillip look up. Martin had a scalpel in one hand. But rather than the blade, Phillip's eyes were drawn to the orange beads circling Martin's wrist. A shock of color in a sea of neutrality.

"Hey," Phillip said. "Where'd you get that bracelet?"

Martin pulled his gaze away from the scalpel to look at Phillip. "Want a soda?" he asked, tossing a can to his guest.

Phillip hadn't even seen where it came from. As he wedged his thumb beneath the metal tab, he noticed Martin didn't have one. "Don't you want one?" he asked. Martin shook his head.

"Not thirsty," he said.

Phillip shrugged and looked at the can. It was silver, like almost everything else in the room. There was no label, but Phillip didn't give that much thought. He popped the top and air hissed from the can in a whisper.

"There you are, Phil," Martin said to the sound of sips and

swallows. Phillip blinked, his eyelids suddenly heavy. Martin grinned wide.

"Bottoms up."

Phillip's shoulder blades ached with cold. He felt metal hard against his back. My eyes are closed, he thought. He opened them and went blind. There was nothing but white for minutes. Hours. Eons.

"You're awake," Martin said. He sounded mildly surprised. There was a blue curtain made of paper clamped to a metal post. Its bottom skirted Phillip's neck. He was on his back and could not see what lay beyond the partition. "I knew you must be because your heart started beating faster." Martin's voice sailed out from behind the floating bib.

My heart, Phillip thought. He could not feel anything, or move his body below the neck. He lifted his head as high as it would go, but could not hold the weight of it up for long. His heavy skull thunked against the metal surface on which his body was suspended.

"Please, don't try to move," Martin said. "You can't anyway." Martin's every syllable was gentle.

A spotlight shone icily down on Phillip in what he realized was an otherwise dark room. He wondered if he had strayed into another dream.

"You and I," Martin said, and there was a stretched-out snap that lasted the length of a finger, "are even more alike now. What you were saying before, it's true." Martin's every breath was labored, but what he toiled over was hidden from view. "Which is why I know you'll appreciate this."

Phillip's head lolled, its contents sloshing.

"I do remember what it was like, being invisible. It sucked. Only time someone noticed me was when they were beating the shit out of me." Phillip looked up into Martin's face, painted in harsh black shadows except for his eyes, which sliced the air with their glinting. They were demonic orbs, dangling in nothing. "You are better than how others treat you, Phillip. Remember that." Martin spoke in a way that didn't suit him at all. He sounded like one of their teachers.

"What? What is this?" Phillip slurred. The anesthetic had worn off enough for him to wake, but his tongue was too thick for proper speech, and the fog too dense for proper thought. Martin leaned towards him and, just like on the day they met, when Martin's head had temporarily blocked the sun's rays, so now did it come between Phillip and the florescent light above.

"Miles didn't ask permission when he did this to me either," Martin said. Phillip, still swimming in and out of consciousness, smiled to himself and thought how angry his mom would be if he ever decided to call her Gloria. "He slipped something into my drink on one of the nights he came home for dinner." Martin seemed deliberately to hold his voice flat, betraying nothing. "Most people can't wait to move away for college, but he stayed local. Came home every chance he got. Mom used to think it was because he missed us," Martin scoffed. "He brought me to the grad lab after hours. Drained me." At this, he held up Phillip's tainted soda can and poured its remains out onto the floor. The sound brought visions of crashing tides to Phillip's altered mind. "Replaced the blood with his little *concoction*." Each syllable was a poison. "*I mean, I wasn't trying to kill you! Ha ha ha!*" Martin opened his hand and let the can fall. On impact, it pealed like a clock shop at midnight. "I've been fourteen a long time, Phillip. Now you will be, too."

The words fell on their recipient's ears but, though he recognized them as such, he could not make sense of them. Phillip's mind was a smear on pavement, sliding in time with Martin's speech. Phillip pictured his own insides melting into cream.

Phillip's heart rate climbed higher. Everything that had happened after he spotted the woman in the casket must belong to a nightmare he was still having.

"He'd tried to help me. That's what he said. After the hell I went through at school he said he'd fix it so I could have a do-over. *That's what big brothers are for, right?* So, I had my do-over. But when he tried to reverse it, I'd been living on what he'd made for so long, my body wouldn't accept anything else. Now I'm stuck like this."

Though escape was his greatest wish, Phillip could not deny his gratitude for the mercy of being unable to see Martin clearly as he spoke.

"Mom and Dad were actually happy, having at least one of their kids be a kid again, forever. We'd just move away whenever folks started asking questions about me. Molly actually volunteered to try it, even after she saw what it did to me. Said she didn't care if she was fourteen for the rest of her life. Only, it didn't work. She got older anyway. Plus her body didn't react well to it." Phillip registered Martin's disgust at his sister's unfortunate state. The memory of her hair swinging in clumps at her chin swam to mind. Her bruises were the same shade as the beads on her bracelet.

"Miles was never interested in using the stuff on himself; he just wants to make money off it. As an adult, you're free. More than a kid, anyway."

Everything was mush. Phillip wanted control of his body back.

"He figures since it turned back time for me in such a big way, maybe it could work on corpses, too. But they only wake up for a little while. I was a fluke. He tried to bring our parents back, but they bit it a second time—the day before their anniversary."

Phillip blinked rapidly. *Wake up. Wake UP.*

"But the samples of your blood I've collected all match my old charts perfectly," Martin said. It was his first time showing real enthusiasm. Martin brought Phillip's wrist out from behind the curtain. It was encircled by an orange bracelet beaded in cheap plastic, identical to Martin's. "I had to take more than one, in case the first was a mistake. Sorry to be so rough on you, but there was no other way. You wouldn't have understood if I'd told you the truth." Martin released his grip and Phillip's arm clapped against the tabletop. "I don't know how many times I've told him how sick I am of being alone in this shit life he trapped me in." In one swift motion, Martin tore back the curtain hovering at Phillip's neck. The skin of his torso had been folded away from his middle like the pages of a book. Phillip stretched his eyelids until they could get no wider. "I had to open you up. To make sure everything was working the way it should, and it is. I can't wait to see the look on that jackass's face when he finds out a high-school freshman did what he couldn't."

The boy on the table felt his head judder back and forth. *Nonononononononononono.*

"I don't have friends," Martin said. "Why bother when I know I'm just gonna move away again? But now, no matter where I go, you and I can be friends. Real friends."

"But, I-I don't want this!" Phillip screamed.

"Of course you do, Phillip. Everyone does. To feel known—truly known—by another human being. People search their whole lives for that. A soulmate," Martin replied. "And you're mine."

Phillip sobbed, the tears turning his face to clay. Where was his mother? Likely sat, stiff with anger, on the couch, television blaring to distract her while she waited for him to call. She would be happy, wouldn't she? Her baby would stay her baby for good. Maybe that would be enough to make up for all the things he would never become. Phillip lay back and closed his leaking eyes. It hadn't been a funhouse mirror after all, but a painting whose oil had dried while his back was turned.

Hold Still

My wife is leaning over me when I open my eyes. There's a new cut above her eyebrow that I want to kiss.

She makes a noise like she's been stuck with a pin and can finally be allowed to deflate. Her lips are held together in tight, wavy lines of unspent grief that roll back from her teeth as she starts to cry. Everything on her that can bend does as she lowers herself to the floor, clutching the sides of my bed. A vague awareness that the bed I'm in is only large enough for one hovers near enough to make out, but not to understand. I reach for my wife, but the sickening tug of an IV stops me. I have become something wild and artificial, both. I whisper around the tubes growing out of my throat. She doesn't hear, so I whisper again, but it's pointless; her sobs eat every sound in the room.

She climbs into her chair and pulls my ferreting hand to her chest. I splay my fingers to absorb her heat.

She says the doctors told her they weren't sure when I'd wake up. Or if. The rest of the words fall apart on her tongue and their unsaid bulge presses against my own throat. She leans down close, and I rub the hollow at the base of her neck. The familiarity of my touch is more than enough to disassemble her completely. Worry has already transformed her face into something unmade, pottery not yet fired by the kiln, left to languish too long on the wheel. I hoped I'd never see her like this, though the possibility always loomed. Until now, there's been no call to weather anything worse than her mother, the widowed Mrs. Oak, staying with us from time to time, and disturbing the peace whenever she does. I wouldn't be surprised if Mama Oak paid that truck driver to mow me down. She probably threw in a little extra to make sure my door got good and caved in. Well, fuck her—I'm alive.

Malinda hasn't stopped crying. I want to tell her not to, but I choke on the tubes and sputter wordlessly instead. She presses a finger to my lips and tells me not to talk. I open my mouth around it and she smiles to let me know it's alright, all of it. In response, I clench what muscles I can, trying to locate the belief that it really is okay that I've been absent from my family for this long—whether through my own failing or not—but it stays hidden. The ghosts of scrapes and wounds cover her like angry brushstrokes. I wonder what I'll find under her clothes the next time we're in bed together. In my head I promise her and God and even Mama Oak that I'll make this up to her somehow.

I ask how Eric is. She says he's fine, but he cried the first time he saw me here. I imagine my eight-year-old son, red-eyed and bewildered. I want to hear that odd rasp in his voice. When he speaks, I always picture a much older, invisible ventriloquist filling his mouth with words that aren't his. I ask where he is now.

She says I've been out for months and sighs theatrically, running a hand over my hair, now thick and overgrown. That explains why her unfamiliar cuts are mostly healed. I remember the impact. My insides crushed against the center console, and me waiting in the seconds of consciousness remaining to feel them squeeze out through my belly button. I heard Malinda scream. Then I was swallowed up. It doesn't take skill or even desire to remember.

But, where is my son?

Malinda focuses on the machine monitoring my heart rate, her pupils responding to the rise and fall of each line. I squint at her, craning my neck. Hoping. Wishing. She finally says that when her mother learned what happened, she offered to come help out for a while. Guess my wishes are all used up.

Malinda watches my crumpled mouth for words. I know she drove here expecting me to fight her on this. I can already see a counter-argument worrying itself into creases across her forehead. There's a lot I could say, want to say, but I hold the words in place before it's too late and I can't take them back.

"Fine," is what I say to her now. Malinda stops wringing her hands to move her body into mine. She can't hug me properly because I can't lift myself enough for her arms to enfold me. She settles for burying her nose in my hair, braving layers of dead skin to breathe me in. I turn my face to her neck and rediscover the scent of her. Malinda. My Linda. As her silk-pressed hair falls like a veil over me, I decide I can deal with Mama Oak every day for a hundred years if I have to.

As if she's read my mind, Malinda whispers that her mother isn't staying forever. She leans back to look me in the eye. She insists that it's just until I'm *up and running again*.

"Up and running?" I pinch her right hip and push my fingers against its fullness. She rolls her eyes as I maneuver into the front pocket of her jeans and reel her closer. Playfully, she pushes away from me and back into her chair. She crosses her legs, tilts her head to one side and laughs. We laugh together. Then everything stops.

I can hear Malinda giggling, but nothing on her moves. Like we're playing "Red Light, Green Light" and I've just whipped around to catch her out. The rim of her ear almost touches her shoulder. Her eyes are closed, her jaws wide.

The sound of my name from her mouth is unmistakable,

but her lips are curved and parted in stiff imitation of a comedy mask. I peer into the darkness between her teeth hoping to catch her tongue in motion, but there's nothing. I reach for her, and something soft and warm blocks my way. Fabric over flesh. Like someone is standing between us. It takes me a minute to realize I can't even see my own hand moving. I can only see the room as it was when we laughed. I try to push the invisible obstruction out of my way and Malinda asks what I'm doing, but I don't know. I push harder and my fingers sink into sponginess and bone. She tells me to stop messing, even though my fingers have yet to make contact with the Malinda statue sitting by my bed. An unseen hand bats mine away.

I frown so powerfully, my face hurts. The intervals between beeps shorten as my chest tenses. I squeeze the rails flanking my bed like they have the power to put the world right again.

Malinda starts to ask me what's wrong, but her words disappear and I feel a hand, her hand, on my face. It jumps to the back of my neck and squeezes. She asks me to say something. Anything. Begs.

I am shaking as much from the cold sweat dribbling down me as from fear. The call button buzzes three times, and I feel my head being clasped to my wife's chest. All the while, a copy of her remains at my bedside, bent-necked and consumed by laughter.

Mama Oak's expression sours when she opens the front door and finds me on the other side. I want to remind her that it's *my* house she's been living in for however-many months, but I breathe deep and count backwards from ten. I tell myself, thinking the words in bold, capital letters, to remember how glad I am to finally be home, hoping it will cancel out the aura of unpleasantness the woman can't help but drag along with her everywhere she goes.

"You back now, huh," she says more than asks, not bothering to hide her disappointment. I guess we do have something in common.

"Yeah, Ma, I'm back."

"What you call me?"

"'Scuse me, Mrs. Oak," I say through gritted teeth. "I apologize." Been married to her daughter long enough to see lace, ivory, and crystal anniversaries come and go; even gave her a grandchild. Every time we meet and clash, I comb through our entire shared history. No matter how I replay and magnify the scenes we've shared, I can't see it. The imperfection. I've tried my best to pin it down, but it fades from view almost as soon as I get close enough to see it clearly.

Malinda asks her mother to be nice for once as she wheels me inside.

"Been raising this man's child for him almost half a year. If that ain't being nice, I don't know what is," the old woman says, not quite under her breath, as she climbs the stairs to the second floor.

"Oh, so because she helps take care of my son for a little while, she thinks she a better parent than me? Even though the only reason I wasn't here is cuz I damn-near died?"

Malinda says I should know not to pay her mother any mind by now. She is clearly exasperated, though whether it's with me or her mother, I can't tell. Before I can start an argument about whose side she's on, I hear Eric's footsteps on the stairs. His eyes brighten when he sees me, and nothing else matters.

He slides down the banister and charges at me, arms wide.

Malinda asks if he has lost his mind. Rather than respond, Eric makes a ball of himself and falls into me. I hug him hard with my good arm, trying to take in every detail: the notches of his spine; the mossy smell of our backyard mixed with his little-boy odor; the smallness of him. I squeeze him tighter, moved by the absurdity of missing things I hadn't noticed before. He squirms in my grip and I let him go.

"What'd I miss?" I ask, putting him in a headlock he worms out of easily enough to dent my pride. He says his soccer team won two games, lost two, and tied one while I was in the hospital.

"Don't worry. Y'all will pull it together before the next one." I pat his head, careful not to disturb the waves I taught him to make. "I want you to win and dedicate the win to me, aight?" I grab Eric and pull him onto my lap. My legs soon start to ache, but I won't let him go. I can feel the weight of every month I've lost in my son. Or maybe, I'm just weaker.

Malinda questions the logic of requesting a dedication, concluding that it would erase the gesture's intended meaning.

"Nope. It'll mean everything to me." I tickle Eric with one arm and watch his corn-stalk legs dangle over the side of my wheelchair, contradicting me. He's not so small after all.

After that episode with the two Malindas, my neurologist suggested I use the chair for a few months. I did break an arm and bang up my legs pretty good in the accident, but since my physical injuries have healed, use of the chair was mostly encouraged because my limbs are weak from disuse, and it's better if I'm already seated when my vision freezes again.

If, Doctor Strauss had insisted. *If* it freezes again, which he assured me was unlikely. The doctors had never seen brain activity like mine before, but conceded that the trauma to my head had been severe. It's not far-fetched that my mind would react to new information like an old computer that's run out of room. Video might seize up on-screen, but the machine hums on. While they readied for additional scans, my vision went back to normal. By the time they scanned me again, the chaos had subsided. Strauss prescribed medication with a name I can't pronounce and all but guaranteed the pills would "calm my synapses" should the need arise. They rattle around in my pocket as Eric flails at my touch. Malinda shoos him from my lap and tells him not to be so rough with me now that they've got me back. I can't help wondering how much good I am to them or anyone right now.

Eric pokes out his bottom lip in a pretend pout, then runs through the kitchen to the backyard. Malinda follows, pausing at the refrigerator to take stock of its contents. I gaze into the hallway mirror and an invalid gazes back. I tell myself that I won't even need this wheelchair in a few weeks. Probably don't need it now. It was all brought on by stress like the doctors said. Relax. I grab the wheels of my chair and push. For some reason, no matter where I look, I can only see my own reflection, stock-still behind the mirror's glass. I roll farther forward, but what I see around me doesn't change. It's like it was at the hospital that day; like time has stopped for me alone. Did I call the glitch back by thinking about it? I try to touch the glass, but instead feel the textured wallpaper Malinda picked out the year Eric learned to walk. Like the first time it happened, my brain refuses to allow new information entry, lingering instead on a moment of its own choosing. Though I feel my fingers slope along the raised, abstract swirls covering the wall, they might as well belong to someone else. Maybe they do. After failing several times to shake the current freeze away, I give up and begin studying my insistent reflection: muscles shriveled from disuse; a coarse afro thick with dead skin cells; lips so dry, I'd clown them if they weren't mine. My eyes are rimmed by sagging rinds. I haven't slept for more than a few hours a night since that strange visit with my wife. The lines around my mouth are deep grooves visible through the rough whiskers on my face. I've never examined myself this closely before. The longer I stare, the less human I seem. I haven't eaten yet today, but my insides begin to revolt anyway. I can't look at this anymore. I tug the pill bottle from my pocket and pop one. "Lin!" I fill the hallway with her name until I hear footsteps approaching.

"What you hollering for?" Every corner of every word from Mama Oak is sharp enough to impale.

The me in my body grimaces, but the one in the mirror continues to stare. "I need some water to help this pill go down," I say to her, or to the area her voice came from. All of a sudden, we're face-to-face in real time. The shock of her so close startles me into a coughing fit.

"Well, don't choke over it," she grumbles, as to a stubborn child. Shuffling in slippered feet to the kitchen sink, she fills a glass with water from the tap. "You'd think your wife would be all over this," she says, handing me the glass. Silently, I agree. "Where'd she go anyway?"

Right on cue, laughter rings out from beyond the back door. Through the window in the door, I see Malinda's head float by. I'm no more than forty feet from them, but I can't shake the loneliness that sneaks up to cradle me in its arms. I flirt with telling Malinda what happened at the mirror simply to enjoy the satisfaction of her shame at not having been there when I needed her. Instead, I watch them from the hallway and sip my water. Mama Oak surveys me from the sink. Even if I cared to, I couldn't decipher the look on her face. A minute passes in quiet. She walks around to the back of my wheelchair and steers me into the kitchen toward the door concealing my wife and son. Her crooked fingers turn the knob without a sound. She pulls the door open with deliberate slowness, leaning her backside against the counter's edge as it nears. I can feel myself teetering on a threshold, trapped between sensations it scares me to dwell on.

Together, our individual longings emanating from us, Mama Oak and I watch the outlines of our offspring blaze with light borrowed from the setting sun.

The next morning, Lin and I are at the kitchen table alone. Eric is at school and Mama Oak is upstairs. After her husband died, it became common for Malinda's mother to be up with the birds and squawking just as loud. She hadn't been very vocal when Pop was alive, so I figured we must be getting all the talking she had saved up over the years. Eventually, mine and Malinda's long-suffering glances at one another became less covert. Mama Oak must have noticed because she began to retreat inward, reverting to her customary, sullen remove.

For breakfast, we have bacon, scrambled eggs, and Malinda's waffles made special with nutmeg, brown sugar, and some other secret ingredient I've yet to figure out. The waffles are sweet enough to rot my teeth to stumps on their own, but with the memory of hospital food fresh in my mind, I take the opportunity to indulge and add syrup. Malinda took a week off from work to help me get settled. With nothing urgent keeping us home, we decide to spend the afternoon at a local art gallery, then get dinner at that seafood spot we always pass by but have never tried. By the time Malinda had set my plate in front of me, the food was already neatly cut into chewable pieces. I told her I was perfectly capable, but she said she was happy to ease my way however she could. It was harder than expected to summon gratitude.

That aside, everything feels more or less like normal. At home, with familiar food in my belly, I'm better equipped to fight off the stabs of longing for my hospital bed that intrude almost as often as I draw breath.

Malinda wonders aloud through a mouthful of eggs what her mother is doing upstairs. She always talks while she eats. I truly believe she forgets the food is in her mouth as soon as she puts it there.

"Maybe she had a heart attack," I reply, trying not to smile. Malinda scowls. "I'm just kidding," I say, almost convincing myself that I mean it.

She stares daggers and sets her fork down. She then

presses her palms to the table's surface, preparing to rise from her chair.

"I'll go," I say. I don't know why. A compulsion to prove myself useful? Or maybe I just want to catch Mama Oak in the act of tearing the person mask from her face so I can see what's really there.

Malinda's expression is somewhere between impressed and confused; she asks how I plan to accomplish this.

"The chair is just for emergencies. My legs aren't broken," I say.

Malinda's lips turn down. She says her mother told her about the brain freeze I had yesterday while she and Eric were out in the yard. While I was watching them run around, I couldn't stop thinking about my little white room in the hospital and how ordinary the state of my body was while I was in it. Even after I woke up, I was fed by either a nurse, or Malinda during her evening visits. My assisted living became rote. And if ever the ordinary gave way to something uglier, I could press a button once and someone would come bustling in, performing their duties without emotion. It was so easy to feel like just another resident.

"Woman, I'm fine," I reply. She doesn't smile, preferring to lace her fingers together and twist them until I can feel the pain in my own hands. I soften my expression. "Really, baby," I say, stretching my better arm across the table. I disentangle one of her hands from the other. She stares through them, eyes unfocused, and I picture her as a little girl.

She nods her assent.

These stairs are my Everest. Like a tortoise, I move one limb at a time, trying not to wince. The upstairs hallway is noiseless except for a faint tittering. Kernels of sound come from the guest room, but no more than that. Once I've made it to the right door, I put my fist up to knock, then press my ear against the wood to listen instead. I hear her voice, but can't make sense of it. It rises and falls, one half of a conversation. I try the knob. The door is unlocked. I inch forward in caterpillar segments partly because of the pain, but also in case she's not decent. Mama Oak sits straight-backed in bed holding the cellphone we gave her two Christmases ago. I feel naked beneath her stare as I shamble over to her like a busted wind-up toy.

"Mam— Mrs. Oak?" I'm ready for her to shoot me one of those dirty looks of hers, but she remains stoic. Her eyes follow me as I get closer. I push the chair next to the nightstand closer to her bed with my foot and ease into it. "Malinda sent me up here to check on you. You doing okay?" I think I see her flinch when I say her daughter's name, but I'm not sure. "Were you on the phone just now? Thought I heard you talking." When my eyes flit toward the phone, she turns it over so that only the emerald-green case is visible. Before she did so, I caught a glimpse of her dead husband's face grinning up at whoever happened to be looking.

"I kept messages," she says. Her face moves begrudgingly, strained with the effort of withholding every possible expression. "For when I need to hear his voice. Sometimes I talk back. Pretend he's listening." She doesn't look at me and I'm glad. I can't think of how to respond, except to restrain my own features in kind.

"I was always pretending. Even when he was here. That man never listened a day in his life. Didn't need to. Just a-skin-nin' and a-grinnin' 'til he made you fall in love." This is the most I've ever heard her talk about Papa Oak. When he was alive, they seemed to occupy different universes entirely, even in the same room. Pop would have us laughing from the time we arrived until we were back home in bed, dreaming about the stories he told. A one-man extravaganza, he could charm the pants off of anyone, and did more times than I can say for sure. But his marriage chugged on. The inverse of her husband, Mama Oak was like a void that stripped cheer of its purpose. Rather than force their energies to cancel one another out, Mama Oak often slipped from rooms, only reappearing when it was time to say goodbye. I used to wonder what voodoo brought the two of them together. Especially when one clearly inspired more joy than the other. But here, firmly within the borders of her universe, the silence is comforting.

"You never cheated on Malinda." It's not a question, but I shake my head no. "Yeah," she says. "You a better man than that. I guess Malinda got it made, huh?"

"I don't know how good a man it makes me to do what I promised I would. It's just decent. If the promise was to keep our marriage open, I'd hold up my end of that, too," I say. "But it's not. So I keep to my own bed."

She goes on nodding well past the statement's end. The depressions encircling the base of her neck are moats defending the sanctity of her reverie. My brain doesn't even have to glitch again—I can take all the time I need to study her. A scatter of small moles pepper her cheeks and chest in a pattern like a stone path. The trail leads to dark brown eyes that are half-closed windows to an echo chamber. One that shouts back at me in a voice I think I recognize. I just had breakfast with my wife. In a family home that I helped create. But Malinda's unease over me coming up the stairs alone, like I'm another child whose development will only ever reignite her anxiety, is humiliating.

I'm not sure when Mama Oak let her eyes drift back up to meet mine. Before I know what's happening, she leans close and lays a hand on my cheek. I have a growing urge to say something, but I don't want to break the silence. Before a new thought can fully form, her hand slides down my neck, coming to rest at the open collar of my shirt. She slips two fingers beneath the plaid cotton and I wrest myself away from her. A flicker of anger contorts her face, then melts away just as quickly. She lets her hand fall feebly to the bedspread and draws it back to herself.

"I don't hate you, you know," she says, hitching one side of her mouth up into something like a smile. I don't know what to say. "And I wish you wouldn't call me Mama," she says, breathing a hard laugh through her nose. "You ain't my son. Having kids ages a woman. I've already had all I can take." She tilts her head to one side and I picture Malinda's unmoving face.

I close my eyes and try to eject the image from my mind.

Mama Oak rearranges her spine against the headboard. I start to speak, but she holds a hand up to shush me. She shakes her head back and forth, lost in thoughts I cannot begin to know. "Just go," she says. If she were a body of water, I'd die trying to reach the bottom.

I go downstairs and tell Malinda everything is fine.

"So I'm supposed to be in my feelings over an empty can?" I say, laughing.

Malinda exclaims that the piece was conceptual, hands open to hold her indignation. Our table is framed by the restaurant's largest window. What little light there is bounces from beneath the lampshades, speckling our silverware and teeth with leftover luster. Malinda arches her back and cackles freely. It's the way I imagine Mama Oak would sound if she were in the habit of laughing. I take in a forkful of grilled salmon and some butter escapes my mouth to coast down my chin. I'm embarrassed, but Malinda dabs at it with a napkin, winking.

"I'm sorry," I say. "A wooden box with a tin can nailed to the top is not any kind of art, conceptual or otherwise."

She assures me, while laughing from some place deep down in the pit of herself, that I just don't know art. She's wearing a black velvet dress with silver stars stitched along every curve. The biggest star begins where her V-neck ends; I glance at it every time she laughs. A waiter orbits our table holding a carafe of sparkling water. By now, we have a routine. He comes by carrying something he thinks we might want. If we do, we nod. If not, we avert our eyes like he is an apparition we can pretend not to have seen. On this occasion I nod, but Malinda, whose glass is still full, slides her eyes away. He fills my glass, smiles, then recedes into the moody darkness.

I appreciate the waitstaff resisting the impulse to hover despite the irregularity of my movements. From the minute we left the house, I've been attracting curious stares.

"What you think Ma would say about that exhibition?" I've been plagued by the question all night and hope my desperation to know the answer doesn't show. Malinda blinks rapidly, obviously caught off-guard. She starts to say something, likely a joke, but stops herself. Thinks. Eventually, she says she has no idea. Malinda has been to plenty of museums and galleries with her parents throughout her life. Malinda's father would regale her with his opinions constantly, but her mother never talked about anything they saw. Lin would apparently stand beside her mother, holding her hand as she stared silently at an object on display. Into it. Malinda laughs remembering how she used to try with all her might to find whatever it was her mama was looking for in each piece. Sometimes, Mama Oak would disappear altogether, reuniting later with her family at the gift shop.

There were moments tonight when Malinda held me to her by my waist, her grip firm, as though she expected me to flop bonelessly to the floor without her support. In the event, perhaps the curator could have supplied her with a label to stick to my lapel. *The Demolished Man: A Meditation on Deficiency.*

She asks if I feel like dessert while staring out the window into the night. I'm stuffed, but don't want our private time to end just yet. I shrug and smile in a way that says, *Sure, if you do*. Our waiter must have our table bugged because he materializes soon after, balancing a tray with replicas of every dessert item on their menu crafted from plastic in the most appetizing colors. My kind of art. When Malinda sees the cheesecake dripping blue and red berries, desire inflates her. Her arm stretches out to it, and the molecules around our table grow heavy. Her pointer finger unfurls and lengthens as she commands the muscles in her face to move. The start of a smile ruffles his lips.

A woman to our right is hunched in the act of getting up from her seat. Her dining partner crawls through invisible tar under their table, one hand on a fallen fork, eyes locked on his companion's crotch. Every diner moves with a sluggish grace, like the entire restaurant is under water. Except for me. This is new. Is my brain's drive space almost full? Maybe the gallery was too much too soon. Too vast a smorgasbord of new information. This isn't like the other times—I can actually see myself moving, and at a normal speed. It's everyone around me who has slowed. The sounds they make stretch like rubber bands, their collective frequency low as they distend. The first couple of times, I was sure it was me who was off-kilter. But now...

I drag Malinda's purse to me with the least ruined of my legs. When it's close enough, I grab it with my good arm and rummage through it. I find the pill bottle trapped beneath her wallet. I have a strong suspicion that if I don't take one soon, the world will stick like this and I'll be trapped on a planet of mannequins. Overlain by a thin sheet of plastic on the wallet's front is a photo of Malinda, me, and Mama Oak standing in a protective row behind Eric. Malinda's hand is on Eric's shoulder, and one of mine is on top of his head—the other curls around my wife's waist. Mama Oak is not looking into the camera's lens, but at me beside her. I swallow a pill, take a drink, and feel the medicine coast down to my stomach on water-bubble wheels. Staring at the photo, I wait for time to catch up with me.

Malinda and I return around 10 P.M. to a silent house. Eric and Mama Oak are in their beds behind doors that are slightly ajar. Behind our closed bedroom door, Malinda swings her hips and unzips her dress in a faux striptease. I see the girl I knew as a teenager—bony, awkward and shy—in the guise of a woman. She helps me into bed, and we celebrate my homecoming properly. When we reach the homestretch, I close my eyes as Malinda bears down against my thighs. Her abdomen tightens and I touch every firm muscle I can find with my fingertips. She lifts both arms, bracing herself for that last, soul-shaking shudder. All at once, I'm caught in it. Color erupts behind my eyelids and I dig my fingers into her hips. I let my head fall back onto my pillow, refusing to open my eyes until I've wrung this feeling dry. Malinda is still tense and compact in my lap, arms rigidly above her head.

"Baby?" I shake her lightly. She doesn't move because the world has stopped completely. I was quick to locate my meds at the restaurant, but now that what I feared is happening around me, I can't help but be fascinated. The world is on pause and the resultant quiet turns my every move into a declaration. The leveling power of silence makes me feel newborn. Without sound or the movement to make it, the living and the inanimate assume equal significance.

Malinda is halfway to looking over her shoulder at our bedroom door. Her brow is furrowed and her eyes are tapered. She's trying to see something more clearly. The pills are back inside her purse. I maneuver out of her as carefully as possible and tip Malinda in the direction of my good arm, pushing what strength I have to the limit. I have to hold onto her as I lay her down so she doesn't smack into the mattress like a brick.

When I get to the door, I realize it's open a sliver. A brown eye glistens as it peeks through the gap. I pull the door open fully to reveal Mama Oak, a gnarled hand held flat against the doorframe for balance. Her other eye is squeezed shut. Moonlight streams through the window at the end of the hallway. She is glowing. Her silhouette is clear and seems to be quivering under the thin fabric of her nightgown, but I know the dark can make you see things. She bulges and sags in places that Malinda does not yet. I stretch out a hand, then pull it back again. I am watching her watch us as though we are art. I wonder if this is the first time she's done this.

I decide to treat her like a sleeping bear, inching around her still form to inspect, but careful not to touch any part of her. I go back into the bedroom and close the door behind me.

The steady tick of the second hand is becoming foreign to me, a precious import that I would guard with iron arms if I could. We are all seated at the kitchen table. Me. Tick. Malinda. Tock. Eric. Tick. Mama Oak...

The only sounds coming from us are the squelches of chews and swallows. The air is stagnant, our movements stiff. Eric tries to catch my eye. When he does, I smile to reassure him but my lips quiver. I'm sorry, son, but no—you're not imagining it. There *is* tension pulling our muscles taut and our brows low. This is the new gravity. Adjust.

Malinda asks her mother without looking up from her plate what time she and Eric went to bed last night. Mama Oak's stare is electric.

"'Bout eight, eight-thirty," she says. Her pupils are dilating. She turns her spotlight gaze on me. I look away.

Malinda nods and doesn't probe further because something in her knows. I didn't tell her about finding her moon-bathed mother frozen in the act of spying on us last night. I didn't tell her I'd had to take another pill either, or about what they have the power to undo. I don't know if I should, or if it's even necessary. I'm counting on her, willing her to figure it all out right now, without me saying a thing.

She asks Eric if he went straight to bed. He replies between chews that he did. Malinda watches him, her lie-detector working. She closes one eye and lifts her chin as if she is peering down the neck of a microscope. Finally, she smiles. Our boy doesn't lie. His only attempt—when he claimed a stray cat had come through the window and made off with the rest of his mother's birthday cake (platter and all)—ended in a tearful confession ten minutes later. No. She knows he's not to blame for all this unwanted suspense. The four of us eat to fill the silence. Tick. Tock. Tick.

After an obscene amount of chewing and swallowing, Malinda tells Eric it's about time he head on to school. Shifting in her seat, she asks Mama Oak if she can drop him off. Her efforts to sound casual makes me ache.

Mama Oak's eyes shrink back into her head. "Why you need me to take him?"

At the same time, my son and I swivel our necks to look at Malinda who says she has some things to take care of at home, and that it would be really helpful. She forces a smile as if metal rods have been shoved into each corner of her mouth.

Mama Oak lays a hand on my wrist and the food I'm chewing gets caught in my throat. I bark out a series of coughs; my mother-in-law pats my back, then transitions to a slow, circular rubbing.

"I'm good, thank you," I say, eyes darting to Malinda.

Mama Oak smears two more loops into my back before returning her hand to her lap. Malinda looks from her mother to me. Mama Oak rises from the table and tilts her head in that all too familiar way, letting her eyes rest on her daughter for three ticks of the second hand. To Eric, she says, "Come on, child." She smirks at Malinda and her eyes are slits. Suspicion dawns, morphing my wife's features.

As he fits his arms through the straps on his backpack, Eric asks his mother what's wrong. Malinda reluctantly tears her eyes away from mine to shake her head and tell him it's nothing.

Eric nods and turns to go, then changes his mind. He jogs over to his mother, hugging her tight. She sinks into the hug, then pinches his nose and kisses him. As Eric hugs me goodbye, he whispers a request to cheer Malinda up. I've never loved my son more than I do right now. Eric waves goodbye and gallops off with his grandmother five steps behind. She leaves the kitchen without looking back. Soon the front door opens. Closes. Malinda's face is granite-hard, but she says my name so quietly that I am tempted to lean in. She's shaking. She asks me what the hell is going on. I reach for her hand but she yanks it away.

I should just tell her what I saw. My mouth hangs open, but I can't make myself speak. Saying it aloud would make it sound worse than it actually was. Plus, I was the only one to see it. There's no way for me to prove to Malinda that I haven't been making these frozen-time scenarios up ever since I came home. After all, the doctors prescribed medication. So I should be good now, right?

She's waiting for me to explain, bending closer, giving me a chance. I close my mouth. I want Mama Oak present when I tell her daughter what happened so Malinda can see her face. That way, she'll know I'm not just making shit up to escape her wrath. I don't say a word. Malinda shakes her head in disbelief and I pray her irritation with me stops short of bringing her to tears. When she cries, it feels like the end of everything. I've always found a way to pull her safely back from the edge of despair, but I'm not sure I'm strong enough to do it just now. How does Mama Oak look when she cries? I've never actually seen it happen. Even at Papa Oak's funeral, her face was closed off against the rest of us. She sat up tall and strong in the front-most pew, right across from her husband's open casket. She didn't even look at him, instead running her eyes over every other surface like a stranger there to observe. Then she was gone, before family and friends could bury her in their sympathies.

If I die before Malinda, I know she won't be strong. She might even be the type of woman who has to be carried out, sobbing and hollering and stretching her body in the direction of my corpse. When I woke up to her in the hospital, her heartbreak was touching. Now the memory threatens to repulse me. She runs up to our bedroom and slams the door. I linger at the kitchen table, counting the minutes.

Mama Oak's return is not silent. She slams the door on her way in and sweeps past the kitchen, pausing when she sees that I am in the same spot I was in when she left. She and I evaluate one another. Having heard Mama Oak's entrance, Malinda flies down the stairs and discovers her mother and I locked in a staring contest. Mama Oak is smiling; I am not. Malinda's face is swollen and wet. Evidently, she's let her imagination propel her toward the worst possibilities.

She asks if there is something her mother wants to tell her.

Mama Oak looks at Malinda like she has no idea where she came from. Her eyelids are at half-mast and her smile has slipped some. "I don't have nothing to say that you need to hear," she says.

Malinda asks what the hell *that's* supposed to mean. The stern countenance my mother-in-law is known for reappears.

"Who you think you talking to like that?" She steps closer to Malinda and I feel the earth move. "I don't need to explain myself to no child of mine."

Malinda insists she does if what she's explaining involves her husband. Her will is already flagging in this very short argument, but she's trying. She definitely wasn't designed with the capacity for anger in mind. Her rage is always gummed up by sadness, never sharp and hot. Regardless of the outcome, I'm certain this argument will change things, though I don't know how much. I want our family to escape without something vital being chipped away but, at the same time, can't bring myself to believe in the possibility.

Mama Oak is not at all impressed by Malinda's flash of courage. "Craig being your husband don't have nothing to do with nothing. I'll share what I want with the people concerned," she replies without raising her voice. "Right now, that ain't you."

Malinda's eyes bug and she looks at me. My stomach goes cold, but I force myself to speak. "Your mother," I begin. "I-I saw her—"

"Watching y'all?" Mama Oak finishes my sentence for me. I open my mouth, but nothing else comes out.

Malinda steps closer to her mother, a look of grim satisfaction on her face. She calls Mama Oak sick and asks what she could possibly get out of watching us have sex.

Mama Oak takes a long, slow breath, exhaling her words. "Don't worry about it, child. Just know," she says, starting to giggle. "You should be proud of yourself. I was never that flexible when I was your age." Malinda's mouth hangs open as her mother laughs. "Maybe your good-for-nothing daddy would'a kept his ass home if I'd wiggled 'round him like an acrobat." With every word, she laughs harder.

Malinda's dam has finally broken, but fury seems to be winning out over grief. She tells her mother to take her own advice about things that don't concern her, including our private lives. Mama Oak lets another laugh tumble free as she gazes at Malinda with something like pity.

"People say all the time their mamas ain't raise no fools,

but I guess I did. Girl, ain't nothing private. Your ups, your downs—your ups *and* downs," she chuckles again and Malinda seethes. She says she wonders whether her mother was more than curious. Asks if she was window shopping.

Mama Oak slaps her knee and howls. "Why? Because when your husband was choking in the hallway, you were out back, running around like a damn simpleton, and I was here where he needed me to be?"

The borders of Malinda's eyes and mouth expand to their greatest width. When they are on the verge of meeting, they abruptly constrict. Under the powerful heat of shame, she wilts.

"Child, boo. This lil boy ain't got nothing I want." Mama Oak wields her words like a mace, and I am disturbed to find myself wounded. "But here's a silver lining for you, baby-girl. Something my own hard-knock life taught me: the bright side is, if he cheats on you, you'll hear about it almost as soon as it happens. And that's excluding the times you walk in on it yourself." With a ghost's assurance, she glides to the nearest wall and raps her knuckles against it, a Cheshire grin bending her face. "Ain't no home enough to withstand prying eyes or wagging tongues. No matter how strong you build it." Time stops. I can't remember where I left my pills.

The silence is like a balm. Without the angst of an argument, the prospect of harmony is easier to imagine. In stillness, Malinda's suspended grief is magnified into something I can study. I am tempted to wipe away her tears but, left untouched, her agony remains acute for us both. I am able to understand it as a thing she feels, rather than a thing I need to fix. Instead of searching for my meds, maybe I should enjoy being the observer for a while. Beyond the reach of helplessness.

A faint rustle of fabric becomes the flapping of bird wings behind me. I turn to see Mama Oak opening and shutting her mouth as if to ensure its hinges haven't rusted. Her skirt swishes with recent movement at her shins. She notices me and smiles kindly at my surprise before rotating each of her wrists in turn. "So you did find it. Never met no one else in here before," she says.

"*In* here?" I ask. "Where are we?"

"Dunno," she says. "But I like it. Don't need to be nothing but what I am in this place."

"And what's that?"

"Alone," she answers without an ounce of irony. She moves around her daughter, like the river would a stone, to the back door, opening it onto a world frozen in place. "No shame in that or anything else here."

I glance at Malinda. Mama Oak's gaze follows mine, and she waves her daughter's inert anguish away, turning her attention back to the yard and beyond. "She'll be alright." On a revolving Earth, I'd peg her words as cruel, but they don't feel that way. Not *here*.

"Do you have pills? How do you get in and out of... this?" I ask. She doesn't turn to look at me this time. I walk over to the back door and fill the space beside her. I want to see what she sees. The world outside is flat but gorgeous without movement. A detailed diorama of suburban backyards, complete with bird decals arranged in an active V, deciduous trees made with real bark scabbing their popsicle-stick trunks, and bits of leaves torn and glued in bunches to resemble birches and maples.

"You can always choose," she says, "when to leave this place."

I take my time considering her words. I take all the time. Because I can.

WHEN I CRY, IT'S SOMEBODY ELSE'S BLOOD

THE FIRST SPECKS OF LIGHT ADORNED THE OPAQUE EXPANSE ABOVE like the sparkling minerals lodged in the walls of the creature's hilltop hovel. On skinny legs it stood, gazing upon the gabled roofs and cloud-spouting stacks of brick below. The village was asleep. Though not a rare event—it happened each time the light faded—it was always a fascinating change from the brighter hours. At those times, the inhabitants were constantly on the move. Sometimes they surged together, a single frightening entity, in the square at the center of their community. At other times, they marched in ordered lines, nearly identical to the tiniest beings who carried clods of dirt atop their glossy, segmented bodies in the grass. The village was cozily ensconced within a group of hills the size of mountains, but cragless and green all over.

Observing the activities of the villagers had become a favorite pastime for the creature who, as its courage grew, left off hiding behind the various shrubs dotting the slope of the hill on which it lived to venture inside their settlement and study them more closely. On one disastrous occasion, the creature was overcome by the lively emissions of a group of younglings. They were superb. Some heads were covered in black, bristly fur, some were capped by curls of various widths and roughnesses, and still others were overlain with a fine fuzz the light color of the knobbly seeds inside the green bulbs that fell from the tree beside the creature's home. The smallest of the bunch had a head full of inky wisps that made the creature shudder with longing as it gripped the sides of the barrel it crouched behind. The young one danced, leaping over a long piece of rope that swished in an ever-loping whorl. She landed first on one foot, then another. The other little ones clapped and made sounds that rose to dizzying pitches and fell so sweetly with the largest openings in their faces—the ones that showed their bones like tiny pebbles in a line together.

The creature widened its own opening and tried, with the aid of its long, blue tongue, to mimic the sounds it heard. It clapped its hands as they did, and was soon drawn out from behind the barrel into plain sight. The creature leapt with its thin, gray legs and landed on one toeless foot before springing into the air once more to meet the ground with the other.

The sounds from the little ones fell away until there was nothing to be heard but the footfalls and grunts of larger humans farther off, bustling to complete the business of their charming lives. After an interminable silence, the little ones let loose piercing shrieks accompanied by a new dance where every limb jerked and thrashed to carry them far, far away. The air became saturated with their screams as they fled. Only the smallest among them remained behind, paralyzed by fright. The creature ceased its imitation of the new dance to circle the little one. The orbs in her face leaked and their resultant sheen only amplified the creature's yearning. It had only ever seen the same color in the pools that sometimes formed on the floor of its hovel when the sky opened up. The hovel was not the creature's true home, but that home was too distant to return to. The creature's vessel had been destroyed on impact, but it had known what it was likely to face in undertaking its mission. To explore was to court danger in some form or other, but it was worth it if it meant learning more of the black beyond. Home would only ever be a memory, and that must be enough.

The loveliness of this human's orbs was unlike anything the creature had encountered in its celestial wanderings. It decided it must have one for its own. In measured steps, it inched closer, arm outstretched. To escape the creature's impending touch, the human child bent its body backwards until, losing balance, it toppled into the dirt. The creature never stopped moving closer, even when the little one's orbs vanished behind tightly wrinkled skin. Finally, the creature rested its fingers on the soft surface of the little one's face. There was nothing to compare it with. Certainly not its own skin, which was pitted and unyielding. This skin was pliant and warm. It was alive.

There was a lovely little bump in the middle of the youngling's face with two small holes. Grasping the strands at the back of the human's head, the creature tugged until the holes were easier to examine. There were fibers, some stuck together with a slimy substance that ran from one dark orifice down to the edge of her face. The orbs were still concealed like a secret, so the creature let go of the small one's strands to use one long finger from each hand to separate the wrinkly skin obscuring them. It was even more lustrous up close. Holding the skin open lest it snap shut again, the creature placed one finger over the black portion of the orb and pressed it, hoping to be shown some private magnificence only a worthy seeker could breach. But there was only noise.

The small human's opening had widened to an impossible degree. From it issued a wail more deafening than that of all the little ones combined. The sound battered the creature's senses so thoroughly that a pulsing ache began to spread inside its body. The creature let go of the human to search itself for the source of the pain, but found no answer. The human remembered its limbs and used them to scurry fast and far. At the same time, larger humans appeared. Those who carried stones hurled them at the creature with great force. One of them had an instrument that hurled small pellets faster than the creature could detect. They struck the creature, but did not break the toughness of its skin. The creature galloped up the hillside, digging its six fingers into the earth to pull itself away from the screaming mass of humans gathered at the base of the hill. As it made its way back to its solitary home, it thought how wonderfully strange humans were, and how intoxicating the allure of their features. Ever since, the creature could think of nothing else. As it stood alone above the dozing village, it remembered the tar-headed human child and resolved to somehow get that close again.

After the encounter with the small human, the creature took care to only visit the village at night. It learned quickly that it could watch them without risk until the sky lit up again. Many of them slept during the dusky hours, and those who did not were often among other humans in large, noisy groups. Sometimes they paired off, alone but for the hungry figure appraising them from the shadows. The pair in question would either press their faces together in passionate appreciation, or pummel each other with hands in the shapes of boulders until they were each smeared with gore. Whenever one attacked too near the orbs, the creature flinched in terror of the beautiful sphere's destruction. Usually the one left standing would poke at the other with their foot. If the fallen human did not move, the victor would shamble off, sometimes glancing quickly back at their unmoving companion. At these times, the creature waited until the quiet had lain undisturbed for an appropriate amount of time. If no other seemed likely to arrive, the creature would sneak over to the unconscious form half in the gutter, and kneel beside it. After making some curious sounds of its own, the creature would pull open the skin around each orb to ensure that it was unharmed. With some difficulty, it wedged the two fingers and one thumb of its free hand into the area between orb and bone and pulled until it heard the pop of separation. Sometimes, the human remained still despite the loss of its organ. If, however, the human reawakened, the creature lovingly pounded its skull until the human was once again at rest.

After the first successful extraction, the creature held the slippery orb up and sniffed with the vertical slit that ran the length of its face. A complex odor came from the juice that dripped from the raggedly torn cord sprouting from the orb like a tail. The creature stuck out its tongue and caught the liquid as it dripped. The taste was much like the smell; both reminded the creature of the shiny, exploding instruments the humans sometimes used to chase it away.

These orbs were precious, and finally the creature had one, which it held to its chest as it slept. It could not bear to set the orb on the ground, for that was where its feet traveled—surely not a place for revered objects to rest. So, the following evening, the creature found an empty barrel like the one it had once hidden behind to watch the younglings, and rolled it up the hill into its home. There was barely enough room for it, but the creature labored to fit the barrel into a corner across from where it slept. From then on, the creature placed each new orb inside the barrel to keep for its very own.

They had seen the gray thing skulking in places the light did not reach. The inside-elbow corners where walls met. Among the long silhouettes of trees that stretched like stockings over and around the village. Behind and inside casks. Beneath bridges like a troll. The thing's speed made it difficult to discern whether what the villagers thought they saw had truly been there at all. But soon, word traveled that this was no ghost, but an Unfamiliar, bent on disturbing the peace. Its victims were easy to identify, for they each had only one eye. Those still in possession of both began staying indoors at night. What did it want with their eyes? They wondered. Did it eat them? Would it move on to their noses, their ears, their fingers and toes? Their hearts?

The creature's intent was never to fill the barrel. All it needed was a receptacle, for storage. In the months that followed, twenty orbs rolled and bumped together over the cask's wooden bottom. The creature did not take them in pairs. It required only one from each human—young ones, old ones, fat ones, thin ones, with skin of every shade—in order to see what secrets each of them held. One of the first orbs the creature tried on belonged to a human male that had been beaten bloody by a larger human female. She had exerted all of her strength in dispatching the male as the creature squatted behind the low wall surrounding their land. The human male looked as if he had spent a great deal of his life being flattened by circumstance. He was economically made, with petite appendages—a fragile being whose last agonizing moments of life took place in a mid-sized rectangle of lawn behind his home. The female, who was already bleeding herself, shoved the male from their tiny cottage and brandished a heavy metallic disk used for cooking. She crushed the male's bones with repeated blows, grunting all the while. When she had finished, she loomed over the male, water dripping from her face. After some time, she let the cooking disk slip from her fingers. She crouched into a ball in the grass and her entire body shook, her lamentations muffled by the hands she held to her mouth. Eventually, she turned away from the mess at her feet, which now soaked and fed the earth, and trudged woefully back to the dwelling she once shared with the dead thing.

When the creature was sure it was alone outside, it crawled over the wall to examine the remains. There was not much to see. What was left was by-and-large a pulpy mixture of viscera and broken bone that made a gurgling soup, one that alternately shone in bubbling puddles and sunk into the soil. The creature stuck a three-pronged hand into the sludge in search of orbs. Its own innards thrummed excitedly when its fingers found a slick bulb that did not belong to the dirt. But its excitement turned to sadness upon finding the orb broken. The creature was not deterred. Encouraged by the knowledge that each human bore two orbs in its head, the creature continued its search until, wiping away the excess, it discovered one that was intact. The color of the central ring was at that point indeterminate due to the gloom of evening. Only after rinsing the orb in rainwater did the lovely hazel circle become visible.

Stretching wide a pore in its own head, the creature linked the torn length of muscle to its own inner workings and forced the orb into place. The black dot at the center expanded and the creature felt its head being ripped open. Projected inside the creature's mind were scenes it did not know. In one instant, the creature was part of a group of small humans who played and made delightful noises and traveled on awkward limbs up and down the hills surrounding the village. In the next, the female appeared. She was giddy and affectionate, with plump fingers that caressed tenderly. In the next scene, there were no other humans—just a cold, empty room where pieces of meat hung from sharp metal hooks and brief clouds accompanied each remembered breath. A profound emptiness overwhelmed the creature, who was relieved when the next memory took place elsewhere. A shopfront where yellow rays of light streamed in and warmed everything. Piles of meat in all varieties, dressed with fake green foliage, sat enticingly under glass. However, the comfort the creature felt was promptly shattered by a new memory in which the female reappeared, older now. Her plate was being piled high by the male with meat. She groaned in discomfort, unable to continue. The male picked up another dripping piece with his fingers and stuffed it between her lips. Another memory came. The shopfront was empty. No customers milling about. No meat in the displays. Just the male alone, tucking one last steak into his satchel, and shutting the store for good. A new scene—a one-room cottage with a window in each wall and a scant amount of plain, wooden furniture. There was nothing but a hunger so pervasive, the male could not be still. He moved into the kitchen, grabbed a knife, and glided like a phantom to his wife's bedside. At the very moment he was about to fillet her already ravaged bicep, she opened her eyes.

"I knew it! You promised you'd never do it again, but I knew you would!" she screamed. Ashamed, but made hungrier by the angry swing of her jowls, the man plunged the knife into his wife's gut. Howling, she staggered out of bed toward her husband. The man cowered before her. She pulled the knife from her stomach and threw it aside. As the man backed away, his wife grabbed the cast-iron skillet that hung above the stove and came for him. The creature raised its arms to block each invisible strike, squishing itself together in fear. Unable to go on, the creature yanked out the orb and let the familiarity of its surroundings wash over. The knowledge acquired from each memory was then integrated into the creature's consciousness. It lay on its back afterward, breathing deeply. How interesting.

As the creature learned more about the humans, they too gleaned what they could of it. Talk circulated endlessly about the eye-stealing maniac, which a number of villagers recalled from an earlier incident with the children while they were playing together at the hamlet's edge. Some even remembered in what direction the creature had retreated. No one had been willing to go after it then, for no one was certain how many of those things there were, nor whether a multitude would attack at full strength if provoked. But the systematic mutilation of so many was too great a crime to ignore. So what if they started a war? They would finish it, too. Thus, it was decided after the latest bloody snatching occurred to seek the creature out and destroy it.

Posters with the indistinct outline of a fiend were pasted to the sides of every building. BEWARE! It was little more than a slightly amorphous portrait with two beady, red eyes and a mouth stacked with pointed, spit-slick teeth. TAKE CARE! The villagers began stealing the blinders from their horses to wear in the daytime, exchanging them for blindfolds at night while they lay in bed. They assumed the creature was likely too simple to realize their eyes were hidden by these articles. They would be safe. They would make themselves safe.

They would win.

Humanity was so captivating. Every person whose memories the creature viewed had been wounded, and wounded others in return. But causing pain was a form of closeness; it was how they shared themselves with one another. One female had been strangled into unconsciousness by a lover; a young male had a hole blown through his knee by a gun; a poisoned female retched in an unlit, narrow passage, clutching herself in agony. It was beautiful, feeling what they had felt; seeing what they had seen.

One night, the creature journeyed back to the village with a plan to obtain the orb of a human child, which it had not yet worn as the children were kept indoors once the sun went down. The creature raced on all fours into town just as a mob of men toting all manner of weaponry surged up the hill toward the creature's home. The creature crept through the mostly vacant village streets until it heard laughter that could only have come from a little one. Beneath a nearby windowsill, the creature waited for the murmurs of woman and child to subside. After the bedroom door creaked shut, the creature forced the window up, splintering the lock, and peeked into the dimly lit space. There was a small bed just below. Tucked within a wad of blankets was a precious imp with black curls. Immediately the creature recognized the child whose orb it had pressed before. Like an insect, the creature skittered inside. Disregarding all but the child, the creature pushed its face quite close, taking in the glow of the little one's skin in the soft, orange light emanating from a far corner of the room. Sensing a strange presence, the child opened her eyes.

Eyes, the creature thought, recalling the term from a memory it had seen. It reached for the girl, who moved her head away, mouth quivering open. The creature pulled its hand back as if stung. "Ahhhs," it said. The child sat up in bed, puzzled and afraid. The creature pointed to her face, her orbs, then at its own slate-gray face. The girl's entire face opened up as comprehension dawned.

"Eyes," she said, placing a tiny hand over each of hers.

"Aieez," the creature repeated, putting three fingertips where its eyes would have been had it been born human. The little girl nodded.

"You took them, didn't you?"

It was the creature's turn to nod. It smiled and tried to mime all of what it had seen, but the girl shook her head and pressed her back against the wall. The creature continued gesturing furiously, but the girl could only tremble.

The creature grabbed hold of her. She tried to cry out, but the creature covered her mouth with a narrow hand. As she squirmed, the creature plucked out one of her eyes in one nimble movement. The shock of it silenced her. The creature then pulled another eye from a pocket of skin in its side and inserted it into the girl's empty socket. She stopped struggling. Her mouth hung slack, the corners drawn slightly up. She then spread her arms, enveloping the room, and the creature knew she was reliving the memories inside the eye. The girl hugged herself hard and cried. Eventually, her breaths came slower until she barely breathed at all. Suddenly, she began to claw at the foreign eye in her skull, scratching red lines into her cheek, her temple, her eyelid. Heavy footsteps grew closer. The creature held the girl's bucking frame in place and removed the eye he had planted in her. The girl's mother burst into the room in time to see her child lying on her side, hair in her face, while the window shade fluttered in the breeze.

She got to her knees, searching cautiously beneath the child's bed and in her closet. She even crawled across the mattress to peer through the open window.

"Didn't I close...?" the woman began, trying to shake the cobwebs from her mind. "Is everything alright?" she asked.

The girl sat up and the curtain of hair fell away from her face. Her mother screamed.

Outside, fire writhed atop the creature's hill. The tree it loved was burning. An angry group of humans swarmed. They made a fence of their bodies to crown the hilltop, and filled the sky with their demented cries. The barrel had been brought outside and overturned. Eyes rolled down the hill as if escaping the flames. The humans had joined together in their distress and found a way to share their pain with one another as the creature had done using their eyes. It could not help but feel joy as it knelt at the foot of the hill it once called home, gathering as many eyes as it could without being seen. Then off into the night, it ran— away from the pain of this place to one as yet undiscovered. The world and all its memories awaited.

INTERMISSION

A FIGURE IS POWDERING MY FOREHEAD TO REDUCE THE SHINE. No face. No words. Only perfunctory movement. They are as inscrutable as my own shadow, and then they are gone. There is no stage. There are no lights. Yet, this is a performance. He comes to me again, the director of these many farces.

You're doing well out there. Better than I had hoped. Perhaps your own hurts have taught you something.

A child's backpack is held up to my drooping body in consideration. A new accessory for a new tale. But are they only stories? What I felt, holding my son to my chest (*you don't have a son*), getting punched and kicked bloody (*you are intact, whole*), and with endless screams from an infinite Hell ringing in my ears (*you are sat at a vanity with only me for company, in a room with no door*)... everything I felt was real. I was in those lives. Living them. Are these not my own hurts? If not, where are the ones they belong to? Have their souls been summoned to perform elsewhere? Or do they only exist for as long as I am forced to fill out their skins?

What is this place?

That is none of your concern.

Though he replies to them, I cannot speak my thoughts

aloud. The mouth on my face only opens to mumble the names Agnes, Martin, and Malinda in sloppy succession. How many beings have been lured away from their own lives to playact in others? And why use me?

Use *you? This is a continuation; you have always played this part.*

I don't understand.

An uncountable number of rings encircle his pupils, whirling like the skirts of dervishes, and I think of Saturn, the ages of trees, a hypnotist's watch. The rings blink in patterns I am able to comprehend as speech. A code. *Don't worry; we've paused your program for now. It will be there when you return.* It isn't really an intermission, because no member of the audience ever leaves. The show goes on indefinitely as far as I can tell and they're concerned. Players disappear through the floors, replaced by others as and when each new story begins. He drifts away to check on the faceless throng, a sea of indistinguishable mounds, gray-dark but for the pinpricks twinkling in their heads like stars.

Sometimes, while delivering my lines, I catch the shadows of spectators jostling for a better view in a prop dish as it dries on the rack, or reflected in a co-star's despairing eyes. Faint echoes of their jeers reverberate through the walls, teasing my ears. My head nearly jerks to locate them properly, but self-preservation kicks in and I force myself to blink it all away. I have to. I don't want his disappointed stare to find and fix me to the spot. Anything but that. Control yourself. Pay no attention to the multitude gathered out of sight.

May fate absolve us all if you shatter the illusion.

IN BETWEEN

A WOMAN STARED AT HER SHADOW AS ITS MOUTH OPENED, YELLOW and empty, like a stencil in sunshine. The sharp corners of its smile rose almost to its eyes. In the rigid manner of a chalk outline, it sprawled in a sea of carpet-fiber braids, each twist of wool stumping off like roughly bitten legs. The woman's legs were barely covered by the hem of something too large to be a shirt but too small not to attract scandalized stares if worn on its own. The shadow's limbs bent in impossible ways as the woman looked on, her own limbs comfortably untangled, for she was the audience, not the performer in this show. Embarrassment crept pleasantly up her neck and she looked away, a coy smile on her lips, as the shadow's angles softened into the shape of a heart. Not a wet and ugly human heart, but the kind that Valentines exchange, with neatly cut edges that open the skin of your palm if pulled too quickly out of hand. The shadow loved her in that outfit. If it'd had any lips to lick, it would have while winking its desperately empty eye.

Returning to a shape that was mostly human, the shadow beckoned. Isley spread her thighs and dug her knees deep into the carpet on either side of the shadow's would-be-waist. She unfurled onto all-fours. The shadow stretched its torso in a compass circle around one side of her until its flat head rested between her legs. She lowered and wound her backside above the carved-out mouth as if to let it taste her. She touched herself until she bucked wildly above the shadow's face. The shadow raised its arms and mimed stroking her legs as Isley shivered against her own dexterous fingers. The shadow wanted so badly to touch her with its own hands, but had promised not to. Instead, it expanded its chest in a parody of inhalation, pretending to take in the scent of her before shrinking back to a shape that resembled a life-sized cardboard cut-out.

Isley bowed her head until her nose rested where the shadow's would be. She laid a hand atop the one that waved up from the floor, bringing the tip of each finger down to touch its two-dimensional twin with slow and deliberate tenderness. She pressed her mouth to the one made of light on the carpet, mushing her lips against the floor in a Hollywood kiss. Specks of lint and hard dirt stuck to her lip gloss and she left it there the way she would the saliva of an eager lover so as not to shame. It was too bad, really, that their latest bridge hadn't lasted long. He was a slick-tongued bartender who had been so bold as to ask Isley if she would be free at the end of his shift. She had thought his boldness must bode well. Turns out it didn't. Isley and Avery had not even made it to the end of their foreplay before he had gone limp, unable to handle Avery's presence inside him. No human being was the same; some were heartier than others. This one had unfortunately been one of the others and now sat, chopped up and stuffed inside a bag in their basement. She hoped today to find another.

The warmth of a human being always helped Isley imagine more fully who her shadow lover might have been in the stretch of time before they had met. Avery had only been inside her twice, and that had been more than enough. It was a level of intimacy that still frightened her. But sex, that was easy. A human act. And she very much expected their next human connector to end up like the last. It was troublesome doing things this way, but it always turned out to be necessary. The two of them had learned long ago that compassion had its limits; what you did when you reached those limits made the difference between joy and despair.

"Was it good for you?" she whispered. Warm, wet beads rolled down from the space between her thighs.

The shadow cocked its head and widened its harlequin eyes, smiling up at her with a mouth full of sunshine.

Isley and Avery first met when the former was ten years old. She did not have any close friends, but got along with her classmates well enough. All except one, who often glared with a hatred so matter-of-fact it was almost boring. Tabitha Crenley was a recent transplant who did not care to make friends, with anyone. All she wanted in this whole stupid world was to reveal Isley's true nature to the idiots at school. No one had noticed. It would be hard to if you actually played during recess. The constant tangle of bodies and voices was a perfect distraction. All anyone had to do was look, *really* look, but no one ever did. No one but Tabitha.

One afternoon, Isley found herself alone with Tabitha. Each of them occupied a separate bench on opposite sides of the school's entrance. The other kids had all either been picked up or were killing time in the air-conditioned cafeteria until their parents arrived. Though late afternoon approached, the sun washed brightly down the face of the building, including where the girls sat in ghost-town silence. Tabitha scanned Isley from kinky head to down past her skinny legs, eyes lingering on the area beneath Isley's dangling feet. Isley was too far away to see it, and engrossed in a chapter book besides, but a vein throbbed like lightning along Tabitha's forehead. Isley often read alone, not playing with the others unless expressly invited. She was the only Black kid in her class, one of just three in the entire grade, but it didn't bother her. It was enough for her to occupy other worlds and form one-way friendships with the kappas, wizards, and extraterrestrials she encountered there. The book she was reading followed a young girl on a sea voyage who had just discovered a stowaway. Ten minutes passed with only the sounds of bees carrying their fuzzy bulk from flower to flower. Finally, Tabitha added her own voice to the outdoor noise.

"I know what you are."

Isley couldn't be sure at first that her classmate had spoken. She watched Tabitha's mouth for more words.

"You're the Devil, aren't you?"

"The Devil?" Isley didn't understand.

"Fine—a demon minion; whatever."

Isley frowned. She looked over one shoulder, then the other, straining her ears to catch the giggles of the classmates who had masterminded this joke (if you could call it that). Would she get pelted by water balloons or smacked in the back of the head? Would someone dump their nasty cottage cheese from lunch into her lap? No matter which way she twisted her neck, she couldn't see anyone. "I don't get it, Tabitha. Sorry," she added, in case it was her own failing that kept her from seeing the point of whatever this was. She returned to the page she had been reading.

"You. Are. From. Hell," Tabitha said in a deadpan that pinned her features down at the sides. There wasn't a single sign of laughter for Isley to see when she looked up again. She scoured her memory for any bit of meanness she might have shown, to Tabitha or anyone, but came up empty. She could not think of anything she had ever said or done to upset Tabitha enough to call her these things. Isley wasn't even altogether clear on the Devil and his doings. All she had ever heard was that he'd disappointed God and been sent away forever to a place where he could take out his anger on the bad people who ended up there. The worst thing Isley could remember doing was sneaking out through her bedroom window without her mother's permission to get a good look at the moon. But the only person to suffer that night was Isley, who'd been laid up for months with a broken leg after falling off the roof.

"Why you keep saying that?"

From that distance, the movement of Tabitha's eyes wasn't easy to catch. She went from looking at Isley to staring at the space beneath the bench Isley sat on. The shadow of the bench was funhouse-long and stretched away like an inky specter. But where Isley's feet swung, there was nothing. The slats between the wood, which should have melded together darkly where she sat, were separated on the ground as if no tiny back and bottom pressed against them. Though the bench held an occupant, its shadow-self did not.

"You don't have a shadow." Tabitha, eyes cold and hard, prepared herself for Isley's tearful apology, the begging for her terrible secret to be kept.

"So?" Isley said, shrugging. She had noticed a long time ago. As far as she was concerned, it was just one of those things that happened to be true. Though slightly baffled, her curiosity ebbed when she realized no one else had noticed. Well, almost no one. Her mother had known all along, but she'd said it was nothing to worry about. Isley's mother had never gone to church and didn't start even after her shadow-less baby was born. She always told Isley that she was a good girl, and that this was all that mattered. Isley had never met her grandparents, though. Sometimes she wondered if they would disagree with what her mother had told her. Clearly, Tabitha did. Her face was twisted into a vile knot of disbelief.

"*So?* People have shadows! *So*, whatever you are *isn't* a person!"

"Well, I look like one," Isley replied, holding out her arms and legs for inspection. She crooked them this way and that before jumping off the bench to wiggle around in front of Tabitha, shoulders shimmying. "I can't go through walls, so I'm not a ghost. And I don't got scales or claws or fangs," she said, yanking her bottom lip down so Tabitha could see her teeth. "I must be a person." Isley slid the soles of her sneakers along the concrete in a faux moonwalk.

Tabitha's left eye twitched.

It was then that Isley's mother arrived at the curb. As they pulled away, Isley turned in her seat to watch Tabitha's angry stare recede to a point beyond interpretation.

"Ma," Isley asked later that evening, "am I a demon?" She held her hands behind her back and crossed one leg over the other.

Isley's mother shut off the television and shifted on the couch in their dimly lit living room, her face inscrutable. "Why would you say a thing like that?"

"This girl at school said I must be."

Her mother chuckled. One could almost be convinced she was at ease. "Hmph. What, she mad you get better grades than her or something?"

Isley was sure her mother knew exactly why Tabitha had called her a demon. She also understood that her mother, whose voice had been the frequency of bedtime stories and too-loud laughter, of songs hummed late at night, and of *I love you* her entire life, had hoped to shield her from this very situation. Worry lay just beneath her mother's smile. In the story Isley was reading, the main character had run away from home because her parents refused to expose her to the harshness of life at sea. Parents wanted ease and happiness for their children, this Isley knew. But she wanted the truth this time, however hard.

"No, ma'am," Isley replied. "She said people have shadows, so I must not be a person." She watched the jiggle in her mother's leg grow more pronounced. "Is that true?"

Isley's mother seemed to hold a whole host of words inside her chest. She leaned forward, the urge to speak written plainly on her face. In the end, it felt to Isley as if many minutes had passed before she did.

"I don't know. What you are." She would not look at Isley. Could not. "I knew your daddy wasn't... right. But I liked him." She squeezed her hands together tightly in her lap. Isley waited for her mother to say more about the man who was half-responsible for her existence, but she didn't. "I never wanted you to feel bad about not having something so silly and useless." Her voice had abandoned its quiver. "It never stopped you being smart. Being kind, or good. And you are," she said, divorcing her clinging hands to grab Isley's. "I can't ever believe you don't belong here with me."

Isley watched her mother without speaking. She didn't trust her to provide answers that did not hide more questions. Outwardly, she nodded her agreement not to worry what anyone said at school. She would keep being good. In her room at night, she sunk back into the seafaring tale she had been reading. In the back of her mind she wondered, if she ever stowed away, how long she could last before getting caught.

Weeks passed, and the discomfort of that evening pushed itself further back in the minds of mother and daughter. Isley never again brought up the thing she so conspicuously lacked, and neither did her mother. Nearly every teacher within earshot assumed a childish rivalry was to blame for the tales Tabitha spun. Isley's teacher, Ms. Hollis, had in fact noticed the girl's shadowlessness around the start of the year. But because she was among the best-performing students in the grade, she thought better of drawing undue attention to Isley's... condition. Isley was well behaved. Why make her pay so dearly for something she could presumably do nothing about? Therefore, anytime another teacher's eyes began to linger on the child, Ms. Hollis was quick to ask them the time, or to mention the incredibly disappointing date she'd been on the night before. It always worked. But though the attentions of harried adults were easy enough to lead in new directions, Isley's schoolmates, hungry for any mention of the bizarre, would not be swayed. In a surprisingly short time, Tabitha turned them all against the demon girl with no shadow. She remarked on Isley's strangeness whenever the sun was high, whispering to whomever would listen.

The things they did to her were never done up close. The fear that she would tear their skin from their bodies and lick the insides like a candy wrapper was strong enough that no abuse could come from one of them alone. They had the instinct to protect each other from her. And so, it took the form of anonymous notes that made fun of her monstrous ugliness. *We know*, the notes implied, *what you really are*. And the cafeteria potato salad, coleslaw, or anything that was more wet than dry, would get tamped into balls from their trays at lunchtime to be flung in Isley's direction. Whenever she turned to see where it had come from, a sea of smiling faces drowned out any single indication of guilt. Chunks of starch got caught in her hair and hung there like rotten fruit, sometimes dropping to the floor in class because the school nurse, the only adult on staff with a similar curl pattern, hadn't been able to free every piece from her tangles in the bathroom. Isley would gather her hair, frizzy from sink water, into a single puffy bun, always tucking the soiled sections deep into the center before it was time to head home. Her mother was none the wiser since Isley had begged the nurse not to tell, and was unable to point the finger of blame in any specific direction besides.

. . .

On the swing-set alone at recess, Isley hung listlessly one afternoon. Everyone else yelped and roared at the other end of the playground, which may as well have been the other side of the world. No one would ask her to play anymore, even if they didn't believe every one of Tabitha's accusations; it was enough that maybe everyone else did. The rumors about Isley had grown jungle-wild. She became all manner of creature depending on the speaker. A mutant bat that sucked the jelly from unsuspecting eyeballs; a mirage that disappeared when you tried to touch her; a hobgoblin in the clever shape of a girl.

The metal links chaining her chosen swing in place burned hot against her forehead. Isley toyed with a plan to keep her eyes closed until the end of time. Maybe then, when no one else was left, the awful sickness that tunneled through her every morning would go away for good. She turned her face away from the searing chain-link when a breeze swept by. Abandoning her resolution for the moment, she opened her eyes. A dark shape like a leg mirrored her own on the ground and her heart sprung to her mouth. Was she... normal after all? Maybe her shadow had been lost and only needed time to find her. As she pondered, the dark shape rippled like a disturbed reflection and billowed into a much larger, human-shaped thing in the sand.

Her leaping heart plummeted.

The shadow waved. After looking around to make sure no one had strayed too close, she waved back. The shadow bent itself into letters that spelled *My name is Avery*. The letters fell together nicely as she read them. The shadow then pointed at her, an outline of negative space distinguishing its hand from its body.

"I'm Isley," she said. But before the polite spill of words she had been taught to say next could come out, she decided to ask what she actually wanted to know. "What are you?"

The shadow beckoned her closer. Isley got to her knees, absentmindedly plunging her fingers into the sand. The shadow reached for her with its own hand and she smiled at the sweetness of it. As the shadow-hand approached hers, nubs breached the dunes, gathering speed as they neared. Before she could do more than let her mouth fall open, a hand like a black hole emerged to hook its fingers around her wrist. Trying to move was pointless. A shock of something white-hot hit her as needle after fine needle began to prick her like frigid drops of rain. She felt the shiver of every piece of information she had ever received being combed through, and saw herself from below, irises a blur as her eyes rolled in one thousand directions. The ambivalence of her bare legs against trillions of grains of sand, while she was also suspended within the shadow's own unsettling dimension, sent her into throes of terror that usurped every supposed nightmare she had ever had. She saw herself and she saw the shadow. They were not separate, had never been, would never be.

When Avery released Isley, she buckled in the wake of a powerful emptiness. She was alone in her body again. Loneliness withered her into a fetal mound in the sand. She held a hand above her face, flexing her fingers and blocking out the sun.

"What was that?" she whispered.

As Isley lay there, she became aware of new memories. A story emerged in which Avery had been torn from its human self and told to wander until it found the one who needed it most. Isley asked Avery if its human had been a man or a woman since time had degraded the memories too severely to reveal their identity to her. Avery shrugged; that knowledge had never been essential to its purpose. Avery had apparently wandered for ages in search of companionship. The shadow suddenly swiveled its head from left to right. When it faced her again it shrugged once more, its negative scrawl of a mouth a drooping line.

"Oh. Everyone else is over there," she said, jabbing a thumb in the direction of her schoolmates. "No one likes me anymore. They think I'm a demon or something. Since I don't have a shadow."

Avery smiled wide, shapeshifting to explain that everything would be alright now. Avery could be her shadow. And no matter what, the two of them would always be friends.

Isley started to smile, then her stomach began to froth. She brought her knees to her chest and held them there. It was all so strange. She remembered what it had felt like to be one with Avery, and held herself tighter. If that was what the shadow did to everyone it met, she thought she knew why it had been alone for so long. "I don't know," she said.

The shadow raised a finger, triumphant. It warped until it was a perfect reflection of Isley in her tense pose of contemplation. A giggle escaped her as she stretched out one leg, then the other, and the shadow did the same, a mirror image in the sand. Maybe it *could* work. If the others saw Avery pretending to be her shadow, the bad stories about her might stop. She clambered upright and made sure the silhouette on the ground looked exactly as it should. Then, she took off running.

With cautious optimism, Isley reintegrated into the social fabric at school. Most of her schoolmates were immediately satisfied by Avery's advanced game of pretend. Tabitha, on the other hand, continued to keep her distance despite the other children's willingness to move on. Though she returned to being alone with a book more often than not, Isley's aloneness was no longer amplified by isolation. She was able to enjoy herself again without the question of her humanity separating her from everyone. However, if she turned her mind in its direction long enough, Isley could just make out the thickening layer of resentment that kept her from accepting any new invitations to play. At such times, her stomach knotted as she watched them run after one another, their shadows overlapping to create mutants, without a single thought of being eaten alive by the one they chased.

Isley's mother was ecstatic when she showed off her new shadow. Immediately, she was on the phone to her own parents, who would apparently be pleased as punch to get a visit from their grandbaby. No matter how she tried, Isley could not find it in her to share in their joy, which she now knew was conditional when it came to her. In her room, Avery asked why she hadn't told her mother about the bargain they'd struck.

"She doesn't tell me everything either," was Isley's only reply. She asked Avery more about itself. "Who made you leave your human? Was it a witch?"

Avery did not know what or whom the creature responsible had been; only that they could look human if they chose, but knew more than Avery's human could have ever hoped to learn in several lifetimes. Frightened, Avery's first act as an independent soul had been to flee. Avery spent its years alone, slithering into corners to spy on lives it had never witnessed before. It learned a lot by watching, and sometimes imitated the more interesting humans it saw. Until it was discovered. Avery tried to befriend humans many times, but fear always took hold as they watched Avery move without a corporeal body. Some even set fire to places where Avery had been seen, hoping to cleanse the abomination from public memory.

Isley considered how her classmates had treated her. Sure, they hadn't used fire, but it wasn't hard to imagine how it might've felt if they had. "I wonder why people are like that," she said.

Avery shrugged. *They don't understand*, it said. *They don't want to.* Isley sat for quite some time as silence filled the room. The shadow held its form patiently, a painted figure on the floor. Eventually, Isley let her eyes rest on the face of her alarm clock. The digital numbers blurred into a many-jointed creature that glowed red.

"What if we made them?"

"Tabitha!" Isley made a beeline for her original heckler as soon as recess started. She had bided her time all day, mulling over how the conversation might go as Ms. Hollis corrected someone's math at the whiteboard. Tabitha played alone, hunkered at the surrounding forest's edge with a trio of dolls. The one in her hand wore a dress that looked homemade and her hair was glued on crooked. She glowered at Isley, who tried to catch her breath. "Look!" Isley shouted, pointing at the ground. There, commingled with Tabitha's, was another girl-shaped shadow. Its feet began where Isley's ended. Tabitha stared at it, willing it to turn into a five-headed goblin whose teeth grew past its eyes. She looked back up at Isley, but said nothing. "Can I play dolls with you?" Isley asked when her tolerance for the quiet finally faltered.

"No," Tabitha said. "I don't play with demon spawn."

"Tabitha, I'm not! I don't know why I didn't have one before, but I'm normal now. Avery's helping me."

Tabitha squinted at Isley, unsure of what she had just heard. "Avery?"

Isley pointed at the silhouette on the ground. "Avery is my shadow. We're friends."

Tabitha sneered. "Shadows aren't friends, moron. They don't have names. God, you don't even know what people do."

Anger spasmed in Isley, and her friendliness began to wane. "I'm not talking about people. I'm talking about me. *My* shadow's name is Avery." Avery waved frantically with both hands, but Tabitha did not see. She had already gone back to playing with her dolls, shaking her head at the poor simpleton blocking her light. Heat spread through Isley, flowering into a collar at her chin. Tabitha wasn't even trying to understand. And fear wasn't to blame. Isley looked down at Avery. "You were right," she said softly.

"Duh," Tabitha said without looking up. Isley didn't bother to correct her.

As she turned to go, Tabitha's arm shot out to her, doll in hand. Isley paused. She looked from the doll to Tabitha, whose arm shook. As Isley reached for the doll, Tabitha made a sound like a sob and gagged as if something were climbing up her throat. Isley stepped back.

"Tabitha?"

Her body had gone rigid, stuck in a permanent squat. With difficulty, she twisted her face up toward Isley's, grunting through clenched teeth. Tears streamed down her cheeks. Isley backed away and Tabitha shuddered hard, struggling to open her mouth. Without warning, her eyes rolled back into her skull and she thudded to the ground. The kids playing nearby froze. Seeing Tabitha so still made one of the other girls scream. Ms. Hollis could only stare helplessly upon arriving at the scene. Another teacher stopped short behind her before yelling for someone to call an ambulance. Ms. Hollis looked to Isley, a question in her eyes.

"Ms. Hollis, I didn't do it! I swear!"

Her teacher did not respond, but Isley thought she felt a partition rise between them before Ms. Hollis jogged away to consult with the other teachers. Isley looked down at Avery and found the shadow, a little girl no more, but instead a hulking shape with a cut-out grin.

Isley fled to the swings, but nowhere was far enough from the memory of Tabitha's blind stare amid the dandelions. Avery leered up at her. "You did that?" Isley asked. The shadow's mouth stretched wider. "Why?"

Slowly, Avery's smile shrank to nothing. It was déjà vu when the shadow reached its fingers up through the mountainous sand. As the others swarmed in panic in the distance, their hive well and truly disturbed, Isley knelt to lace her fingers through Avery's.

She deserved it.

Isley heard the words inside her head, but could not be certain if they were hers or Avery's. When Tabitha did not return to school, Isley was careful to hide her delight.

Thoughts of Tabitha Crenley had pumped Isley full of nostalgia that set her jittering for someone with a hometown feel. The one she found in the end was a cashier at her local grocery store whose name tag innocuously read *Ben*. Isley had known he'd be easy because he never glanced at a single item as he swiped them across the scanner—his eyes were locked on her and the beautiful, brown strip of belly that peeked out from beneath her baby tee whenever she raised her arms, her laughter like a wind chime. Isley caught Ben's eye and slowly rolled down the top of her shorts so the lines of her hipbones could not be missed. Ben wiped the sweat from his boyishly bare upper lip and did his bagging in slow motion, giving himself ample time to take in the rest of her. The middle-aged man in line behind Isley coughed, more uncomfortable than irritated. Upon hearing what she owed, Isley handed Ben a wad of cash, and a torn slip of paper with her phone number on it.

Avery was impatient by the time Ben arrived at their place. Isley enjoyed the boy's sweet admiration for only a few minutes before his eyes suddenly rolled up into his head and back again, their darkness now infinite. At Avery's command, Ben's fingers were thrust inside Isley to wriggle like two fat grubs in the knothole of a tree. Isley clutched the bedsheets and clenched around them. Avery moved Ben's other hand under Isley's shirt, pinching and plucking to the delight of them both. Ben's tongue writhed, first inside of Avery's mouth, then Isley's as the three of them held fast to one another. Isley cried out, as she often did when her pleasure mounted, and stared into the pair of eyes being held open by Avery's spectral fingers to look at her. Ben's were gray and wide, like someone had come up from behind and plunged a needle into his backside. When all was said, done, and done again, Ben swayed, drained, at the center of the room. He had witnessed it all, but from far away. The fog in his brain was almost dense enough for Isley to touch as she watched him try to recall the thing that had trapped him so completely. He noticed something moving at his feet, and looked down.

Ben had two shadows, equally distinct. One stretched his own profile tall and seemed to observe the other... which looked up at him with cut-out eyes. Ben screamed and the sound wavered as the harlequin eyes on the floor expanded with glee. Isley petted Ben's arm and shushed him, then cupped the back of his head. She told him it was alright and asked hadn't they had fun? They could do this all the time if he wanted. Ben shook his head and began inching backward. The mouth was like a massive, quartered slice of apple that Ben feared would swallow him, and so he continued to scream. Isley sighed as shame passed over her like a slow-moving cloud. She stared at Ben, her eyes desolate, yearning—then she blinked the emptiness away. With a smile as beatific as the one on the floor, Isley bent down and pulled something from beneath her bed. Ben's throat burned. He was too worn out to go on yelling. He bowed his head to cry, and noticed Isley had no dark underline bringing her into stronger relief. He raised his head and watched her glow in the tide of sunlight that poured in through the windows. His last thought was of Wendy sewing Peter Pan's shadow to his feet before Isley struck him with the hammer in her fist.

Isley had planned to shower immediately after getting off with Avery this time, but instead she sat with her legs crossed beside the heap of carved-up sinew that was once called Ben.

She gazed through the window at the passing world below, unseen and perfectly content. The sun was far too bright for anyone to have a clear view of the unlit room. Ben would have to be disposed of, along with the bartender, before the mice ate through the bags and let their smell out, but it would be okay to sit for a little while. Avery slid away from Isley to creep up the wall behind her. From there, it could pretend to lean, observing the same slice of life as its beloved. It did not matter to either of them, in moments like these, how legible they were to those who moved through their days, mindlessly mimicked by the featureless doppelgängers at their feet whom they believed to be nameless.

HOMUNCULUS

"Her hair was blonde, but more white-blonde than yellow, see?"

Charles focuses on where the man's shaking finger stabs the photograph. Its subject is wrapped in a red sundress with daisies vivid enough to be real raining diagonally across the fabric. Strands fly loose from her ponytail like wisps of raw cotton in the wind. Her mouth is bright with laughter, her green eyes mushed into semicircles by full, pink cheeks. She'd had a nice face, a kind one, that was likely quite plain and smooth as milk when not decorated by a smile. He wonders where the photo was taken. Clearly not within city limits, as there are no stacks belching white mist, or tinkerers flogging robotic limbs made to replace those lost in the Great War. Only hills that seem to rise and fall infinitely, back and back and back, under a sky so clear of smog it almost hurts to look at it. Charles pinches the bottom corner of the photo between index finger and thumb, attempting to take it for reference. The man resists for a moment before letting the picture slip from his grasp. His fingers extend briefly before curling in on themselves.

"Can you do it?" the man asks.

"Of course," Charles says, a bit flippantly. Then, seeing himself reflected in the man's eyes, he says, "Yes. Yes, I can."

The smile given in response—full of relief and hope—might have been enough to sate a man with no cares to speak of. But Charles has a home to maintain, and is thus forced to ask for payment.

The bodies slump in the corner, their empty eye sockets gaping at nothing in particular. Arms, legs, fingers entwine. This immobile audience oversees Charles at his work, silently critical. He presses the faux skin to its muscle and bone gently, gently. He must wear gloves. It is paramount that the ridges in his fingertips do not infiltrate the surface of the doll; the figures must at least *appear* to be of nature's making. After completely clothing one arm in a pallid sheath of fake skin, Charles removes one glove and shakes the open hand with his eyes closed, careful not to squeeze too tight. Yes. He could indeed be palm to warm palm with an actual young lady. Success. Now, on to the rest of the body.

"You can't keep doing this," Esther says. She peeks over Charles's shoulder and gazes at him from the creased corners of her eyes. Ebony hair jumps loose from her generously pinned head to fill the space between her eyebrows. She uses a finger to bury the mutinous strands more deeply inside the bouquet of coarse curls straining to blossom from her head.

"I know," Charles says, but keeps working. His client had made a down payment after all.

"It won't help him. In the end," she says. Her vacant eyes rove his workspace. Bins brim with synthetic hair. Eyes made of resin nearly spill from an open drawer, their glossy irises brown, blue, hazel, green, and gray. Charles fingers the bodiless arm delicately. It is coated in a self-heating substance, with firm rubber muscles swaddling plastic bones. Charles uses a time-tested mixture of additives with silicone sourced from specialty retailers. It had taken him over a decade, but he'd finally hit upon the perfect combination of ingredients to make the skin of his creations feel eerily human. The earlier models were passable, but this is a level of realism he never imagined achieving. If he had not forfeited most of his too-long life to this trade, which could only be whispered about in deserted rooms and alleyways narrow enough to be missed by the peering occupants of airships, he could almost feel proud. As it is, he feels only a penetrating weariness.

Esther turns her head on her thin neck to look at Charles. She rests her round, little-girl chin upon his shoulder. "Did it help you?" she asks.

"I'm not lonely anymore, am I?" he answers. He presses a plastic fingernail hard against the drop of glue meant to fasten it in place. Esther watches an angry pink glow through the viewfinder of Charles's thumbnail. He releases the pressure. The pink softens to a pale peach. "I can't imagine my life without you."

A slow grin crawls into place beneath Esther's nose. "Of course you can." She kisses the hard salt and pepper stubble on his cheek. If she had any blood, her pricked bottom lip would grow a single bead for her to lick away. "That's why I'm here."

Like every day since the one on which her eyes first clicked open and locked onto his in recognition, Esther is right. She is always right.

In bed at night, his body yearns for hers. Running a hand across the sheets, he imagines catching hold of her warmth, but Esther has her own room downstairs. She does not require sleep, but enjoys her privacy nonetheless. She is not the one who once shared his bed, whose hips and shoulders wore the neon outline of the sun so elegantly every morning when he opened his eyes, so Charles does not—will not—allow desire to rupture the borders of his own body. Sometimes, when he passes her closed door, Charles hears Esther speaking softly to Madeline, the doll he made for her out of burlap stuffed with handkerchiefs after months of Esther crying for a companion of her own. With every stitch, jealousy had eroded him further. Was he not enough? That's not what she meant and he knew it, she'd said. So he finished cobbling Madeline together out of the least appealing materials he'd had to hand in hopes that Esther would feel the lack and crave his touch instead. But Esther was quite satisfied with Madeline as she was. He would have made Esther a doll out of his own mottled skin had she asked. He would have done anything. Absolutely anything.

"Thank you! Oh, *thank* you!"

"Hello, Daniel," the doll says to the overjoyed man. Her hair is more white-blonde than yellow, and her unsmiling face is as smooth as milk. She looks like the woman in the photograph as a child on the cusp of womanhood, and always would. The adult-sized models never functioned properly for long, so Charles stopped making them in favor of smaller models with longer lifespans. The people who came to him did not mind, for they were so hungry for a glimpse of their lost loved ones that any version of them would do. His latest creation looks upon her new guardian with eyes unclouded by mistrust. Her clockwork heart is too young to doubt—him, or anyone.

"I can't begin to thank you," Daniel says to Charles.

Would it help him in the end? After the initial burst of joy at his beloved's return subsides, Charles knows that, in time, a new platoon of emotions will creep in under the cover of Daniel's cheer. Questions he never thought to ask will claw up to confront him, no matter the excess of unspent love he showers upon her to distract himself. Now that she's here, what will you do with all that pain? Is it best saved for later? Because the doll *will* die. But what will happen to her if it's you who goes first this time? What does she want to happen? However close the resemblance, she is not Her, and you can never know this heart so well as the one you buried. Will you look back on this day and those that follow with ecstasy, or regret? Over many years, Charles had prepared three answers to that last, most important question: the one he would give a customer, the one he would give a colleague if he had one, and the one he knew in his heart to be true.

Well. One can hurl *shoulds* into the wind forever.

"I'm... glad you're satisfied," Charles replies. He dons a small smile like a costume. Let Daniel figure out the answers on his own. Who knows—maybe they'll be different. Charles will never know either way.

Daniel hands Charles a pouch heavy with coins and leaves the café, arm-in-arm with his new, old friend. She laughs as the bell above the closing door tinkles.

He had assumed he would forget her eventually. The mockingly large eyes, a brown as light as decaying autumn leaves. The way she held utensils when she ate. Laughter that was always hesitant to be heard. Dark hair like wool that somehow always sprang loose to fall into her eyes regardless of how steadfastly she pinned it. The deep slant of her vowels rolling up out of her full-lipped mouth. A slant that had regrettably straightened out with each new pair of vocal cords. Surely the finer details should fade over time. But everything she had been is still as crisply imprinted upon him as on the day they first met—the lines and colors sharp enough to sting — and he refused to let them wink out of knowing. Those who learned of his occupation and requested this service of him were only ever allowed one doll. When it died, that was that. He refused to let anyone else live out their days in the particular Hell he had cultivated for himself until it bloomed, soft, agonizing and infinite. Infinite because every time she died, he rebuilt her.

"Esther," Charles says later that night. "Do you wish for another life?"

"No," she answers, to his great relief. "I can't imagine a life other than the one I have."

"You can have any life you choose," he says. His words are jagged. Pained.

She stares at him with the fourth pair of eyes ever to look at him that way. An eternity elapses. "I choose this life," she says finally. "I know you feel an emptiness, and I am happy to fill it."

Charles's mouth contracts to its smallest point. "I don't need you to fill my empty spaces. I want you to be happy," he says. Maybe, if he repeats the words often enough, they'll become true. Wood into flesh. No puppeteering required.

"It's alright," Esther says. Her voice is flat, but not unkind. "I don't mind that you need me."

This he cannot deny. The missing will never reach its end, because he will never let it. "I'll give you anything you ask for," he whispers, his misery and ecstasy enfolding one another in a consumptive embrace. She brings her elfin hand up to his face and smiles.

"I ask only for this life. With you."

TAKE IT FROM ME

THE LIGHTS WERE OFF BECAUSE THERE WAS NOTHING TO SEE. DUST had settled in snowdrifts onto every chair and bookcase, every window ledge and side table. The carpet lay under a blizzard of grime. On her few trips from room to room, Imelda deliberately made her steps heavy enough to leave footprints behind. In bed, she closed her eyes. The sun pierced her memory, then radiated its warmth and light outward until, finally, the entire scene dripped into place behind her eyelids, uninterrupted.

She had agreed to meet Evan that day because she had thought, hoped, they would finally have the long-awaited discussion that would set things right. She had come prepared to bare all, to be open about every way he had hurt her, which she was certain he had not done on purpose, and all the ways they might start to work on things. Getting herself to their meeting place had been Herculean. She moved slowly, on crutches. The errant elbows and handbags that occasionally collided with her made it nearly impossible to get along without support. Sure she was bandaged, but any activity rubbed them against her flayed areas and the pain doubled her over every few steps. Each time, she was certain she wouldn't make it. Eventually, she stood heaving beside a park bench where Evan sat looking vaguely irritated.

He did not stand to greet her. Instead, she swiveled into place, resting her lopsided bottom onto the farthest end. The blue birds—her mother had taught her that the space between words was vital as these were not bluebirds, only birds with blue feathers—shrieked admonishments at one another, or maybe the reproach was meant for all present. She mused, during a lull in conversation that was quickly tilting into awkwardness, about what the birds must think of the humans who roamed this patch of greenery endlessly. The only reply was silence, so she stuttered on about the ways in which scrub-jay husbands probably greeted their wives when they got home. Those chirps must sound different from the rest, she'd said. Evan looked at his watch. *"Honey, I'm home! I know we usually grab dinner together, but I thought I'd be proactive and pick some up myself. On my way back, though, I flew too low and a flying squirrel clipped my leg! I was so surprised, I dropped the bug I'd found for us. You know how clumsy I can be. But omigosh, you should've seen the size of that thing!" And his wife would roll her eyes because he was always exaggerating about something. Then she'd pick up a twig with her beak and reveal a stash of leftover acorns and he'd be so relieved.* And she had laughed, too loudly, hoping to elicit a smirk from him at the very least. Instead, he glared into her eyes with a withering heat.

They're just birds, he'd replied. He brought his hand to her face, then up to her hairline. He tore a large strip of skin away from her forehead, which he tossed to the ground. All manner of birds rushed over at once to peck and pull at the discarded scrap. A banana fold of skin drooped at the bridge of Imelda's nose and she whimpered. Each time she tried to push it back into place, rubbing hard in the hope that it would stick to the blood pearling there, she would wince at the pain and feel her papery skin detach again. She felt something wet roll down her chin, but couldn't be sure whether it was tears or blood. She refused to check.

Evan's nostrils twitched. *Look, I think we're just wasting each other's time now, don't you?* A pigeon swooped into the fray and swept the dominating jay aside with one flapping wing. *We've been doing this for a while now, and I realized you're just not what I'm looking for. I think I tried to go against type and make it work, like... broaden my horizons, keep an open mind or whatever. But if I'm honest with myself, we just don't really... fit. You know?*

When, she asked, had he realized that?

Months ago, he'd said, exhaling his reply like a martyr ready to die-just-die-already. When the conversation finally shriveled to a close, Imelda struggled to her feet. The arm of hers that had been nearest to Evan came away with a gooey snap as she stood. The two of them stared at it as footfalls and laughter from other park-goers continued all around them. Eventually, Evan picked up the arm, opened his backpack and stuffed the limb inside. Once bent at the elbow, it fit quite nicely. *I'm sure I can use this. You don't mind, do you?*

Imelda shook her head. No. No she did not.

She had given up a lot of herself during whatever it had been with Evan. She no longer felt confident enough to classify it as a relationship. He hadn't even seemed prepared to admit knowing her intimately by the end. Maybe if someone had held a cocked gun to his head. Or a hatchet to his throat. Maybe not even then. Technically, she hadn't lost as much as she had, say, to Vince—even her family had hardly recognized her after that—but a lot. All told, Imelda had lost an arm, her right buttock, and seventy percent of her skin. (It was probably closer to sixty-eight percent but she tended to round up in these situations.) A foot had broken off at the ankle on one of her recent trips to the kitchen. She'd been thinking about him too much. No, not just about Evan, but Vince, and her first, second, and third loves, too, because everything, every failure, all the *hims* were irrevocably connected. She had to be careful. She stared at the ceiling, focusing on those spots where the nails rebelled a little more each day, pushing against the layers of paint that struggled to keep them hidden. A slow go at freedom. She'd had her buttock surgically reattached fairly quickly as life had been *severely* inconvenient without it, but her foot was put away in the cabinet under the bathroom sink. When she felt well enough to believe it would actually adhere, she would give reattachment a try. But not now. Now was hopeless.

She heard a knock at the door, but didn't move. Maybe if she pretended it hadn't happened, the memory of the knock would dissolve like everything else in her life and the perpetrator along with it. But why should she suddenly get lucky now? The knocking went on until Imelda, forgetting her footlessness, dipped off-balance and thunked heavily into the wall en route to the front door. She crawled the rest of the way and sat by the loafers, refusing even to look through the peephole in case whoever was on the other side witnessed the distorted blink of her eye. Imelda held her breath, listening. Eventually, she heard the scratchy click of something left at her matless entrance, and footsteps as the leaver walked away. She froze there a bit longer, forehead pressed to the ribbed doorframe. She wondered if she had the strength to open the door, if she could withstand the sight of the world she had chosen to pretend didn't exist for a while. The light gave her an instant headache. She tried lifting an arm to shade herself, only to be hit with a fresh wave of shame when she remembered the lonely nub of joint left there to work itself to no end. There was a wicker basket on the ground. She waited for its contents to move or cry, but no orphaned baby mewled to her from within.

Safely resealed in her apartment, she lifted the basket's lid and found what looked like a blanket folded up inside. She pulled it out, then yelped when the "blanket" unfolded into the unfinished shape of a man. It was skin that had been neatly ripped away from hairline to hipbone. She dropped the partial human sleeve to the floor and looked around, suddenly afraid the person the skin belonged to would jump out from behind her armchair, demanding it back. Who would give her this? She glanced at the basket expecting no answer. A note as neatly folded as the quilt of skin rested at the bottom.

Hey Neighbor,
   Thought you could use this.

There was no signature. The question of who'd left it was only half-answered—a neighbor—but at least the why was guessable. They must have witnessed Imelda's walk of shame after her disastrous talk with Evan. She couldn't remember running into anyone. In fact, she had waited behind the dumpster downstairs, flies landing on her open wounds, until the coast was clear. Then she'd hobbled up the stairs and into her apartment as fast as she could. She had heard a couple of voices before her moment came, but couldn't assign them to anyone because she hadn't bothered making small talk or even introducing herself to the other people who lived there. Imelda had been certain she and Evan would end up moving in together before long, so why bother making flimsy connections with the neighbors when she wouldn't even remember their faces a year from now? Recalling her own short-sightedness threatened to shrink her into a sheepish ball. She squatted to retrieve the skin. It was close to her shade, but also the raw pink of animal flesh in some places as if sunburnt. Its bloodlessness had firmed its texture to rubber. Imelda forced the skin back into the basket without folding it and left the entire package on the living-room floor, turning off the lights as she returned to her bedroom. As long as she couldn't see it, she could pretend it wasn't there, just like everything else.

It was hard to sleep. It had come so easily in the weeks immediately following the conversation. Her brain had seemed happy to shut down for several hours, too exhausted at first to even run a reel of dreams. When eventually the dreams came, they were bizarre and painful. In one that had glued itself to her mind, Evan and Vince had gotten together to compose a letter illuminating all of her faults, which they delivered and read to her in person, each wearing a top hat and sparkling trousers, while riding giant tapirs. Once they had given her the message, the two men leaned dangerously on the backs of their respective beasts to shake hands, then rode away on what had become two manatees while she wasn't looking. Even dreaming, Imelda's cynicism embittered her on behalf of the manatees, which she had always considered thoroughly feminine animals, with their patient grace and sweetly blunt faces. Imelda, who had first stood paralyzed at the railing outside her apartment door, unable to flee despite how badly she'd wanted to, ended the dream in a dinghy with a hole in its bottom. Helplessly, she sunk into the sudden ocean as each of her exes made for the horizon on the strength of a new creature's love, whooping like cowboys who'd been quickest on the draw.

When she woke the next day, it was more like coming out of a trance. She had only dozed since the finding of the basket at her door. She was drawn back to it like something brainless reeled into her living room by a string. She knelt by the basket and removed the bulk of skin awkwardly stuffed in its mouth. She held it to herself like a dress and it grabbed her, fusing as though it had always belonged to her. The patches of her that were missing did not match this donation exactly, but it didn't matter. The skin sunk right into her. Briefly, it was like suffocation of a bearable kind. A too-tight hug. She closed her eyes. When she opened them, the new skin had filled in the sections of hers that were gone and it was somehow exactly her color and she felt... safe. Deviant bacteria would have to work harder to invade her. No flailing limb could clip her in a way that caused immediate and lasting pain. She ripped her bandages away and waved her remaining arm above her head, smiling for the first time in a long time. She did a one-handed cartwheel, after which she clunked a shin against the armchair, and fell on her ass without a second foot to balance on. It didn't hurt much since her leg muscles were no longer grossly exposed. She laughed with abandon and lay on her back, wriggling to make the imprint of an angelic amputee in the silted floor.

Imelda had grieved the loss of her skin most because it was what let others recognize her as human. Most of the people she encountered were missing something. Even the ones in long-term commitments were regularly robbed of chunks of themselves by arguments and small betrayals. But they tended to heal up more quickly than the ones who were still in the "figuring it out" stages with someone. Imelda was not only among the latter, but serially so. With great swaths of skin gone, her crusting muscles and cartilage exposed, she had been like a grotesque exhibit others strained to keep their eyes averted from. Even covered in bandages, her bodily fluids had soaked through as a reminder of what was underneath. Many were desperate to conceal their greatest losses, so they went to the clinic to have things replaced as soon as possible. It was always best to at least *look* like a competent adult who let life roll idly off their mentally healthy, well-adjusted back. It didn't matter that losing body parts was normal; people always, *always* looked—privately comparing their woes to passersby. The ones who had lost high percentages of themselves because they'd been fired or laid off or lost their homes couldn't necessarily afford to hide the impact of such a shakeup with a well-timed visit to the clinic. Those who grieved the death of a loved one had even less hope of instant recovery, often resembling unfinished statues more than human beings. Most health insurance plans didn't cover it as it was considered cosmetic and therefore unnecessary. Never mind that the wrong infection could kill you. If that happened... well, you should have been more careful.

As someone whose earnings were average at best, Imelda couldn't afford the clinic either. Fixing her butt had depleted her savings almost entirely. So this time, she had planned to stay sequestered in her apartment until she'd made enough money to have new skin installed. Now, she wrote a grocery list with her remaining hand, using a small sculpture of a woman's headless torso she'd gotten as a gift to pin the paper in place as she wrote. When she went out the door, crossbody bag in place, she actually smiled and said hello back when one of her neighbors greeted her on the stairs. They were dressed a bit heavily for spring in Southern California, and the shades and bandana worn over nose and mouth did make them look a bit like a bank robber, but they seemed nice enough. It wasn't until she reached the first-floor landing that she wondered if they were her mystery donor.

The Ralph's was only twelve minutes away on foot which, because one of those feet was under the bathroom sink, stretched out to an even thirty with a crutch. By the time she got there, much of Imelda's cheer had melted away to be replaced by an all-too-familiar anxiety. She found herself choosing her destination, not according to which items were where, but by how many people occupied the aisle in question. She circled endlessly, ducking into random food alleys to cut short curious stares. She shambled quickly down the one with the garbage bags and toilet paper to avoid the gaze of a man pressing his thumbs into the apricots to check their firmness. With every corner she rounded, she imagined coming face-to-face with Evan, his dull stare too unmotivated even to pass through her. Eventually, she nudged her shopping cart to the front with her crutch and chose the one register without a line. The cashier was missing a cheek. Even though she had just spent the last hour and a half dodging other people's eyes, Imelda's darted to the gaping hole in his face every time his teeth clicked shut on certain words. She was proud of herself for being only mildly jealous of how little he seemed to be missing. Then again, he was fully clothed; who but he could say what was (or wasn't) underneath? She didn't end up buying much since she had only half as many arms to carry it all with. She could, but would not use a car service or bus to get home. Most were automated due to the risk posed by a human driver's spontaneous loss of limb, but every vehicle took on multiple passengers at once. She knew she would only spend the ride wondering how many were sneakily tracing the shape of the armless lump at her shoulder as she gazed out the window pretending not to care. She found herself hiding behind the dumpster again upon her return. As soon as she made it inside, she dropped her bags and tackled the door closed. She fell back into bed without putting anything away.

She awoke to melted ice cream and warm olives. Another unfortunate dream about Evan had left her brows and lashes on the pillow above the tip of her nose. She swept these snowman remains into a pillbox and threw it into her underwear drawer. What was it about her exactly that had turned him off? Was there something she could have done differently? She was on autopilot when she found herself at her front door, wishing he would come and just tell her. Even if he was out there with Vince on tapir-back, at least she'd know. The worst thing was realizing she had missed the signs of his growing disinterest. Remembering how he'd been at the park, a total 180 from the shy, kind man she'd met wandering down Melrose, she couldn't understand how those cues had passed her by. She had been right there. The whole time.

Imelda shuffled about, putting things away, trying not to think. As she opened the pantry to store her new pack of paper plates, there was a knock at the door. For the longest few seconds she had ever lived, she could not decide whether she wanted to answer it. Finally she twisted, rather abruptly, and nearly brained herself on an open cabinet door trying to get to the knocker before they left. When she opened the door, she just caught the back of a sneaker as it disappeared around a corner in the walled stairwell. At her foot was a mid-sized, plastic tub. It slid easily inside when she used her calf to draw it to her. Upon opening the tub, she found an arm folded up at the elbow with a note taped to the lid.

*Easier to carry groceries with one of these...*it said.

This time she knew there was nothing to fear except maybe the fact that someone was keeping tabs on her. Somehow, that didn't bother her much, even though she registered that this arm must have come from a different source than the skin she now wore. Was someone stealing body parts for her? She was actually kind of grateful, beneath the layers of doubt, that someone cared enough to see what she was up to and try to help. Imelda stuck the donated arm to where hers was missing. When she let it go, it fell to the floor. She tried again, and the same thing happened. She had gotten by alright without her other arm, but would have liked to have it back in place just the same. Why had the skin glommed immediately on, but the arm hadn't? She held it up and turned it about. Seemed fine. Freckled, which was interesting. Clean fingernails. Immaculate, really. It reminded her of Aaron, another ex. She remembered her sister teasing her about her boyfriend's freakishly perfect hands.

No way someone with the digits of a god would be seen holding that raggedy-ass paw of yours. He's gonna dump you for a nail tech. Turns out she was right. But not about the nail-tech thing—the woman he dumped her for was actually an ex of his who regularly gnawed her own cuticles. Imelda crawled on hands and knees to the bathroom and removed her foot from under the sink. She held it to her ankle for at least thirty seconds, pushing firmly all the while. When she let it go, the foot stayed on for five glorious seconds before peeling away to thunk down onto the bathmat.

It occurred to her that, though the relief of once more having two arms to use was still... er... out of reach, this could be an opportunity. The foot, being hers, she replaced under the sink. The arm, she folded back into the tub, and brought the note into the kitchen. After some thought, she scribbled her own message on the back:

Thank you for the gift. Sorry I can't accept it. Well actually... it won't accept me. But thanks for thinking of me. Who are you anyway?
   —I.

With furtive glances in either direction, she left the tub out front, note taped conspicuously on top. She decided she wouldn't open her door again for anything but an answer, and prayed to no one in particular that it wasn't something annoyingly vague, like *A friend.*

If she were completely honest with herself, forcing her way through the unpleasant stabs of hopelessness that arose at the realization, she would have to say that eight-years-old was the last time romantic love hadn't felt to Imelda like being looted. She and Mateo were the same age. Her mother became fast friends with his as soon as they discovered that their families had emigrated to the United States from neighboring towns in the same coastal province of Spain. Both had chosen Delaware as opposed to its flashier cousin for its beaches—despite both patriarchs having lost bits of themselves to the sand and sea—and for its lower population, hoping to recreate some small aspect of their old lives even as they braved the unfamiliar. The cold eventually forced them all away: Imelda's family to California, and Mateo's to Florida. But for almost two years, the expats regularly visited New York City together in lieu of traveling the world. Back in Wilmington, the parents would share a garlicky gachamiga, wine, and raucous laughter on their front porches as their children played in the snow. Though their kids were still very much kids, the mothers joked easily about who would arrange what for the wedding, and which of their engagement rings Imelda would wear in the hope of passing it down when the time came. Neither ring was very expensive as the risk of losing it along with its finger made spending thousands impractical. But many families made a game of seeing how long a worn heirloom could continue through the generations without falling victim to someone's suffering, and being surreptitiously replaced.

Mateo was tall and sturdily built, with large brown eyes that always smiled just before his mouth did. While Imelda's sister Anaís and Mateo's sister Patricia were joined at the hip —as middle-schoolers with their own mysterious concerns— the younger siblings got to know one another and grew close. Not once did Mateo ever tease Imelda for being too scared to touch a dead animal, or for crying as holiday fireworks exploded above them. Once, when Imelda's anxiety over the patriotic noise reached its peak, her ears fell from the sides of her head like flower petals. Mateo picked them up and put them in his shirt pocket for safekeeping, then wiped the streaks of tears from her face with gentle strokes of his thumb. He told Imelda that his mother had told him that the first time his father had stepped between her and a swerving car on a busy street, wrapping her in his arms, was when she knew he loved her. Thus, Mateo held Imelda's hand, protecting the dark, star-shaped birthmark near her head line, whenever and wherever they walked alone together—alone because he knew their parents' joking embarrassed her—and always placed himself between her and any possible harm. He was the very first to take her love, fluttering and new, into his waiting hands with a mixture of seriousness and joy that suited him entirely. It had been a grave business when they were young, watching over things that could not watch over themselves, and Mateo had minded Imelda's heart as though it were a fine-boned, living thing incapable of surviving on its own—an amount of care no romantic interest had shown since.

Back then, Imelda had heard from a classmate that as you died, the people you once knew and loved most who were already dead showed up to shepherd you into the afterlife. So she decided, right after Mateo kissed her with sticky lips inside the jungle gym, that she wanted him to be her guide, and promised in her head to be his if she died first. But thinking on it now, she realized she had no idea who she'd be getting when the time came, and neither did he.

After moving away, Imelda hadn't lost as much of herself because she'd assumed they would all see each other again. However, life had rolled on, and her family spoke of his less and less. There's no need to contort yourself into the shape someone likes best when what they like best is you. To be chosen for doing absolutely nothing but existing as you are; Imelda chased that experience in every person she met. It wasn't about needing another person to make her whole. It was about together becoming a fortress for the world to crash broken against when it tried to break you. You. Singular and plural. Imelda plus one. The one whose arm would hook into hers, building scaffolds with their bones until the soundness of their combined structure was a foregone conclusion. How long would it take to get there? With Matty she seemed to begin at that end, the foundation already firm beneath their feet; girders settled, unmoving. But in the years that then intruded, no interaction was ever genuine enough to reassure her that she was playing her part correctly. So she began to bend and twist in response, each time assuming it would be worth it when this person saw how much it meant to her to be cherished by the one she adored. And when they didn't see it, as in *really* see—beyond what the untrained eye read as desperation or neediness or the kind of damage with the power to infect—Imelda's body bent further, this time under the weight of her own failure to inspire devotion.

The reminder always came clanging like a bell whose ring reverberated long after the sound had disappeared: there was something missing from her. A thing that a select few did not need in order to love her, but most others apparently did. Imelda never figured out what the love of her fledgling life had admired in her so greatly. She wondered if he, too, had made a pretzel of himself over the years. Maybe they would both be too crook-backed and angular to recognize each other. Even in that shadowy space between life and death where you suddenly knew the things vitality had meanly hidden. Or worse... maybe he'd been forced to amend himself into a Vince or an Evan; someone serrated enough to thrive.

Imelda was only made aware of her expression by the ache of holding it in place. Grief had crimped her every muscle. She wondered if maybe they'd stay that way, even as she began massaging them loose.

Her sad routine resumed. She lived in bed, but kept herself awake with assignments from work and memories of herself as a happier person. She did doze—she couldn't stay awake forever—and ended up back in that familiar, zombified tumble through her days. She wasn't sure anymore that it mattered who had left the skin and the arm at her door. One hadn't attached and the other hadn't been enough to make her feel whole again. Matty would guide her in death, but who would guide her through this? It was enough already, this constant loneliness, inflamed anew whenever something else didn't work out. Lying in a rumpled heap of dirty sheets —because who, in grief, had time for laundry?—Imelda drooled without wiping her mouth. Why not let it all go? If Evan saw her now, he'd be disgusted. That made her laugh. She pushed more saliva from her mouth and smiled as it rolled viscously down into the sheets. Fuck that guy. I'll do what I want.

A knock at the door broke her filth-baked reverie in two and she pounded the mattress with her flailing body. Every. Single. Time she settled into a new way of thinking, of coping, someone knocked and interrupted everything. Imelda rolled out of bed too fast and burned her knees on the carpet as she scrabbled to stand. She hopped, clawed, and scowled her way to the front door. When she opened it, the person on the other side had their fist raised to knock again. She couldn't tell who it was with the train-robber bandana and giant shades obscuring most of their face. Through the magic mirror of her doorway, Imelda looked them over and watched them do the same to her. The tub with the arm was gone.

"What happened to your eyebrows?" they said, voice muffled and deep.

"Bad dream," she replied.

"Am I... catching you at the wrong time?"

"There isn't really a better one," she said. She leaned against the doorframe in her bra with the torn cup, and her favorite panties with the alien emoji repeated all over, rolled at the hips, clutching at her irritation like a life ring. No more caring what anyone else thought; it's not like caring ever got her anywhere. She would live as she pleased. In solitude. Half-naked in filth. Who could stop her? Who would care to?

Someone else came up the stairs and peeked at her over her visitor's trench-coated shoulder before walking on.

"What's your deal? Is this stuff you've been giving me yours?" Imelda asked.

"I haven't given you anything yet," her caller replied, holding out a gloved hand full of envelopes, useless fliers and coupons. "Your mail was in my box. Thought I'd hand it to you instead of leaving it here to get picked through."

"Oh," Imelda said, her stoicism deflating a little. "You... haven't been dropping body parts off for me?"

Even with their face hidden, Imelda could tell by the way the bandana shifted that they were confused. They looked her over again. "From the clinic? I don't work there, if that's what you mean. I've been there almost every day for the past couple of weeks trying to get some skin so I can take all this shit off," they said, lifting their covered arms and raising a sweatpant-covered knee. "No dice."

"They don't have your shade in?"

"Not at first, so I said I'd wait, but that doesn't even matter to me anymore. I told them I'd take anything, but nothing they try to attach stays on. The last one actually scrunched away like a fucking caterpillar. Gave me nightmares."

"Somebody's been leaving me stuff," Imelda said. "The skin stayed on, but the arm didn't. I even have my own foot inside," she said, pointing with her elbow, "but that wouldn't attach either."

"Leaving you stuff? For free? Somebody must love you." Her neighbor shook their covered head. "The clinic is hella expensive. You heard about them getting large donations in lately? I wonder if there's some kook out there taking people's parts. I've heard they won't attach if they didn't come off... naturally."

"Why can't I reattach my own foot, then? It's not like I cut it off."

The person at her door shrugged. "You could ask down at

the clinic. They should know. I say *should* but, hell—the doctors don't seem to know much more than we do."

Imelda thanked her mysterious neighbor for her mail and watched them go, then sealed herself indoors once more.

Over the next few weeks, the dust continued to build in her apartment until even air stirred by a single blink made Imelda sneeze. Unable to go on, she cleaned until it looked like an actual person lived there, instead of a lovelorn husk in an aging wedding gown with a heavily cobwebbed meal stuck on display in her dining room; but she did not leave. Not yet. As she dusted, she unearthed photos of happier versions of herself that she had lain face-down in their frames. The only men in any of them were her father, uncles, cousins, and friends, including one of her and Mateo. Every photo of her and her partner of the moment had always been deletable, saved only in her phone or laptop. As she blew away the film that covered her own laughing face, squished between other faces she loved, she thought that maybe her unwillingness to frame photos of her exes meant something. She used to believe the immediacy of having those images stored in something she used all the time spoke to their preciousness. Now, what struck her was her own relief at being able to wipe them from her tech, and eventually her mind.

In time, she began to slide the back door open, sit on the concrete floor of her balcony, and gaze between the metal bars. In SoCal, there were no deciduous forests for her apartment to back onto. Instead there was a sea of Spanish tile, swaying palms, and the pale outlines of mountains painted on a not-so-distant backdrop of sky. In the light of the sun, she flexed her toes. Impulsively, she tried to bend the toes of her missing foot and felt nothing, but it was okay. No surge of grief welled up inside her—just a dull-edged melancholy. The thought of her arm jammed into Evan's bag still had the power to drag her halfway to misery, but she had steadily improved at pushing that feeling away until it took longer and longer to return. With rain so rare in her part of the world, she even fell asleep one night in the big squishy chair she kept outside. She awoke the next morning feeling a little lighter than the day before. She could not remember whether she had dreamed, and wasn't eager to know either way.

She decided to try replacing the tip of her nose. It was small, its absence negligible, so if it didn't work, she figured it wouldn't bother her as much. Imelda held her finger to her face and counted out a full minute before letting go. It stayed on. Leaning in close to the bathroom mirror to check for lines of separation, Imelda noticed the stubs of her lashes and the cactus prickle of her eyebrows returning. "Hey there," she murmured to the face in the mirror. "I know you."

A few months passed before the last note came.

There had been no knock. Imelda was on her way to an appointment at the What's Mine is Yours clinic in Valencia when she heard the crinkle of paper underfoot. She stood on both feet, having successfully reattached the one that had come off. Her stomach leapt when she caught sight of the handwriting. She glanced around, not really expecting to see anyone.

"'Melda! You're among the living!"

Anaís took the remaining stairs two at a time and pulled her sister into the sort of strong, perfume-heavy hug Imelda had missed so much. She hadn't noticed what was in her sister's hand until they broke apart. It was an arm. Imelda stared at its loosely gesturing hand.

"Oh! I almost forgot!" Anaís held the arm out to Imelda. It looked familiar. "This is yours."

An impossible number of questions raced to fill Imelda's head. She chose one. "Mine, as in you got it for me?"

"*Yours*, as in it came off your body."

Imelda glared at the arm in shock. It looked like it could be hers, but, "How do you know for sure?"

Anaís grinned and turned it so the palm was open. A random blotch of melanin, darker than the rest of the arm and in the vague shape of a star, was clearly visible beside the head line. "Anyway, the nails look like a badger's been chewing on 'em, so if the birthmark hadn't tipped me off, your woodchipper manicure would have."

Imelda frowned, but couldn't hold the expression for more than two seconds before starting to laugh so hard her stomach hurt. "Where did you find it? Was it donated?"

"No. Would've been better if it was." Imelda frowned in earnest this time. "I got it from Evan."

She didn't want to react, but she fell against the doorframe before she realized what was happening. Absentmindedly, she flexed her ankle. It creaked. "What, did you break into his house and take it?"

Anaís rolled her eyes. "As if I'd risk jail over that creep. I went to his door and asked, very politely, for it back."

Imelda raised a regrown eyebrow.

"Fine—*mostly* politely. Anyway, you wanna know what that freak said to me? *Take it. I'm almost out of room anyway.*"

"Out of... room?"

"There were so many *parts* in there, 'Melda. All from different people. You dodged a fucking bullet there, baby." Anaís shook her head and shuddered. "I don't think that guy was even this—" she pinched her thumb and forefinger together as tightly as possible "—invested in being in a relationship. Like, ever. He just likes to feel like hot shit, the fucking ego-maniac." Anaís lowered her angry fist to look at her little sister, whose face was strangely blank. She moved closer, prepared to rub Imelda's shaking back as she cried. "I'm so sorry, baby. I didn't mean to hit you with all that at once. But I'm a million-trillion percent sure this all turned out for the best. You deserve so much better."

Imelda stared at the sky beyond the balcony, remembering Evan and his poor manatee from her dream. She let her eyes refocus on Anaís and smiled.

"Are you... okay?" Anaís asked.

Imelda held the note out to Anaís.

"What's this?"

"I don't know. I haven't read it yet. Here, I'll trade you."

Anaís blinked at the sheet of paper, eventually understanding. Grabbing the letter with one hand, she gave Imelda the arm in her other hand. Imelda pushed the arm against her shoulder, and waited. "Well?" she asked, nodding in the note's direction. "What does it say?"

Anaís smoothed the wrinkled paper as much as she could and read aloud:

'Hello again, Neighbor,

Was worried about you. I almost called the fire department to come kick the door in and make sure you were still alive, but then I saw you out on your balcony. Don't worry, I'm not a stalker—promise. I was on my way somewhere when I spotted you. Your eyes were closed, but I don't think you were asleep. You looked so peaceful. Maybe it sounds stupid since we don't even know each other, but seeing you like that made me feel... lighter. Like the world isn't just a ball of garbage hurtling through outer space. So, I guess you're good now, huh? Or at least getting there? I hope so. If you're up for it, maybe we could meet irl one day and laugh about how terrible things can be. Or possibly something happier. In any case, I'll keep my eyes peeled for a reply.

(Maybe) see you soon.'

. . .

Anaís eyed the note with suspicion. "Who wrote this?" she asked, turning the page over.

Imelda's smile was soft at the edges as she pressed the returned arm into her shoulder. She didn't know yet whether she would say yes to meeting her anonymous donor in person. Being the one who got to choose, without bending an inch, unfastened her. She could float away. Beyond Earth's atmosphere, she would hold the star in her hand up to what it was trying to be and tell it there was no need.

One finger at a time, Imelda loosened her grip on the once-missing arm. "A friend," she said, shrugging, and let go.

BARROOM BLESSINGS

She had seen him in there every night for a year. Same drink in his hand. Same stain on his shirt. Same smile on his lips. She thought he might leave on his own, that she would not have to get involved. But if the need did not exist, then why did she? Her dress lay snugly upon her, shimmering. The black satin swished at her ankles as she slid through the lacquered doors. A din of voices jangled in her ears as she passed table after table of merry friends and lovers. The shrunken heads at her waist knocked a little song no one could hear above the chatter. She would come for these people, too, eventually, but would worry about that when it was appropriate. For now, she focused on the open collar of his button-down; the bobbing of his Adam's apple; his neighing laugh. His mouth was in constant motion, yet no one bothered to react to his terrible jokes and meager observations. This barman's rule for obnoxious customers was to let them be until they crossed the line into belligerence. However, when it came to this customer in particular, the barman, like everyone else in the room, obeyed the rule without effort. She took the empty seat beside the laughing man. She sat and sat.

"Aren't you gonna order something?" The man spoke to her in the offhand way of someone expecting to be ignored.

"Not thirsty," she replied. The man turned to her and stared. Her face was hard to keep hold of. It was the velvet dark of a starless sky and smudged at every edge like an incomplete painting. Her expression remained unchanged; it was his impression of her that shifted constantly. She played the game with him until he gave in and looked away, down the lines of her body. His eyes stopped at the row of heads. Absently, he swirled the drink he had been nursing indefinitely.

"I can't stay here anymore, can I?" he asked, his eyes still on the heads. He watched them as if he were imagining his own, sucked dry of moisture, teeth eternally bared.

"I'm afraid not," she said. There was no trace of a sneer or even pity in her voice. It was a fact. "There's no room."

"I don't take up much space," he said, kicking the mahogany bar with the toe of one battered, black loafer. Gone were the robust laugh and drunken confidence of invisibility. He had become sober and childlike in her presence. "I don't take up *any* space, really."

"You know that's not true," she replied. No one else ever attempted to sit on his barstool, but they didn't know why. It had never occurred to anyone to think on it. The ones who came close felt the chill of him and moved on to another stool or unoccupied table. His presence bothered no one because no one realized he was present. No one but her. And the greater powers who had neither faces nor names. "Cosmic space. You're taking it up. You don't belong here."

He slouched himself into a question mark, laying an elbow on either side of his glass. She caught herself watching him with a fond curiosity, as a mother would her child, and encouraged her own gaze elsewhere.

"I just wanted... to be part of things, you know?" he said. "I want to see what happens next. I hate the idea of the world spinning on without me."

"But why here? Your surviving loved ones don't frequent this place. In fact, no one you know does," the woman said. The man continued to slump at the bar, not asking how she knew these things. If she could see him, then she probably knew everything.

"It's life. Not my family's lives—that'd just make me feel left out. But here," and he opened his arms to the unwitting crowd, sending stray fingers through the man beside him who shivered and pulled his jacket tighter. "Here, I can be ignored and still feel like I'm part of it all. Everyone only ever talks to the people they came with, but it doesn't matter. It's enough to be someplace where everyone around you is having a good time. You don't have to know them," he finished, letting his arms rest once more on the surface of the bar.

"But you aren't part of this. You are neither seen nor felt. By anyone." She allowed her fingers to drift through his chest and come away soot-covered. "And if they *do* happen to feel you..." Without warning, she pushed him, suddenly solid at her touch, backward into the man beside him who leapt up, trying frantically to rub heat back into his torso.

"What the—? Are you okay?"

"Yeah, yeah, I just... got a bad chill. Fuck's sake."

"No worries. Hey! Can we get another Scotch over here?"

The man no one could see watched as the man he'd bumped into laughed with his companion, the biting cold in his bones already forgotten. Neither man glanced in the ghost's direction. "Hm," he said.

"Can you truly be satisfied," she asked, "knowing that this is your only effect on people?" The incline of her body toward his was too slight to be noticed by anyone but her. If he had marked it and been calculating enough, he would have played on her sympathies. Just then, it wouldn't have taken much.

The realization struck her and was stifled in a single, uncountable fraction of time.

"I can handle it," he said. The falsehood plucked at something in her that she was not fully prepared to acknowledge. "It's worth it anyway. Anybody would agree," he said. At that, she looked about her, and he seemed grateful to join her in doing so.

It was lovely. Red velvets and golden filigree combined to create a cradle of lush radiance that would immediately warm any poor soul wandering in out of a downpour. The staff always kept one eye on the entrance in preparation to lavish every newcomer with an enthusiastic welcome. Rich gravies intermingled their fragrance with the sharp florality of fresh broccoli and roasted carrots. The taste of tender meat falling apart on your tongue began well before a plate had been put in front of you. She could see why he had chosen this place. Every single person was apparently having the time of their life. She did not know what that felt like.

"I'm sorry," she said. She laid a hand on his chest before her will could desert her.

"No. Please!" he screamed.

The woman's hand glowed white-hot, and he exploded into a cloud of ash. Silence fell like a guillotine. Forks paused midair. The man who had felt frigid at its touch stared at the place where the offending apparition had been and watched as flakes of soot dirtied the now empty stool. Others looked to the unfathomably high ceiling for a leak or a burning light fixture. With no explanation forthcoming, the low murmur of voices steadily climbed again to a comfortable roar, the interruption already growing fainter in their minds. The barman's wolfish eyes fell upon the woman in black as she rose from her seat.

"Leaving so soon?" he asked. She allowed herself a lopsided smile.

"I think I've done enough here," she replied.

"Only your job," he said. "But now it's done, and with none the wiser. Why not stay for a drink?"

"What drink would you say suits this occasion best?"

Emil put a hand to his finely manicured chin in pretend contemplation. "I'd say... a Manhattan Runaway." He pulled out a contraption with a long tube attached. "With a bit of smoke." The two of them glanced from the contraption to one another wearing identical smirks. As he mixed her drink, she ran a hand across the surface of the soot-covered stool. The ghost's remains fluttered down to season the carpet below. As she again got comfortably seated, Emil added the last of the bitters to a shaker. He held her gaze as he put a hand in his own pocket and pulled out a vial of black liquid.

"What'd you do to that one?" she asked, dipping her head in the vial's direction. Emil uncorked it and poured the viscous liquid into the shaker.

"A little electrocution. Some parasites. Nothing too gruesome," Emil answered. "I didn't want to lose too much of this beautiful blood to torture." He covered the shaker and shook it vigorously.

"How *conscientious* of you," she said, rolling her eyes.

Emil poured the now chilled drink into a cocktail glass. He tossed the shaker into a sink at his waist before grabbing the machine that had so amused them both. He held the open end of the tube above the lip of the glass and flipped the switch on the infuser. "While your sarcasm is almost suffocating, you'll applaud my fastidiousness once you've tasted this." Emil turned off the infuser and raised the tube with a flourish as the last of the smoke seeped out. From behind the bar, he pulled a small jar of dark red cherries and a shot glass crowded with skewers. Carefully, he chose the plumpest cherry he could see and impaled it. He set the decorated skewer across the top of the glass and sighed. Rather than slide the glass into place in front of her, he lifted it by thumb and middle finger alone, dramatically extending the fingers that remained. In the restored din, it was impossible to hear the tap of the glass as he set it before her. The woody smoke reached her nostrils, curling into them. She picked up the glass and swirled its contents.

"It's not wine," Emil said, grinning.

"I am well aware," she answered. "I want to watch the smoke move." The bitter cloud dispersed into smaller clumps that orbited, unwilling to stray too far. She inhaled deeply, hoping to hold the flavor of the smoke inside her as she sipped. The liquid warmed her immediately. Though the blood was black, its color dissolved into nothing once it met alcohol. "Varrennian?"

Emil touched the tip of his nose with a spindly index finger and pointed at her. "You're good," he said. "Then again, I taught you everything you know."

"Hardly," she replied, and took another sip. It didn't take much talent; once you knew, you knew. The flavor of Varrennian blood is distinct. It has the salt-sour tang of Worcestershire sauce, but with an acrid aftertaste particular to the atmosphere of Varren. The atoms there are arranged in a way she well knew from many moons spent exploding souls there. The whiskey's bitterness wound about the blood's in an elegant dance. Normally, she wasn't a whiskey fan, but the blood cut and blended with the flavor of the alcohol in a way that made the whiskey more than tolerable. Holding the skewer to her lips, she slid the red fruit free with her tongue. The sweetness of the brandied cherry became almost mellow at the center of so many acute sensations. She rolled the fruit around her mouth in a lazy way until its sugar coated her tongue. She pressed it to the roof of her mouth and felt it flatten. Another sip melted the candied intensity of the cherry further and restored balance to her taste buds.

"Good, isn't it?" Emil asked. She laughed primly.

"I wondered how much time would pass before you could restrain yourself no longer."

"Well, isn't it?" he pressed on. She dipped her head in a solemn nod.

"It is indeed. One of your finest."

A wide grin cut Emil's narrow face nearly in half. His expression turned wistful as he picked up a glass recently washed and dried it with a clean towel. "Was he anything to write home about?"

"Not really. He was an average human who missed the sensation of life. Nothing out of the ordinary."

Emil surveyed her with a naked openness. "Wouldn't you?"

She paused to stopper the reply pressing uncomfortably against her lips, mining his eyes for an answer that could only come from her. Before her lips could part, she smiled and sipped her drink.

"Oh, come now. Don't be coy; it doesn't suit you."

"I'm not being coy. I simply don't understand the question."

Emil watched for a crack in her veneer, but none showed itself. He clarified, "Would you not miss life?"

She wanted to ask how one went about missing something they'd never had. Her *life* had only ever been this. She would occupy all of time— that is, until the Great Forces decided that she too had become obsolete. Then, she would be obliterated in much the same way as the unfortunate loiterers assigned to her.

"Ours is not much of an existence, is it?" she asked in return. She made a stormy sea of the amber left in her glass, winding the tumbler in a continuous circle. A small whirlpool formed.

"No," Emil conceded. Both she and Emil operated within the realm of despair—he in matters leading up to death, and she in the afterward. "Who was your first," he asked, "under the Revision?" The rag in his hand swirled on and on, doing little to enhance the bar's shine.

She could not see their face in her mind, only her own shaking hand as she laid it upon their soul. The wrongness of it—this being, who trusted her completely with itself, believing in her ability to guide them to wherever was next. When next was oblivion. She had closed her eyes as the soul stared down at its shell, freshly flung from the back of a wild animal to break apart inside its corporeal sleeve.

She had turned her head from the sound of disintegration as it was happening. She did not want to see the teaspoon depressions, where eyes should have been, contort in shock. Unbelieving, even until the last second. The scorched flakes of their remains then caught on the wind, some stippling the brim of her hat. She had held out her hands frantically to catch more, and held the fragments to her chest like a loved one's wet and frightened face, whispering apologies. She cannot now remember shame's last appearance, or even when it first began to give up its hold on her. She took another sip of her drink and closed her eyes, as if trying to recall. When she opened them again, they were blank.

"It's gone now," she said, each word pricking her throat on its stubborn way out. "They. They're gone."

Her friend could not quite parse whether she meant from memory or from existence. "Do you believe?" he asked.

Death stared at him, uncomprehending.

"In Them. In their... warnings," he specified.

The question burned all reason away, for she truly did not know. She had trusted the Great Forces—did, still—and yet she could not be certain they knew anymore about what was best for the universe than she did. She had indeed wondered how it could be possible for an expanse that she, in all of *her* expansiveness, had never seen the edges of to "run out of room." In the beginning, and for countless revolutions after, she had worn the question like a yoke about her neck. But she did not dare ask, for they would doubt her loyalty, and thus her usefulness. In her most maudlin moods, she imagined what it would be like: her self struck from eternal record. She knew she deserved it—oh yes, she did—but no matter how deep into the doldrums she descended, she was not ready to be ended. Not yet.

She shifted in her seat and felt the heads on their raggedly-torn necks accent her movements with their own. They were a constant reminder of the anguish she, Emil, and all who followed the Forces' dictates peddled. She took far less pleasure in it now, and would never forgive herself the exultation that had at one time, and for too long, lit her from within at the moment of another soul's ruin. So she began to keep those whose demise she had enjoyed most with her, their sewn mouths and puckered eyelids eventually coming to signify reproach, which she gratefully accepted. It was sublime, this emotional flagellation. She realized that imagining her own bloody elimination whenever she looked at those dead faces was the closest thing to joy she now knew.

"Why'd you wait so long to retire that guy anyway?" Having finished with the final glass, Emil had moved on to wiping down another sticky patch of bar near her elbow. "No one's tried sitting on that stool for years."

The last customers began to trickle out, their thank yous and goodbyes to staff as heartfelt as an airport farewell. *We will absolutely be back. Remember our faces.* Perhaps they would indeed. Of course, no one would remember hers.

"Because he made me feel—" she began. She blinked... then concentrated on choosing her words carefully. "It's been a long time since I've met one who only wanted to watch things continue."

Emil stopped what he was doing to look at her. "How would you know? How often do you hear them out before annihilating them?"

Her brow pleated in shock before she could get hold of herself. Emil did not react, but let his eyes bore into hers until she looked away.

"I sensed no selfishness in him," she said, trying to recover. "I thought—hoped—I might learn something."

"Wanting to remain behind *is* selfish," Emil countered. "Regardless of the reason."

"There was no malevolence in it, however pitiful his want may have been." She let her eyes drift over the many necks of bottles behind the bar. Could this really be the first time she had truly considered her purpose? She had always prized the hard-won stolidity of her own mind. It was that which she credited with her continued success; or, at the very least, what she believed made her universal function bearable.

"Oh, my," Emil muttered to the taps as he wiped away the leftover froth bearding their nozzles. Mercifully, he chose to observe his own progress instead of her face. "Don't tell me you were *touched*."

She stared at her palms, basking beach-flat on the bar under a florescent sun. They had blackened permanently from the soot of trillions. If she closed her eyes and focused, she could feel them covering her with their souls' squirming remains. They were determined, even now, to persist. "I was... curious." She glanced up at her friend. His expression might have been mistaken by the gullible for an innocent one, but she knew better. He had mixed a drink that had ironed loose the secret creases in her mind without her realizing it. It was true that earthly alcohol worked this way on humans. Now, she knew what that felt like.

She would have glared at him, but it felt too late for that. She stood and smoothed the wrinkles from her dress.

"You don't have to go."

"You're closed, are you not?"

"Ah, but for you, I would remain open indefinitely."

She favored him with one last look of genuine affection, in spite of her discovery, and turned to leave. Before taking another step, she swiped her glass from the bar and downed what remained. "Do you believe?" she asked. She did not look at Emil as she lowered her empty tumbler to the bar. Who knew what truths he might catch swimming across her eyes if she did?

"Only in my own continuance," he answered playfully. "What else is there?" Yes. That was what bound them all and propelled them forward. Who could say which way was the right one? Perhaps what was "right" was merely that which allowed you to go on.

She nearly laughed, but instead exited without a word. Emil watched until he was unable to distinguish her outline from those that made up the world outside.

If he was worth his salt as a barman, the drink would continue its work long into the night, and on this he privately congratulated himself. The Great Forces had never had the privilege of his trust. But then his kind, unlike the Reapers, had never been revered, so no one cared what he thought. But he cared what *she* thought. He had noticed her unease almost as soon as the announcement had been made. Her pride in her role as guide to what came after had been all but stamped across her skin in the old days. The time in which he had come of age was vastly different from this one. But then, so much had changed.

Every light but the ones over and behind the bar clicked off as his juvenile coworkers headed to the back to clock out after performing their final sweep. The absent light took with it the warmth that had so recently reached its tendrils out the door to draw customers in from the cold. His actual colleagues never failed to mention the oddity of Emil choosing such a jolly place for his base of operations. But tonight, the bar had served its purpose well. Though his universal function was, for reasons that were surely beyond his understanding, to torture until death, a bartender's job was to attend to woes that were unfit for other ears. He regretted not having performed that duty altogether honorably this evening, but he trusted that his friend was wise to his intentions. After all, she had always known his heart and evaded his questions. He hoped that, in time, she would forgive this transgression, though if she did not, he would not blame her.

If nothing else, perhaps, with the veil of ambivalence lifted for a night, future wayward souls might be allowed to idle a little longer in the glow of what they have left behind. Even, if only, under the watchful eye of their eventual destroyer.

Mr. Hide

The great skyscraper leaned with dangerous nonchalance. Citizens gathered at its base, awestruck and afraid. Would this be the moment it finally fell? Mr. Bumblebee gripped his young daughter Frizzy's hand. Ms. Margo clutched her giant tomato to her chest, worried that if the building did topple, it would crush the Big Food Emporium two doors down. A stiff breeze blew hard. Sections of the building wobbled and the windows rattled. An unconventional structure, the skyscraper was made of a series of large rooms stacked one on top of the other, unwelded. The boss of the construction firm responsible was also the architect and very creative. He had assured the city's inhabitants that this skyscraper would bring in tourists from all over, boosting the economy and driving the profits of local businesses through the roof. The apparel shop, Klose, had begun a roaring trade with out-of-towners, as well as the souvenir shop around the corner, which now sold tiny replicas of the precarious edifice.

What do you think, Mr. Hide? Will it stay up?

Everyone in the city held their breath.

"Darius?"

Suddenly, the sun was blocked by something no one could

properly see. A dark silhouette floated slowly through the sky toward the leaning building. A giant index finger, bigger even than Big Food's County Fair line of over-oversized produce, stopped just shy of the fiftieth-story block. It pointed ominously at the crooked unit, then pressed the outer wall like a button. The mouths of the onlookers below stretched wide in wailing terror.

"Dear God, NOOOOOOOO!" Mr. Bumblebee cried as he pulled Frizzy backward into the screaming crowd.

"Darius!"

Frizzy held her chubby arms aloft and screamed with delight at all the commotion. Toes were crunched underfoot. Some townspeople stumbled and were trampled beneath others while fleeing the tumbling blocks, which scattered in an almost elegant formation into the air, like migrating birds, as they fell. Then, finally...

BOOM!

One by one, the blocks slammed into the street. One crushed the legs of local news anchor Tom Twinkletooth, as he crawled along the ground grabbing after the rolling bottle of custom hair gel that had been knocked from his hands. Another block did make a crater in Big Food the size of the Grand Canyon into which cars, bicycles, and the ice-cream truck all fell. Luckily, Ms. Margo was too busy running for her life to notice. She would have time to mourn later, when she was safe in her living room, twenty miles away. In the end, buildings, cars, and people had been flattened by about thirty block-apartments.

Elliot the Dog Man ran on all fours to the park to tell his girlfriend, Janet the Dog Woman, and their friends what had happened. The other survivors looked around in amazement.

"Darius, what the— You better answer me when I'm calling you!"

The little boy turned around and looked at his mother with innocent eyes the shade of black coffee. The neighborhood on his play-table looked like a bomb had struck. Plastic trees lay on their sides along with a smattering of brightly painted, wooden alphabet blocks. A plastic tomato rocked back and forth in the wreckage, refusing to settle. Darius frowned as his mother walked up to him.

"So, this is what all that hollering was about?" she asked.

"Block Tower fell," Darius replied simply. "It was an act of God."

His mother's eyes darted to him. "Where you hear that, D?"

"What?"

"Act of God."

Darius shrugged. He had just turned five. His mother often wondered what he thought about, as he rarely spoke. Well, to her anyway.

"Mr. Hide tell you that?" she asked.

Darius nodded.

She didn't want to prod further, but couldn't help herself. "What'd he say it means?"

Darius looked up at her and recited as from a cue card, "An extraordinary and unforeseen circumstance beyond the realm of control." This was a sequence of words that she had never taught him. Mr. Hide told Darius lots of things. He was the boy's imaginary friend, which, in Myra's mind, meant he was the convenient scapegoat for all of her son's odd learnings and doings. He was a seven-foot-tall cat-monster with a long, vertical mouth that looked like a puddle of melted cheese at the bottom. His teeth were predictably sword-like in their length and sharpness. His fur was a retina-sizzling combination of hot pink, purple, and neon orange that grew in moppish ropes all over his body. He had three clawed paws (one had apparently gotten blown off in a fight with a nuclear mole-person), but the claws left were so sharp you wouldn't even realize he'd used them until you looked down and noticed you were short a few body parts yourself. Myra had asked Darius months ago, when he first showed her a drawing he'd done of Mr. Hide, why his claws were so sharp.

"For defense," he'd answered. Myra opened, then closed her mouth.

"Well, how can you hug him, D?" she asked then, recovering. "Won't his claws get you?"

"No," Darius said. "He likes me."

Myra had raised an eyebrow in reply and studied the drawing once more. Maybe he should be able to turn invisible, too, she thought. That fur is so bright, astronauts would see it from space.

Now, Myra surveyed the destruction done to the playtable neighborhood Darius had dubbed Ectoplot. None of the town's residents were alive, yet somehow they all managed to buy food and clothing, construct new buildings, and participate in all sorts of lively events, like getting maimed or injured. Myra kept all of this to herself whenever her parents called to check on her and the son she'd had at such a young age. His father had been a brilliant loner. A researcher in the field of physics at the local university. Myra hadn't asked him much about his work over the months they'd spent together, though she admired greatly anyone who not only studied science but was smart enough to be paid to do so. He had kept a great deal to himself, but had never shied away from showing her affection, which is all she really cared about. He had never made her feel stupid, even though he was who he was and she was just a first-year undergraduate with no idea what she wanted to do. When she got pregnant, she was so afraid he would leave her, perhaps after agreeing to toss a few dollars her way for the kid. But when she finally told him, a slow smile had spread across his face and her anxiety had vanished instantly.

"You hungry?"

Darius did not answer, but looked at his mother expectantly.

"I made your favorite."

And then it happened, the thing she lived for: Darius smiled at her. A white crescent moon through which the ghost of his father radiated. They shared other things: cocoa-colored skin; tight, spider-silk curls in a brown that was almost black; somber eyes that always seemed to watch her. But when her son smiled, Myra knew her romance with his father had been real. Darius's existence was not proof enough, for this child might have materialized from anywhere. It was that smile that tied him to the history of this planet, and to her life in particular. Darius rarely acted like a child, so when he threw his hands up and yelled, "Yay!" Myra's heart felt squeezed inside his tiny fist.

Darius plunked himself down at the café table in their kitchen and laid both palms flat on top, steeling himself. Myra set his plate onto the red plastic placemat in front of him and could swear she saw him swoon. The bacon lardons in the boeuf bourguignon were his favorite part of the dish. He always began by picking them out one by one, and sucking the gravy from them until he was left with nothing but the salty flavor of the pork. He chewed each piece ten times before swallowing. By the time he was done with the bacon, the beef had cooled to its ideal temperature. He cut the meat and mushrooms apart with care, and scraped up some sauce with them before welcoming each bite into his mouth. Darius never seemed more adult than when he was eating. He made Myra feel like a toddler as she gobbled down hunks of food that had only been cursorily chewed. They sat at the table for about an hour. Myra had finished her food fifteen minutes in, but she liked to watch her son eat because the calm surrounding him at mealtimes inevitably found its way into her. The steady rhythm of his chewing encouraged meditation. It was the ideal opportunity to take inventory of the life they now led.

Things were alright, really. She worked from home doing data entry for a hospital. Sure, it made her lonely sometimes, being the only grown-up in their rented duplex. Some nights she lay in bed and couldn't help thinking of it as a raft she would have to crawl to the edge of someday and paddle toward the wall with one hand. If she made it, she could open the window there and shout the certainty of her existence to passersby. Perhaps another adult would hear her and send help in the form of a friend ready to tell her off for looking so raggedy even at home, because you never know who you'll run into, girl. Or maybe a plumber with muscular forearms and tools that hung heavy in his belt would see her and ask if he could come in and have a look at her waterworks. She would surely have to send Darius outside to play while the plumber got down to business maintaining her...

Myra shook her head. That kind of foolishness only happened in porn. Hell, she'd even take an Avon lady's relentless pitch as hard up as she was for adult conversation. Sure she could, and did, talk to Darius, but it was often like trying to waltz with a brick wall. The silence that hovered as he worked through the last of his food was the usual soundtrack to their time spent together. It could be peaceful or maddening depending on her mood. She had already made the decision to homeschool Darius when the time came because it was clear that his was a brain in need of constant occupation, and she didn't trust most teachers to know how to deal with him. As it was, she could look after her boy and bring money in without setting foot outside. It was the ideal setup, or at least it had seemed to be at first. But soon, she had begun to feel her *I like* and *I don't like* slip away in favor of what Darius did and did not like. She had become less and less important in her own mind. Whenever Myra's mother called, she never failed to ask if Myra had been out lately, or made friends with any of her neighbors; and she never failed to sound disappointed when her daughter answered in the negative yet again.

Darius had finished eating. He rose from the table and took his mother's plate to the sink with his own.

"Thanks, D," Myra said. Darius pulled his stepladder over to the sink and climbed. She watched his legs move and realized, not for the first time, that she could wrap her fingers around his shins and calves, and the tips would touch. Darius set to work on the dishes, humming a song that hadn't existed until now. He lathered one of the plates with soap and rinsed before holding it over the dish towel that lay off to one side. He opened his hand.

Myra gasped, already half out of her chair.

The plate hovered for two whole seconds before landing on the covered countertop.

"Wha—?" Myra frowned at the plate.

Darius turned around. "What?" he asked.

Myra didn't respond, instead waiting to see what would happen to the plate her son now held. He furrowed his brow in confusion and set the clean dish down beside the sink. Myra realized she had been holding her breath. She exhaled, whistling low.

"Nothing. Don't—don't worry about it," she said. Darius watched her closely as she staggered to the refrigerator and groped about inside. She pulled out a bottle of wine and took it with her into the living room. Her son's tuneless hum resumed.

Myra and Darius watched a black and white film from the 1950s together after the dishes were put away. A giant, atomic lizard terrorized a city of screaming people. Darius loved that movie. He had a toy version of the lizard in his room. Its disproportionately slight arms stuck out as if to grab, and it screeched its distaste for all that got in its way whenever the button in its back was pushed. Sometimes, as one of the more temperamental members of the community, the lizard visited his (yes, *his*) wrath upon Ectoplot, but in the end he was always redeemed. He and Ms. Margo had become good friends. In fact, she was often thoughtful enough to pick up a giant zucchini for him during her visits to the Big Food Emporium because apparently they were his favorite. If he ever got angry, he was nonetheless careful to skip her house when stomping out his rage.

After the movie, it was bedtime for mother and son. Myra followed Darius up the stairs to his room. She never had to fight him on whether or not he could stay up another hour. Darius took every opportunity to be alone, including bedtime. Myra watched him pick out his pajamas for the night. Black and covered in tiny white stars with rocket ships blasting this way and that. His bed had remained neatly made since that morning. Darius took great pleasure in making the bed. It looked like he used a ruler to ensure the exact same amount of fabric was tucked into envelope folds on either side of the mattress. Myra's pillows lay like broken eggs on the floor of her bedroom. She assumed she had a habit of thrashing in bed, but always woke up in the center of the mattress with her arms stiff at her sides. She had even begun to find rips in the sheets.

"Mama," Darius said. He was situated comfortably among a cluster of faux-fur cushions. He liked to have as many as possible because it let him pretend to be a sleeping cub in a pack of wolves. "Do you want to sleep here tonight?"

Myra had been leaning in to give him a kiss. Her lips remained stuck in a pout even as her eyebrows zigged and zagged.

"Why would I do that?"

Darius stayed silent for a few seconds. His eyes slid to the open door of his closet and back to his mother. Myra looked at the closet, but could only see a colorful row of t-shirts above a row of shorts and pants in beiges, blues, and blacks. A shelf above the shirts held Darius's hats; below his bottoms were pair upon pair of sneakers. No item of clothing had escaped its militaristic arrangement. In fact, there was nothing out of place... except for the fact that she could see the clothes at all. Myra would have sworn on her life the closet door had been shut when she'd first entered and turned on the light.

"You looked... lonely today," Darius said.

Myra sat up straight. "What d'you mean?" she asked. She met her son's probing gaze. Had she been speaking her thoughts aloud?

Darius cut his eyes to somewhere over her shoulder, then looked at her again and shrugged. "It's just how you looked," he said.

"According to who?"

Darius pressed his lips together to keep the words from escaping, but she knew what they were.

"What else did Mr. Hide tell you about me?"

Darius looked down at the bridge his fingers made in his lap. "He said you want more grown-ups to talk to. That you feel left out of the world." Darius wrung his hands, demolishing the bridge. "That I take up a lot of space. There's no room for anyone else now."

Myra felt cold air on her tongue as her jaws sunk open, but felt no urge to close them. She wanted to do so many things just then, but could not decide whether to gather Darius into her arms, kiss his forehead and laugh in a way that carefully concealed any latent bitterness, or openly weep onto her son's blanketed knees.

"Oh, D," she began. But where could she go from there? So many other words begged to be said, but tears also threatened to follow. She swallowed them all down with the painful lump in her throat. Then something cool lay upon her hand. It was Darius's small palm. His hand was as steady as his stare when she met his eyes with hers. His unwavering concern made the tears come at last. She did not wipe her eyes as the droplets slid from pore to pore on their way to her chin. She sniffled in an ugly, graceless way, but felt no shame. She was safe there with Darius. They were both safe. Another person was unnecessary. Whomever it was might ruin the perfect equilibrium she and Darius had created.

"Don't worry about me. You don't take up any space I don't want taken up," she said. The words were not wrapped in cheap, unsteady laughter; there was nothing in them to disguise. "You have my whole heart, just like you should, okay?"

Darius nodded, not taking his eyes off his mother. He looked like he didn't quite believe her, but said nothing. Myra held his hands in hers and squeezed.

"Really, D," she said. She kissed his hands, one at a time, got up, and walked to the doorway. A deep depression remained in Darius's comforter where Myra had done her convincing. Because the weight of her had not evaporated, the comforter immediately plumping to erase the imprint she had made, she felt she could trust the truth of her own words. She turned out the light and left her son alone to dream his wolf-cub dreams.

The TV set in Myra's bedroom had been donated by her parents. It was a floor model encased in cherrywood with vines and grapes carved into three-dimensionality on either side of the screen. It looked like it had been stolen away from a history museum. Or maybe out of Myra's memories. It was the television she had watched growing up. There wasn't much on air that held her attention these days, but back then, she had loved so many shows. Mostly cartoons. Myra had loved anything that might help her escape the dull reality she often found herself in. But as an adult, television was part of that dull reality. News, news, and more news. Myra found it hard to care about anything happening beyond her front door because the world out there did not feel real to her. For all she knew, the symptoms, treatment, and insurance information she entered into the hospital's database every day were all made up. Who were these people? She never saw their faces. They were words. Numbers. The images that played across her computer and television screens were composed of billions of microscopic pixels. Who was to say where those data points originated? They might have been pumped out of a massive supercomputer that at that very moment rumbled beneath Myra's feet in a secret, underground hollow. The "people" on-screen might not be people at all.

Myra climbed into bed, turned off her lamp, and settled herself within her own nest of pillows. She had never imagined herself as a wolf cub, but she did often think of floating up into the sky to rest among the clouds. She closed her eyes and adjusted her body, replacing the bed frame with a hammock in her mind as it creaked. A hammock in the clouds —why not? The ancient television murmured its white-noise lullaby of unfamiliar voices. Myra floated on the waves of indistinct sounds, drifting in and out of wakefulness. The ceiling blurred. A warm drop of water hit her cheek, then her forehead. Rain. Myra strained her ears to hear its patter. She must have slipped into a dream. She turned her head, but could hear nothing. Another warm droplet pelted the top of her ear. Myra hummed in confusion. Another drop hit her eyelid. Her eyes rolled to meet the disturbance. She felt a soft weight on her stomach. Something like a mittened hand pushed her nightshirt up to expose her belly. Myra arched her back and turned onto her side. She pulled her limbs into a fetal ball. Once more, something plush pushed her shirt up. As something rough and wet scratched at her exposed waist, she opened her eyes. Spheres hovered in the air above her. Yellow, with gaping black holes at their centers. Myra squinted. The spheres narrowed into oblongs, squinting back.

Eyes. They were eyes.

Myra screamed with such force that she began to choke.

She scrambled to the other side of the bed and heard something slice through the air behind her head. She strained to move forward, but could not. Her nightshirt was caught on something. Myra did not look back, but instead pulled her body more insistently in the opposite direction. The more her nightshirt tore, the harder she pulled. Her arms ached. She wrenched herself to the edge of the mattress and pulled with all her might, gasping for breath, until finally the fabric snapped and she crashed to the floor.

She didn't want to look. Pressing painfully against the heavy wood of her nightstand, she watched for the reappearance of those horrible shining disks. Or a sinister hand, hooking one clawed finger at a time over the edge of the mattress. After what felt like an eternity, Myra unclenched her body and moved, slow and silent. She pushed her fingertips into the rumpled bedclothes with as little force as possible and pulled herself up onto her knees. She rose just above the peaks of the disturbed sheets to look around, but could only see harsh shadows playing chicken with the dim light buzzing from the television. Though exaggerated, none mimicked the shape of the monstrosity she had glimpsed in the haze of half-sleep. Marking the spot where she had seen the eyes, Myra cast about madly for the lamp on her nightstand. She turned the knob until it clicked and light flooded the room.

Nothing. Only the faded glow of an infomercial advertising some new and somehow improved way to chop vegetables. Vaguely, Myra wondered how many ways there were to do that before hoisting herself up onto unsteady legs. She truly did feel at sea as she wobbled around the room, checking behind the television, inside the closet, even under the bed, the dreaded den of monsters everywhere. Finally, she sat at the foot of the bed and ground the heel of each hand into her eyes. She must have dreamed the thing up, whatever it was, but her brain had forgotten to wipe it away as she woke. Myra fell backwards into the swirling mess of fabric, her terror deflating. The flatness of the ceiling reassured her that all was as it had been in the days, months, and years leading up to that moment. The sound of her breathing melted into the unintelligible murmur coming from the TV set. Though it had been rattling her ribcage only seconds earlier, the drumming in her heart slowed. She was coated in a film of anxiety she could not scrape away. But why? Hadn't she decided it had only been a trick of her own mind? She turned her head until her cheek met the sheets and saw... a frayed piece of fabric. Myra reached out and ran her fingertips along it. The sheet was torn. And where the previous tears were more like punctures, this was a full-on gaping hole. Myra bent her neck and pulled at the hem of her nightshirt. It was ragged. Strips flapped unevenly in her hand. She sat up and spotted the missing chunk of fabric cast near her bedroom door. Her heart rate began a steady climb back to its earlier, panicked tempo as she rushed from the room.

She clawed at the light switch in Darius's room until it flipped. Her son did not stir. He hardly seemed to breathe at all. Myra ran to his bedside and crouched before the altar of his placid face.

"Darius," she hissed. She was afraid to touch him. His face was so relaxed, it might slide from his skull. Myra pressed a finger into his shoulder.

Darius's eyelids opened immediately, like he'd been switched on. He hadn't been asleep; she knew it because she knew every inch of this child, physical and metaphysical. She tried to stop herself glaring at him, but his having been awake was a betrayal. He watched her without sound or movement.

"Did you hear anything just now? In my room."

Darius's lips lay as serenely as the rest of him, but there were no gaps between them. He did not want to speak.

"Tell me," said Myra, his mother, who had loved and cared for him every minute of his life, who monitored every moment of his existence for any sign of discomfort that she could work to dispel, who did not show loyalty she did not expect in return.

"I heard you moving around. Walking around. I heard something fall on the floor."

"That was me," Myra said. "I fell on the floor. Because I saw something with huge yellow eyes. Look at my shirt," she said, and yanked the torn hem higher so he could see. Darius flicked his eyes in the direction of the nightshirt, but said nothing. He did not seem concerned that something dangerous might be in the house. On the contrary, he seemed more concerned by his mother's anger.

"Maybe it got caught on something when you fell," he said, impossibly rational. His bottomless stare made no attempt to bear the weight of her fear. The explanation was simple and she should go back to bed. Why did it always feel as if he were parenting her?

"It got caught on something I was tryna get away from. Did you see anything? Are you alright?" That last question held a lie. She knew he was fine, and only asked after him because it was expected of her. He indulged her playacting with a nod. She laid her palm on the top of his head. She had not seen anything Darius-shaped in her room that night. What happened hadn't had anything to do with him. But he was too calm. He should wear at least some indication of upset. Widened eyes. An intermittent stutter. Goosebumps. But Darius lay completely unperturbed. He stared on, like a cat, unblinking, until she told him to go back to sleep.

There was a heavy knock on the door the next morning. When Myra opened it, an arm reached out to pull her into an embrace. Bristles scratched at her temple like tree branches against a windowpane, and she looked up into her father's smiling face. Myra's mother peeked at her over her husband's shoulder. Myra peeled one arm from around her father and reached for her mother's hand. The fingers were thin, almost breakable, but their warmth radiated all through Myra. She took her father's hand and ushered her parents inside.

"Where's —?" But Myra's mother hadn't even finished her sentence before spotting her grandson in the kitchen archway. She bent her knees and opened her arms to him; he ran until he collided gently with her middle. The sun seemed to set and rise again as they hugged each other tight.

"Alright, now, that's enough. I want some love from my grandson, too!" Myra's father cried. Darius pulled away from his grandmother and ran to his grandfather. Instead of tackling his grandfather's knees, he stopped before him and waited. His grandfather extended an open hand. "Hard as you can," he said to Darius.

Darius raised his own hand and brought it down to meet his grandfather's with a slap. The pair of them grinned widely enough to devour the Earth.

"How's it going, little man?"

"I'm fine, Pa-Pa. How are you?"

Pa-Pa's eyes softened as he got to his knees and scooped Darius into an embrace. "I'm doing just fine," he said, dipping his nose into Darius's springy curls.

When he was back on his feet, Darius asked his nana if she wanted to see his play-table.

"Oh, I'm not invited, huh?" Pa-Pa said, feigning disappointment.

"I promised Nana in my letter that I'd show her Ectoplot," Darius said. "You can come, too, if you want."

Nana frowned at Myra for a clue.

"The town he made," Myra said in answer. Her mother closed her eyes and nodded quickly so Darius wouldn't see.

"Nah, I'll stay down here with your mama for now. Y'all go have fun," Pa-Pa said.

Darius grabbed his grandmother's hand and towed her up the stairs at once.

"So how's it going, baby-girl?" Myra's father asked. He lowered himself onto her loveseat as carefully as he could, but it groaned under his weight nonetheless.

Oh, you know," she replied. "The same." Her father tried to keep his face clear of any expression as he leaned into the cushions at his back. "We're fine," Myra added. She knew that answer ultimately wouldn't be enough to satisfy him, but she also knew her father would not pry. Not directly, at least.

"Everything good with the hospital?" he asked, moving on.

"Mhmm," she replied. She still hadn't sat down. She had guests. Even if they were her own parents, they were from the outside world. She had to be ready to prove that she knew how things worked and could be a competent hostess. "You want something to drink, Daddy?"

"Just some water if you can spare any," he said. "So, you not bored working from home, cooped up in here every day?"

Here we go. "Daddy, it's fine, okay? I'm paid enough to take care of us. And D's still little; it's good for me to be home with him, don't you think?"

Myra's father raised his eyebrows high and nodded slowly. His beard covered his face in a forest of gray and brown that made him look like the wisest man living. It was hard not to bury his every word like a seed inside herself. "Course it's good for you to be together. Lord knows the boy probably wouldn't do well in kindergarten," he said almost to himself. "He's too smart." Myra wished he had kept that thought to himself, mostly because she was constantly trying to stop thinking it herself. "What you got him watching and doing in here every day?"

"D doesn't watch a lot of TV. He'll sit with me when I watch the news, or we'll watch movies together sometimes," Myra said. She walked back into the living room and handed her father a glass of water. He took the glass as well as the opportunity to look her in the eye.

"Since when you watch the news, Myra?"

Damn. She needed to be careful. One too many memories immediately sprang to mind of Myra's father turning on the evening news, and Myra asking, over her shoulder as she strode away, why he insisted on watching that depressing mess.

"Everybody should keep up with what's going on," she said before retreating to the kitchen once more. The loveseat faced the archway that separated one room from the other. Myra stood at the sink with her back to her father and grabbed a dish from the drying rack. She turned on the faucet and ran the clean plate under the water so as not to look at him.

"Yeah, they do," he replied silkily. "Think I've told you that once or twice. Never thought you heard me, though."

Damnit, damnit, damnit. Myra had thought she should mention the news in case Darius brought up some obscure piece of intelligence he'd received. She had hoped her own steadfast refusal to watch the news had somehow escaped her father's memory. Evidently not. "Well, I did," she said. "It's just hard to process all the crazy stuff happening out there. Depresses me. But you right—I need to stay up on what's going on—so I've started watching sometimes."

Myra kept her back to her father. She could have moved into the corner near the back door, out of sight, and pretended to look outside at the woods that began not six feet from the house. The row she lived on was hemmed in on both sides by nature. It shut out the sound, and made the world all the more like a distant fiction her mind had created. She didn't have much of a backyard to look at, though the occasional raccoon could be heard picking through her neighbors' unguarded belongings at night. Sometimes, she thought she heard the faraway screeches of foxes in heat. Either that or their ankles had been painfully crunched inside a trap. Myra often thought about what that must be like. She was sure she would scream like a fox in heat if ever her leg were caught in the grip of metal teeth.

"Well, good for you," her father replied. Myra could not even remember what remark of hers he was responding to. "You heard from—"

"No, I haven't," she said before he could finish. She didn't want to hear his name, not from anyone. Ever again. "We're fine. I make more than enough for us, so it doesn't matter."

"It does matter," her father said softly, but not too softly to be missed.

"They said they'd never heard of him, that he never worked there. What am I supposed to do? Clearly, he don't wanna be found." Myra had been polishing the same clean dish dry for the last five minutes. She gripped the dish so tightly, its round edge bit into her skin, but she wouldn't let go. The rag swirled on, its task long over, its tail swishing in an endless loop. She loved when her parents visited. They were her only tangible link to the outside world. But she hated when they asked about him. She didn't want—

"Mama?" It was Darius. She heard the light patter of his feet on the stairs, then the slap of his sneakers on the kitchen linoleum. "Where's Nana?"

"What?"

"She's not upstairs."

"Well, our house ain't that big. Daddy, you seen—"

But he wasn't there, though his half-full glass remained. Myra shook her head and walked over to the loveseat. Her father's bulk was impossible to hide behind any furniture she owned; he nearly filled her couch with his entire body just by sitting on it. Yet, Myra pulled the loveseat away from the wall and searched there, knowing she would find nothing.

"You look in the bedrooms?" she asked Darius.

He nodded. If nothing else, Myra thought, he finally appeared as unsettled as she felt. They couldn't both have snuck out without either Myra or Darius noticing, could they? Myra opened her front door and scanned the area. There was no sign of them or their car. Maybe they had parked a ways down the street. Myra walked down to the sidewalk out front and stared first in one direction, then the other. None of the vehicles she saw resembled her father's dirty, brown pickup. Back inside, the phone rang. Myra didn't move. She was determined to understand the joke. Her parents would never leave without saying goodbye, so they must have hidden themselves somewhere.

"Mama!" Darius called. She did not answer, so he called again. When she looked at the house, the front door seemed to open into nothing. She could not see the outline of a single shape belonging to her living room. For all she knew, it might not be there anymore. "Mama! It's Nana!"

Myra hadn't realized the plate was still in her hands until she let it go. It hit the sidewalk and shattered as she ran.

"Ma...?" Myra held the phone a few inches from her head. She didn't know what would happen, and wasn't sure she wanted to.

"Myra? What's the matter? Darius asked who I was like he really didn't know." The voice reverberated through the earpiece in a way she recognized. The easy laugh throbbed in Myra's ear, a place it knew. The voice sounded like her mother's.

"Ma, what the—? Why'd y'all leave like that?"

Silence on the line. Myra wondered briefly whether they had disappeared again.

"Baby, what're you talking about?" Myra listened hard for lies, but could not discern any suspicious syllables hiding in and among her mother's words.

"You... you and Daddy," Myra replied, suddenly unsure. "Where'd y'all go?"

"Oh, we ain't been nowhere today, gal. I been sitting here trying to get this sweater finished for Darius. I know I keep saying I'll give it to him. Should be done by the next time winter rolls around," Nana said, giggling as her needles clicked. Myra waited a full beat after her mother's laughter died to let a weak chuckle echo into the electric void between them. "Your daddy's been in the garage tryna straighten up his tools and all. I just took him out some lemonade. He got the door up cuz it gets so hot in there, but it's hot outside, too, so I don't know that the open door's really helping. How y'all doing?"

"Is this..." Real. That's the word Myra wanted to say. Instead, she let it drown in her mother's questions about how she'd been and how Darius was getting on. "I'm fine," Myra said. "We're fine. Everything's fine."

It's not just me, is it? Myra practiced asking the question with varied levels of casualness in the bathroom mirror. She could not decide whether she should actually have that discussion with Darius. The prospect felt like opening something forbidden. A box with a rusted lock. Myra shouldn't be consulting her five-year-old son on the nature of reality. But he was the only person other than herself who had witnessed the strangeness of the day before. He was the only one who could prove she wasn't crazy or mistaken, despite what her mother's nervous laughter had implied. Myra had spoken to her mother for a while longer, then her father, before passing the phone back to Darius. By the time the receiver had returned to him, his composure had been completely rebuilt. He spoke to his grandparents as if everything were as fine as Myra had said it was.

What is wrong with him? She shouldn't be asking. And whenever she did, she made sure to spend at least ten minutes mercilessly berating herself for having asked. Who thinks such things about her own child? And he was a child. Just five.

Barely a person. How dare you judge him as you would a fully-grown man? He doesn't deserve it. In fact, no matter how old he gets, he'll never deserve that from you. Only love. Because you brought him here. You. He did not ask to be here. To be birthed into reality. She had never really thought of bringing a child into the world. Lee. She had only thought of Lee. But he didn't exist according to his colleagues at the university. One day, he just... poof... vanished. And yeah, part of her had been relieved. Because it's hard making space in your life for someone else. Even harder to make space in your heart for an all-consuming love when there was still yourself to think of. She didn't know if she was capable of that, but she would do her best. And just as she had begun to come to peace with that reality, another great love had appeared for whom her body had already made space. And so Lee left, without Myra ever having voiced these concerns to him. Perhaps he had known her fears like he knew so much else and had taken it upon himself to relieve her of the burden he presented. But I did love you, she thought every single day afterward. She hadn't wanted him to go, not really. But she knew her thoughts and heart had worked in tandem too efficiently for her to take that fleeting feeling back. Sometimes you had a wish and it happened, and there was nothing you could do about it.

So now, here she was with this boy from Elsewhere. This child who reminded her of the love she'd lost before it could fully take root. Now her love for Darius had rooted itself in her reality, and there was no taking it back. Not that she ever would. No. Of course not.

She was dusting when they came. A couple of horrors from the outside world. They must have been watching her for God knows how long. It was the only explanation for the assured way the one in front had held Myra's door open when she'd sensed danger and tried to slam it shut. They'd already known there was no big strong presence in her home to fend them off. Two young men in masks. They wanted something she could not give: valuables. The only valuables she had were her son's life and her own, and she wouldn't give them that—they'd have to take them, like everything else. But they held her between themselves nonetheless. One left to case the upper floor and Myra's heart jumped to her throat. She wanted to cry out, but thought it best not to. If Darius had found a place to hide, she did not want to alert them to his presence in the house. Yes, their entire life was in this house, but these two couldn't have watched them long enough to know that. It wasn't the sort of information that was relevant to someone looking to be instantly gratified. Perhaps someone who hoped to injure Myra's pride, thoroughly break her down inside until she was pliable enough to serve up every piece of useful information—bank account, social security number, any person who had ever provided her with monetary gifts and might be willing to do so again—would have watched her longer. Such a person would have indeed made note of Myra's particular loneliness and capitalized on it. These two just wanted whatever they could carry in their arms. The one who stayed behind to hold her in place did not look at her much. His eyes jumped from the cabinets to the loveseat and its single cushion sewn into the body of the couch, to the potted plants by the door. Despite her rapt attention to the utter hollowness in her stomach, Myra sensed his disappointment at the question, which had occurred too late, of whether they should have chosen a different house. His eyes were all she could see through the homemade balaclava. They were uninterested, dull. His grip on her wrists was firm, but not urgent. The two of them stood like statues by the coat closet—her, not wanting to move in case it inspired an abrupt bout of rage; him, not caring to, or so it seemed—waiting for someone to scream, "Green light!" or "Action!" But no command came.

Even so, she felt her guardian would never lose the game. His stillness was absolute, even as his eyes struggled to alight on something that would make this act of criminality worthwhile.

Eventually, the second intruder descended from the insubstantial upstairs with his hands on Darius's shoulders. Darius made no fuss as the strange man led him down to the living room. The man pushed Darius over to Myra, who hugged him gratefully to herself, and his partner took this as an opportunity to separate himself from her.

"There's a hella old desktop up there. Ain't nobody gonna give us shit for that. There's another TV, too, but even if you help, we can't move it."

"What about the one down here?" The man who'd held Myra in his aluminum grip pointed at the set in the living room. This black plastic TV sat atop a bookcase and was much smaller than the one upstairs. There were no flat-paneled televisions in Myra's home. Most appliances were things that had been given freely to her by relatives she rarely saw, almost as a form of apology for their disinterest in visiting.

"Sure," the other bandit said. He wasn't truly invested in this heist anymore. Probably hadn't been since he'd walked through the door. The one who'd led Darius downstairs took a few tentative steps toward the living room, then looked over his shoulder to make sure his partner was behind him. The one who'd been keeping an eye on Myra glanced at her; she shifted her face into the appropriate expression, a tacit agreement that she would not make trouble for them. If she were honest with herself, underneath the glaze of sweat and the intermittent trembling of her arms and legs, Myra could admit to feeling unafraid. In fact, part of her was disappointed she could not give them a better success story. Silently, as one robber carried her pathetically outdated television through the front door his partner held for him, she wished them well. The one who'd blandly held her prisoner looked back at her.

"Any cash in the house?" he asked without any real enthusiasm. Myra shrugged apologetically and shook her head no. He nodded to himself as if to say, *Of course*. He offered a limp-wristed wave, and closed the door behind him.

That night, Myra lay in bed unable to sleep. When she put him to bed, Darius had seemed as untroubled by the thieves as she was. She couldn't even count on a robbery to spice things up. Perhaps her property acted as some sort of vacuum that blunted the edge of every single thing that entered. Perhaps it could have been more interesting had she put up more of a fight. She wondered if the man who'd stayed downstairs with her had found her at all attractive. She had no idea whether or not he was attractive; his mask had obscured everything but his eyes, which were light brown with green halos circling the irises. The skin of his eyelids had been the color of wet sand. She suspected his hair curled in larger ringlets than her own, and was softer. She imagined the feel of it beneath her fingers.

"Hey."

She sat up fast, her chest nearly splitting open with the strength of each breath. Had she been dreaming? The TV persisted in murmuring its infomercial overture in an effort to send her back to sleep. Myra's eyes drifted from the screen to the too-dark corner of the room beside the front door. Where the ceiling met the walls, the shadows wore normal shades. But as her eyes descended to the height of the doorframe, the shadows became impossibly black. Someone was there. "You awake now?" they asked.

Myra's stomach throbbed in anxious pain. She clutched the sheets in what was becoming a nightly ritual of terror. Myra searched for impossibly large, yellow eyes, but saw none. There was only the deep gulf between the walls. "Who are you?" she asked. If no answer came, she vowed to lay her head down and go on pretending. Silently, she begged for that chance at denial.

The darkness shifted, then fell forward all at once in a repulsive tumble, like the footfall of a slug with a thousand feet. She pressed herself against the cheap headboard, buttons stapled into pillowed squares that made jutting knots against her spine. The eyes were human. The body tall, muscular, attractive. Familiar.

"You."

He wore no mask, yet he looked ready to hold her with the same moderate sternness as before. His partner was nowhere in sight.

"What are you... doing here?"

He cocked his head in a way that might not have been disturbing in a brightly lit room, and grinned. "Well, I'm not here to give you your TV back," he said. "Not that it'll do us much good either."

Myra laughed, then wondered if she had gone insane. This man had robbed her, or at least had watched with indifference as his partner carried her thirteen-inch television out the door, yet she felt relaxed enough to laugh at his tasteless joke. Clearly she was lonelier than even she had guessed. In no time at all, he was perched on her mattress. He extended his hand, fingers reaching like tentacles to touch the edge of the silk scarf wrapped around her head. He pushed his fingers forward until they slipped beneath the fabric. The scarf slid back until it fell onto her neck. He gathered the cloth in his hand and threw it aside, not waiting to bury his fingers in her naked coils. Myra did not flinch away as he brought his face forward to lay his mouth against hers. His lips were barely there; she pressed her mouth more firmly into his to show him it was alright. He mashed against her and she held desperately to his narrow torso. His body was a tree trunk in a flood, and she did not want to drown in this, her first sexual encounter since before her son was born. Myra's hands jumped from shoulder blade, to bicep, to the crease down the middle of his back. She dug her fingers in to feel his spine. She was being kissed, seen, appreciated by someone to whom she did not in some way owe her life. She rolled him onto his back and climbed astride him. She shucked her nightshirt and wound it in a circle overhead before letting it fly somewhere behind her. He reached up to grab handfuls of her, and she felt like treasure uncovered. She dipped down again for the salty taste of his mouth... but got the wind knocked out of her instead.

He shrank as she flew backward. She crashed into the TV and a rope of saliva hit the floor between her splayed legs like a dropped snake. Myra gulped down air, her brain hungry for oxygen. Before her eyes, neon triangles, squares, and splotches shivered in and out of focus. Figures wrestled on her bed. The larger of the two was hulking; her almost-lover had been completely overpowered. His stick and hay limbs flailed beneath the powerful, trunk-thick arms of the other. Myra was so dumbfounded she nearly forgot to speak.

"Hey! Stop! Get off him, you—!" And at that moment, the head of the dominant creature swiveled in her direction, alighting its bright yellow eyes on Myra. Her blood ceased its flow and all the words she might have spoken shriveled into non-existence. Nothing moved. The eyes hovered like satellites near the ceiling, an impossible distance from Myra's rumpled mattress below. She did nothing and the thing she was looking at did nothing. Even the robber froze, extremities jutting like tree branches in all directions. A cog creaked into motion as she recalled her working body, and crawled to the door. As she scrambled to rise, snatching her shirt from the floor, the creature made for her instead. Rather than open her door, she ran to the light switch and thumped her palm against it. The myth-loving child inside her believed the light would make this nightmare and its bulbous eyes disappear like so much smoke, and she would be left to laugh with abandon in a quivering heap on the floor. She flipped the switch.

"Stop!" Darius screamed. Myra blinked at the sound of his voice. That familiar tone was out of place in this craggy scene of fright, paralysis, and the tragic snuffing out of her first romantic attempt in a lifetime, his lifetime. The light fixture above her bed was attached to a ceiling fan which hummed to life in concert with the lightbulbs. One of the bulbs was dead. A sepia glow spread across the ceiling and dripped down the walls. The shadows cast had rounded edges that did not match the aloe vera spikes of arms and legs extending, still as stone, from the whorl of sheets, or the twitching triangular ears of the creature, one of which was aimed at Darius. The shining eyes never left Myra. Fur fell in thick, matted strings from its pointed ears to its clawed feet. One of its arms was missing, but that did nothing to lessen her fear. The other arm still reached for its quarry, claws kneading the air above the robber's torso.

"Mr... Hide?"

The end of the creature's long tail flicked and, mercifully, its eyes closed in a prolonged blink.

"But..."

"Leave him alone," Darius said, but not to Myra. The little boy stared at Mr. Hide with a sternness that made the cat bow its head. Shock and pride swirled in Myra's belly, fighting for dominance. Mr. Hide had terrified her, but Darius ruled him.

Suddenly, Mr. Hide's claws elongated to puncture the robber's abdomen. A sound like a pool toy's exhalation issued from the robber, who had been glued to the spot ever since Mr. Hide had turned his full attention to Myra. Her breath caught in her throat. She would finally witness injury, perhaps death, before her very eyes, and on her very mattress. Mr. Hide's claws slashed the stomach of the unmoving man. Myra's eyes bulged. She searched for a spurt of dark blood and her ears nearly bent in their hunt for a howl of pain that never came.

Myra released the breath trapped in her chest and, as she did, the robber disappeared in a puff of black soot that shimmered, then faded without trace.

Myra took a step forward, then remembered Mr. Hide. She curled her toes into the carpet fibers to hold herself in place. Her brain ripped itself in half trying to understand.

"He's jealous," Darius said. "Because he was here first, but you ignore him."

The skin around Myra's mouth and eyes became heavy. She could not feel the muscles to move them.

"You don't remember him."

"From your drawings? Yeah, I... I know who he is," she said, voice trembling.

"No," Darius said. "You made him."

For the first time since the light switch was flipped, Myra tore her eyes away from the three-legged cat to stare at her son. He searched her eyes for some sign of knowing. She wanted desperately not to disappoint him, but this was beyond her in every way. Darius's shoulders drooped; he looked exhausted.

"Nana and Pa-Pa weren't here before. Like that man," he said, pointing at his mother's empty bed. His finger, like his voice, held steady while Myra's skin rippled like a wheat field in the wind.

The hairs on her body rose as her eyes skated between the two most frightening entities she had ever seen. Mr. Hide yawned wide with his sideways mouth and Myra saw herself impaled between his teeth. She wondered if there would be blood or a smear of black dust. Myra swallowed to soothe the dryness in her throat. "I made them?"

Darius nodded. "Mr. Hide thought if he nursed, you'd remember you were his mom, too."

Myra folded her arms tightly across her chest and collapsed. She knew deep breaths could calm, but no breath she took went deeper than a stone skipped across a pond.

Shaking, she crawled over to Darius. Her eyes skimmed the carpet, unseeing, until they fell upon her son's toes. The way they squared at the ends like unused blocks of clay. Like hers. Like his father's. A lightning bolt struck her mind and she slowed her crawl. A sting began in her nostrils and climbed to the corners of her eyes. "Are you...?" That it was even a question pained her beyond any bruise or break; beyond being sliced navel to collarbone by Mr. Hide's claws. Myra's chest heaved as she sucked in all the air she could. She did not bother to stem the flow of tears. If she could not have him, could not trust his presence, her reason for confining her life to this domestic island, then she would rather cry herself dead.

Darius bent over her, and rested his hand in his mother's hair.

"I'm real, Mama," he said.

Myra did not dare open her eyes as she reached up to cover his hand with hers. She pulled him to her and buried her soaking face in his chest. The floor shook as Mr. Hide's weight fell upon it over and over. He crouched onto his haunches before them and curled his tail around the family of two. A rumble issued from somewhere deep inside him.

"But," Darius continued, "I don't know how."

Myra froze. She did not want to open her eyes, knew she shouldn't. Nonetheless, she raised her face to his. *Please. Don't say it.*

"You never met anyone else who knew him, did you?"

A wish can be a powerful thing.

"No," she whispered.

Darius shut his eyes and did not pull away when Mr. Hide stooped to groom the top of his head with his barbed, serpentine tongue.

She tucked Darius in and left Mr. Hide to watch over him. The large cat climbed into bed beside the sleeping child with practiced care. She could still hear purring long after the door had shut.

She went to her bedroom and locked herself in. Lights off, she stood at the window and stared down at the street below. She clenched her muscles tight behind her skin and clutched at the windowsill until loose paint chipped and lodged beneath her fingernails. The silence of the night became a ringing in her ears, but she would not stop. A spot of pain grew between her eyebrows, and still she persisted. She pressed the balls of her feet into the carpet and thought of Lee. She was disappointed by how hard it was to picture his face, but the sensation of being loved by him was indelible. The blue-black night was only occasionally broken up by streaks of red and white from the cars that sped beyond the line of trees out front. A thick tree trunk swayed in the wind. Myra gazed, wondering if her mind was also powerful enough to move things. The trunk danced maddeningly forward, and she was too in awe to be afraid. Under the light of the streetlamp, the trunk stepped. It was no tree, but a man whose features could not be seen clearly in the midst of so many shadows. His face rose until his open eyes glinted in her direction. Myra's heart beat faster as he raised his arm, and waved.

EPILOGUE: AND NOW, BACK TO YOUR REGULARLY SCHEDULED...

The power's back on!
  Oh... yeah, it is.
  Lawd. What's wrong now?
  Now? You don't—? Remember.
  Remember what?
  ... Nothing.

She is moving now, and so is the world. The electricity hums once more, reassuring us that everything's been put right again. The circuits in my brain all seem to react at once. I am as ready to sob as I am to laugh or vomit. I want to bend every joint in my body at least ten times each just to make sure they are back under my control.

It's okay if Denise can't remember. In fact, I'm sure it's for the best. I wish I couldn't. Maybe, if anyone out there cares about my sanity, the memory of this ridiculous night (year? decade? age?) will merge with other fragments of memory and dreams until I'm unable to distinguish it from the rest. I must have seen her in there, met her as someone different each time, but I'll never know which parts she played.

The devouring eyes slurped up every scene, and at the end of each story we starred in, we were forced to dip our heads in acknowledgment of their adoration. It is their chosen purpose, to watch until they grow bored enough of cosmic births and deaths to switch the whole thing off. I wonder if I should feel grateful to have received their roses—ardently tossed at my feet as we took our final bow—despite my inability to choose whether or not to try and earn them. Maybe it's being chosen that I'm meant to feel grateful for.

Denise's hands flap through the air to punctuate her every word. She's oblivious, and I'm not mad at her.

It's over, and we're alive.

I laugh with something greater than relief. This feeling, that life has resumed, is like nothing else. I hug Denise and can tell she's caught off-guard, but she hugs me back anyway. That's when I see them: nighttime shapes flitting across the glass of a picture frame. I lift my hand from Denise's back and peer at the tips of my fingers. I try to follow each string's dangling path to its terminus, but it fades somewhere near the ceiling.

Acknowledgments

Many thanks to my UK agent, Charlotte Colwill, for finding my US agent, Penelope Burns. Penelope, thank you for being so relentlessly hardworking. You didn't give up until we found the right Stateside home for this book and I appreciate that more than I can say.

Thank you Christoph Paul for remembering the conversation we had back in 2017 at AWP DC, and for making good on the interest you showed in my work back then. Your enthusiasm to include this book in CLASH's lineup was palpable. I'm really looking forward to what's ahead.

Thank you Kaitlyn Kessinger for communicating so openly and for making the publishing process feel impossibly easy.

Thank you Joel Amat Güell for the beautiful cover art. I love your style!

Thank you to my pals all over the globe who've helped get me through the rough and the terrible to this place of bringing a dream to fruition. I love you all, whether you came and went or are still making your goodness felt in my life. Special thanks to US-based pals Jessica Pennell, Adrianne Greene, Sierra-Nicole Qualles, Bridgette Robinson, and Katy Dycus for allowing me to continue growing alongside you.

Thank you Auntie for never being shy about how proud you are of me. Thank you Met for making it feel like I had a brother even though I technically didn't. Thank you Nana and Pa-Pa for your endless love and concern for your family's wellbeing (and for being "hoops")—I love y'all.

Thank you Godmother and King Moe for always supporting everything I do and truly making me feel looked out for. It's like I have three moms; how lucky am I?

To my actual mom: it's always been the two of us holding each other up, and it always will be. Thank you for EVERYTHING, because what you've done for me is unquantifiable.

Dad, I'm almost certain you'll never read this—and if you do, you'll probably forget—but I love you.

Thank you Neal and Choko for being my constant, furry sources of unconditional love, no matter where in the world I dragged you to. I'll always miss you, Neally.

ABOUT THE AUTHOR

Gianni Washington is an American writer with a Ph.D. in Creative Writing from The University of Surrey. Her writing can be found in the *Chicago Review of Books*, *West Trade Review*, on <u>Litromagazine.com</u>, and in the horror anthology *Brief Grislys*, among other places. She resides somewhere in the ether with her cats Choko and Neal.

ALSO BY CLASH BOOKS

EVERYTHING THE DARKNESS EATS

Eric LaRocca

INVAGINIES

Joe Koch

THE BODY HARVEST

Michael J. Seidlinger

LETTERS TO THE PURPLE SATIN KILLER

Joshua Chaplinsky

VAGUE PREDICTIONS AND PROPHECIES

Daisuke Shen

DEATH ROW RESTAURANT

Daniel Gonzalez

THE BLACK TREE ATOP THE HILL

Karla Yvette

THE LONGEST SUMMER

Alexandrine Ogundimu

THE KING OF VIDEO POKER

Paolo Iacovelli

WE PUT THE LIT IN LITERARY

CLASHBOOKS.COM

FOLLOW US

IG

X

FB

@clashbooks

9/24